40
LOVE

ALSO BY MADELEINE WICKHAM

A Desirable Residence

The Wedding Girl

Sleeping Arrangements

The Gatecrasher

Cocktails for Three

40
LOVE

Madeleine Wickham

THOMAS DUNNE BOOKS

ST. MARTIN'S PRESS

NEW YORK

This is a work of fiction. All of the characters, organizations, and events portrayed in this novel are either products of the author's imagination or are used fictitiously.

THOMAS DUNNE BOOKS.
An imprint of St. Martin's Press.

40 LOVE. Copyright © 1995 by Madeleine Wickham. All rights reserved. Printed in the United States of America. For information, address St. Martin's Press, 175 Fifth Avenue, New York, N.Y. 10010.

www.thomasdunnebooks.com
www.stmartins.com

Library of Congress Cataloging-in-Publication Data

Wickham, Madeleine.
    40 Love / Madeleine Wickham.—1st U.S. ed.
        p. cm.
    "A Thomas Dunne Book."
    ISBN 0-312-14053-3
    1. Married people—Fiction.   2. Tennis players—Fiction.   3. England—
Fiction.   I. Title.

PR6073.I246 T46 1996
823'.914—dc20   95026162

ISBN 978-0-312-56275-5 (second hardcover edition)

Originally published in Great Britain by Black Swan Books,
a division of Transworld Publishers, Ltd.

First published in the United States by Thomas Dunne Books,
an imprint of St. Martin's Press

Second St. Martin's Press Hardcover Edition: September 2011

10   9   8   7   6   5   4   3   2   1

For my parents,
David and Patricia Townley

I would like to thank Araminta Whitley,
Sally Gaminara and Diane Pearson,
and above all,
Henry Wickham

CHAPTER ONE

It was the sort of warm, scented evening that Caroline Chance associated with holidays in Greece; with glasses of ouzo and flirtatious waiters and the feel of cool cotton against burnt shoulders. Except that the sweet smell wafting through the air was not olive groves, but freshly mown English grass. And the sound in the distance was not the sea, but Georgina's riding instructor, intoning—always with the same monotonous inflection—'Trot on. Trot on.'

Caroline grimaced and resumed painting her toenails. She didn't object to her daughter's passion for riding—but neither did she comprehend it. The moment they had moved to Bindon from Seymour Road, Georgina had started clamouring for a pony. And, of course, Patrick had insisted she should be given one.

In fact, Caroline had grown quite fond of the first pony. It was a sweet little thing, with a shaggy mane and a docile manner. Caroline had sometimes gone to look at it when no-one was about and had taken to feeding it Ferrero Rocher chocolates. But this latest creature was a monster—a huge great black thing that looked quite wild. At eleven, Georgina was tall and strong, but Caroline couldn't understand how she could even get onto the thing, let alone ride it and go over jumps.

She finished painting her right foot and took a slug of white wine. Her left foot was dry, and she lifted it up to admire the pearly colour in the evening light. She was sitting on the wide ter-race outside the main drawing-room of the house. The White House had been built—rather stupidly, Caroline felt, given the English climate—as a suntrap. The stark white walls reflected the sun into the central courtyard, and the main rooms faced south. A vine bearing rather bitter grapes had been persuaded to creep along the wall above Caroline's head; and several exotic plants were brought out of the greenhouse every summer to adorn the terrace. But it was still bloody freezing England. There wasn't much they could do about that.

Today, though, she had to concede, had been about as perfect as it could get. Translucent blue sky; scorching sun; not a gust of wind. She had spent most of the day getting ready for tomorrow, but luckily the tasks she had allotted herself—arranging flowers, preparing vegetables, waxing her legs—were the sort of thing that could be done outside. The main dishes—vegetable terrine for lunch; seafood tartlets for dinner—had arrived from the caterers that morning, and Mrs Finch had already decanted them onto serving plates. She had raised an eyebrow—*Couldn't you even bring yourself to cook for eight people?*—but Caroline was used to Mrs Finch's upwardly mobile eyebrows and ignored them. For Christ's sake, she thought, pouring herself another glass of wine, what was the point of having money and not spending it?

The riding lesson was over and Georgina came bounding across the lawn, long blond rivers of recently plaited hair streaming down her back.

'Mummy,' she called, 'Dawn said my rising trot was more controlled than it's ever been! She said if I ride like that in the East Silchester gymkhana . . .' She looked impressively at Caroline. Then what? thought Caroline. Then you'll win? Then you'd better give up? She had no idea whether a rising trot was supposed to be controlled or utterly abandoned. *'And* my jumping's getting better,' added Georgina.

'Oh good, darling,' said Caroline. Her voice was husky, roughened by cigarettes and, lately, a bottle of white wine nearly every evening.

'Nail varnish,' said Georgina. 'Can I put some on?'

'Not on those filthy nails,' said Caroline. 'You need a bath.'

'Can I when I've had my bath?'

'Maybe. If I have time.'

'I want bright pink.'

'I haven't got any bright pink,' said Caroline, wrinkling her nose. 'You can have this pretty pale pink or red.'

'Red, urggh.' Georgina pulled a face. Then she jumped up onto the terrace and swung on the back of Caroline's beechwood chair. 'Who's coming tomorrow?'

'You know who's coming,' said Caroline, carefully applying a second coat to her left foot.

'Nicola's coming, isn't she?'

'Mmm.'

'Is she better yet?'

'Getting better.'

'Shall I take her riding? Is she allowed?'

'You'll have to ask Annie. I don't see why not. But make sure you take Toby, too.'

'He's too little to go on Arabia.'

'All right, then, he can watch.'

'Can I be in the tennis tournament?'

'No.'

'Can I wear my tennis skirt?'

'If you want to.'

'Can I be ballgirl?'

'You can if you want,' said Caroline, 'but you'll get bored.'

'No I won't,' said Georgina. 'I know how to do it. You roll the balls along the line and then you hold them up and throw them to the people playing. Poppy Wharton's cousin was a ballgirl in Wimbledon, and she saw Navratilova. I can serve overhead, too.'

She threw up an imaginary ball and took a swipe at it, bumping into Caroline's chair as she did so. The nail varnish brush smudged.

'Fuck,' said Caroline without rancour.

'No one's going to see your feet, anyway,' said Georgina. 'Will you put some on my fingers?'

'After your bath. You need clean nails. Yours are all horsey.' But Georgina had lost interest and was doing a handspring on the lawn. Caroline, who had once trained as a gymnast herself, looked up. They didn't teach them to finish off properly any more, she thought; to land neatly and present to the judges with a pretty smile. At Georgina's boarding school, no one took gymnastics seriously. They did it to strengthen the girls for more important pursuits— netball, lacrosse, and always the horses. None of them seemed interested in competitions, show routines, shiny leotards and ribbons—the stuff of which Caroline's childhood had been made.

Patrick Chance, walking up to the house from the tennis court, saw his beautiful, agile daughter turning cartwheels against the setting sun, and stopped for a moment, taking in her effortless grace, her vitality and energy. Was every father as sentimental as he? He found it difficult, talking to other parents, to emulate their easy nonchalance. Whereas they shrugged off their children's achievements, he could not resist cataloguing Georgina's; could never resist breaking off in conversation to point out that his daughter had just gone into the ring, yes, competing in the under fourteens, even though she was only just eleven. When the other parents nodded, smiling, and turned back to their chatter, his heart would beat with suppressed rage and incomprehension. But look at her! he always wanted to cry. Just look at her! She plays the piano, too, he would say, desperate to win back their attention. Coming on very well, her teacher says. We thought we might try her on the flute.

Caroline, he noticed, had turned her attention back to her nail polish. It still pained him that she didn't share his fervent appreciation of Georgina—and refused to join in when he began to eulogize about her, even when they were together on their own. Particularly because, to be fair, there was a lot more in Georgina that Caroline could claim as her own than he could. Mother and daughter shared their blond hair, their athletic frames, their tendency to burst into raucous laughter. But perhaps that was why Caroline was so blasé about Georgina. She was used to beauty, physical accomplishment and popularity. Whereas Patrick, short, stumpy and short-sighted, was not.

He continued walking towards the house and Georgina started walking towards him in a crab.

'Hello, Daddy,' she panted, and collapsed on the ground.

'Hello, kitten,' he said. 'Good riding lesson?'

'Brilliant.' He looked up at Caroline.

'Everything under control for tomorrow?'

'The food's on the plates, if that's what you mean,' said Caroline. 'And Mrs Finch went over the bedrooms this morning.'

'Who's next door to me?' demanded Georgina.

'The little Mobyn twins and that nanny girl. What's her name?'

'Martina I think,' said Patrick. 'She's German. Or Austrian, or something.' Georgina wrinkled her nose.

'Why couldn't it be Nicola and Toby?'

'Ask Daddy,' said Caroline acerbically. 'He insisted that Charles and Cressida go in the big spare room, so the twins have to go in the one next to you. Cressida,' she enunciated the word with deliberate care, 'likes having them near by.'

'Why couldn't they all go down the passage?' suggested Georgina. 'And Annie and Stephen go in the big spare room and Nicola and Toby next to me?'

'Daddy wants Charles and Cressida to have the big room,' said Caroline, 'because they're very rich, and he doesn't want them to sneer at us.' Patrick flushed.

'Now that's not true at all. I just thought it would be nice for them to have that room. Since they haven't been here before.'

'They probably never will be here, either,' said Caroline briskly. 'What's the betting they phone and cancel tomorrow morning?'

'They can't do that,' said Patrick, too quickly, he realized.

Caroline raised suspicious eyes. 'Why the hell not? That's what they usually do. How long have we been here? Nearly three years. And they've always been too busy to make it to anything.'

'Cressida is a shithead,' said Georgina. Caroline gave a cackle of laughter. Patrick stared at Georgina.

'Where on earth did you learn language like that?'

'Don't be so boring,' said Caroline. 'Why do you think Cressida's a shithead, sweetie? You hardly know her.'

'I liked Ella,' said Georgina mulishly.

'You can't possibly remember Ella,' said Caroline.

'I do,' said Georgina. 'She was really nice, she used to sing me songs. And Charles used to play the guitar.' Patrick looked admiringly at her.

'What a memory! You must have been only about six then.'

'I liked Seymour Road,' said Georgina simply. 'I wish we still lived there.' Caroline gave another cackle of laughter.

'There you are, Patrick, so much for the country life!' Her

blue eyes held his mockingly for a moment, and he stared back with an impotent rage. Her eyes seemed to reflect his own failures and worries back at him, reminding him in a tacit instant of the disappointments and disillusionments of the last thirteen years.

'I must go and draw up the chart for tomorrow,' he said abruptly. For Georgina's sake more than his own he walked onto the terrace and kissed his wife on the mouth. She tasted, as she had done when he first kissed her behind one of the stands at the *Daily Telegraph* personal finance exhibition, of lipstick, cigarettes and alcohol.

'I'll be eighth seed if you like,' she said, when his head came up again. 'I don't rate myself very highly at tennis.'

'It's doubles,' he said, irritation rising.

'Mixed doubles,' said Georgina, who was once again in a crab position. 'I could play with Toby, and Nicola could play with one of the twins. And the other twin could play with the nanny. How about that, Daddy?'

But he had gone.

As Patrick entered his study, he felt rather deflated. Caroline's last dig about the country life had touched an unexpected sore spot. Life at Bindon had not turned out quite as he had wanted, and he, too, often felt a secret nostalgia for the days at Seymour Road. He had decided that they should move into the country really for Georgina's sake. All the smart little girls that he met at her school seemed to live in villages, in old rectories and farmhouses, with dogs and horses and sheep. None of them lived in red-brick villas in the suburbs of Silchester.

So they had sold 24 Seymour Road, moved to Bindon and bought Georgina a pony. Here, Patrick had felt, they would move into a new level of existence. His mind had been filled, in the few weeks before the move, with images of large houses with sweeping drives, aristocratic girls leading horses out of loose boxes, croquet on the lawn, young boys called Henry and Hugo for Georgina to grow up with.

But Bindon wasn't like that. Hardly any of the families living in the village were what Patrick thought of as 'country.' Many had moved to Bindon out of Silchester, or even London, attracted by the quick rail link to Waterloo. They made Patrick shudder, with their whining London voices, so different from Georgina's clipped schoolgirl tones. Besides, they tended to keep to themselves, relying for their social life on parties of friends down from London— and, when those dried up, often moving back to London themselves. The previous owners of The White House had sold it to move back to Battersea, bored with a village life that they hadn't even tried.

For there was a village community of sorts in Bindon. Patrick and Caroline attended church every other Sunday, patronized the village fête, and were on amiable terms with the farmer whose land bordered their own. They knew the old lady whose family had once owned the manor house—and who now lived in a nearby cottage. They knew the fluttery pair of sisters whose brother had been the vicar of Bindon before he died. They knew the rather eccentric Taylors, who had lived in Bindon for generations—and probably married each other for generations, Caroline liked to add. But nowhere had Patrick found the smart, sociable, double-barrelled, Country Life families for which he was looking.

The trouble with Silchester, he had heard another parent at Georgina's school saying, was that it had turned into another London suburb—full of bloody commuters. Patrick, who himself commuted to London, was not offended by this remark. He knew he wasn't the proper thing—neither was Caroline. But Georgina could and would be, if only she could mix with the right people. He was now looking seriously at moving further into the country—Dorset, Wiltshire, Somerset, perhaps. He had visions of a big Georgian house; perhaps ten or twenty acres. If this year went well, perhaps they could start looking.

If this year went well.

Patrick's eye fell on his desk; on the paperwork he'd prepared for tomorrow. He would ask Charles casually into the study after lunch. No hassle, just an agreeable piece of business between friends. Besides, hassling wasn't Patrick's style. Never had been. Even when he'd been a cold-call salesman, he'd always retreated gracefully at the first sign of annoyance, playing it cool and courteous. Always courteous. Sometimes they were intrigued; sometimes he even found the punters phoning *him* back. When he sensed he'd got their interest, he would sometimes switch on the intimate, enthusiastic, I'm-doing-this-for-you-as-a-friend routine. But not if they were sophisticated investors—or, most tricky of all, thought they were sophisticated. Then it would be the smooth, I'm-not-going-to-insult-your-intelligence approach. Selling's all about judging the client, he thought. There's a way into anyone's pocket.

He sat down, put the folder marked 'Charles' to one side, and began carefully drawing out the chart for the tournament. But a doubt kept swimming around in his mind. Charles and Cressida had always managed to cancel when they'd been invited to Bindon before—an ill child; a recalcitrant nanny; once, less believably, two cars that wouldn't start. And although he'd got Charles' absolute assurance that they would be attending the party tomorrow, the very thought that they might somehow pull out caused distress signals to go shooting down Patrick's spine. If they didn't meet tomorrow, there would probably be no chance of seeing Charles for several months.

He sat back in his chair, staring blindly at the bookcase. Was it worth phoning Charles and Cressida to check that they were coming? He rehearsed the call in his mind. A relaxed, unpressured tone of voice—'Charles, old boy, don't tell us you're going to blow us out again. Caroline will never forgive you.' Or, if he got Cressida, some domestic query that would please her—'Just checking that the twins aren't allergic to goose-down quilts.' He reached for his Filofax and dialled the number, fingers trembling slightly.

'Allo?'

Shit. The German nanny. But perhaps Charles was there.

'Hello there, could I speak to Mr Mobyn?'

'He isn't here, I am sorry, is there a message please?'

Fuck.

'It's Patrick Chance here, just checking that you're all coming to the tennis party tomorrow?'

'Tennis party.' The girl sounded doubtful. Patrick held his breath. 'Yes, I think we leave here at ten o'clock.'

'Good, good.' Patrick tried not to sound too elated.

'What is the message please?'

'Oh, erm, no message,' said Patrick. 'Just checking you were all still coming.'

'Shall I ask Mr Mobyn to call you back?'

'Yes. Look, it really doesn't matter,' said Patrick. 'I'll see you all tomorrow, all right?'

'Is that the message?'

'Yes, all right.' Patrick gave in.

He replaced the receiver and closed his eyes. By this time tomorrow it should all be in the bag; signed, sealed and stamped. He picked up the folder and flicked through it a couple of times. But he was already completely familiar with its contents. He put it into his top drawer, closed and locked it. Then he spread out the sheet for the tournament chart and began to write the names of the four pairs across the top. Patrick and Caroline, he wrote. Stephen and Annie. Don and Valerie. Charles and Cressida.

Charles and Cressida Mobyn were attending a drinks party at the house of Sir Benjamin Sutcliffe, before a charity performance of the *Messiah* in Silchester Cathedral. They mingled, holding glasses of Kir Royale, with the most eminent residents of Silchester—many of whom lived, like they did, in the Cathedral

Close—together with a sprinkling of celebrities from around the area and even a few from London. Sir Benjamin's drawing room was long and high-ceilinged, with enormous unshuttered windows looking directly onto the floodlit Cathedral, and most of the guests were turned unconsciously towards the view, looking up every so often as though to check it was still there.

Cressida was one of the few guests present with her back towards the Cathedral. Tall, elegant and queenly, she seemed oblivious of its towering presence; even though she was universally acknowledged as one of the most tireless campaigners for the West Tower Fund. Indeed, her name was listed on the back of tonight's concert programme as one of the hardworking committee members who had made it all possible.

She was talking now to the well-loved radio presenter who would be making a speech at the beginning of the concert. The radio presenter was gesturing flamboyantly at the splendid sight of the Cathedral, and Cressida, looking slightly taken aback, turned to look at it. Almost immediately, she turned back and smiled politely at the presenter. She had, after all, seen the Cathedral nearly every day for the last four years. She did, after all, live opposite it.

Charles, watching her from the other side of the room, could follow her thoughts as easily as his own. After all this time, the combination of her blinkered mind, her rangy blond beauty and her wealth still acted on him like an aphrodisiac. When Cressida, at the breakfast table, looked up from the newspaper and asked in all innocence what they meant by privatization—or what on earth was wrong with insider dealing—he invariably felt an immediate surge of sexual energy. When she opened letters from her portfolio managers, frowned in slight puzzlement, and threw them down beside her plate, he didn't know whether to laugh or cry. Contrary to popular belief, he hadn't married Cressida for her money. He had married her for her complete indifference to it.

The only child of a successful toy manufacturer, Cressida had been raised by her aristocratic mother to live on a stream of chequebooks, shop accounts and credit cards—all to be paid off by Daddy. Even now, she invariably carried little cash. Her portfolio of investments, managed by a blue-blooded investment management firm in London, kept a steady flow of income into her Coutts account, and it was now Charles, not Daddy, who undertook the monthly reckoning up of bills.

The portfolio had diminished rather sharply in size over the last three years. A large chunk had gone on the house in the Cathedral Close, and another on buying out Angus, his former business partner. Charles was now the sole proprietor of the Silchester Print Centre, part gallery, part shop, dealing in prints of all descriptions. When he, Angus and Ella had run the Centre together, it had been different. They had put on lots of exhibitions of new young artists; had held printing workshops; had sponsored an annual print competition at the local technical and arts college. Now, running it more or less on his own, and engrossed with Cressida and the twins, Charles found himself veering towards the safer, more predictable end of the market. Old prints of Silchester Cathedral; prints of watercolours by Sargent; even posters of Van Gogh's *Sunflowers*. He defended this path to himself on financial grounds: the figures weren't as good as they had been; it was time to stop throwing money around on experimental projects and consolidate. When a small voice in his brain pointed out that the figures had only got worse *after* he'd given up on all the experimental projects, he ignored it.

He didn't regret leaving Ella. Occasionally he felt momentary stirrings of nostalgia for their cosy existence together in Seymour Road. But that hadn't been real life. This, mingling with important people in an important house in the Close, was real life. Discussing schools for the twins, instructing Coutts to open bank accounts for them, was real life. Being asked, as he had been today, to be godfather to the Hon. Sebastian Fairfax—that was real life.

Homely, red-brick Seymour Road had simply been a preparation for the real world. He remembered it fondly and still held affection for it—but it was the same affection he felt for his childhood rocking-horse when he outgrew it. As for Ella, he hardly ever gave her a thought.

The lights were on at 18 Seymour Road when Stephen Fairweather pushed his bike through the gate and padlocked it to the fence. The overgrown front garden smelt of fresh evening air and honeysuckle; as he pushed open the front door, this was combined with the aroma of frying mushrooms.

Downstairs, in the cosy basement kitchen, Annie was making a mushroom omelette while Nicola sat at the kitchen table, carefully colouring in a map of Africa. Stephen stood at the door watching her for a moment. His heart contracted as he saw her clenching the pen, controlling the movements of her arm as best she could and frowning with impatience when a sudden jerk sent the green colour shooting outside the black outline of the map.

Colouring was good for her co-ordination, Nicola's physiotherapist said. Anything which used the damaged right side of her body should be encouraged. So the kitchen table was permanently heaped with colouring-books, beanbags for throwing and catching, skipping-ropes, crayons, cutting-out scissors, spillikins, rubber rings, rubber balls, jigsaws. Next to her map of Africa, Stephen saw Nicola's holiday project folder. 'Africa is a continent, not a country,' he read. 'Zambia and Zimbabwe are in Africa. The weather is very hot and there is not very much water. Sometimes the people starve.' Nicola had just been starting to learn to write when she had had the stroke. Now her writing was spidery, with ill-formed letters ground hard into the page. He could read frustration in every jagged line.

She looked up then, and her thick spectacles gleamed with pleasure.

'Hello, Daddy!' Annie looked up from the frying pan.

'Stephen! I didn't hear you come in!' He crossed the kitchen, ruffling Nicola's hair on the way, and gave Annie a kiss. Her cheeks were bright red from the heat and her dark hair had curled into tendrils around her face. 'Did you have a good day?' she asked.

Stephen closed his eyes and briefly reviewed the last twelve hours. An early train journey into London; an hour's wait at the department to see his supervisor for fifteen minutes; a sandwich

at the British Library while waiting for the documents he'd re-
quested; a few hours' good work; a late appearance at a seminar
he'd promised to attend; back onto the train and home . . . He
opened his eyes again.

'Yes, not bad,' he said.

Stephen was scheduled to finish his Ph.D. the next summer.
At the rate he was going, it might just be possible—but still the
thought of marshalling his assorted notes, ideas and theories into
a coherent, substantial thesis filled him with a blank dread. Information that had seemed solid enough when he put together
his thesis proposal, arguments that had seemed weighty and convincing, now seemed to have become gossamer thin, floating out
of the grasp of his mind whenever he attempted to formulate
them in academic English or even find a place for them in his in-
troduction.

At the department, at seminars, even at home with Annie,
he remained outwardly confident, assuming with a worrying
ease the veneer of someone who knows he is going to succeed.
He never articulated his secret fear—that he simply wasn't up to
the rigours of such an ambitious project; that he should have
stayed as he was: a humble schoolmaster with no pretensions to
changing the face of fourteenth-century musical history.

He opened the fridge and cracked open a beer.

'Did I say I had a good day?' he said humorously. 'I must be
mad. Mark wasn't free to see me when he'd said he would be,
my papers took forever to arrive, and I was coerced into going to
the mad Bulgarian woman's seminar.' Nicola giggled.

'Is she really mad?'

'Barking,' said Stephen solemnly. 'She entertained us for an hour with her views on the music that is all around us in nature.'

'Birds singing,' suggested Nicola.

'If only,' said Stephen. 'No, she was talking about trees, and snails' shells, and other completely soundless creatures.'

'Definitely mad,' said Annie. Stephen took a swig of beer.

'And did you all have a good day?' He looked around. 'Is Toby in bed?' Annie grinned.

'Yes, we wore him out with a walk on the downs. We took a picnic up there. It's been such wonderful weather.'

'And then we got everyone's clothes ready for tomorrow,' said Nicola. Stephen looked puzzled.

'What's tomorrow?'

'The tennis party, of course,' said Nicola in tones of amazement. 'You must know about that!'

'He does know,' said Annie. 'He's just pretending he's forgotten.' Stephen shook his head.

'No, this time I didn't have to pretend. It really had gone straight out of my mind.'

'Good thing Mummy remembered,' said Nicola, 'all our things needed washing.' Stephen grimaced.

'I didn't know I had any "things."'

'Old white shorts and an aertex,' said Annie briskly. 'And your racquet's just about OK. A string's missing, but . . .'

'But someone with my talent doesn't need the equipment,' said Stephen. 'I know. What about you?'

'Well actually,' said Annie, blushing slightly, 'Caroline very kindly said I could borrow some of her things. I think she realized . . .' She tailed off and her dark eyes met Stephen's green ones. For a moment, he felt a flash of anger. He knew Caroline's sympathetic, slightly too-loud remarks; her appraising looks; her complete incomprehension as to why anyone would chuck in a perfectly good teaching job to do more *studying*, for Christ's sake. He would be aware of her no doubt kindly meant gesture all day. But to say any of that to Annie would be unforgivable.

'Very good of her,' he said lightly. 'Pity Patrick's such a fat bugger. Otherwise I could have swanned around in his Lacoste. Perhaps I will anyway.' And, hoisting his rucksack onto his back, he went out of the kitchen and up the stairs to put away his books.

CHAPTER TWO

Caroline woke up the next morning to the sensation of Patrick's warm breath on her neck. Keeping her eyes closed, she registered first the fact that a brightness, which must be the morning sun, was penetrating her eyelids with a red glare. Then she became aware that Patrick's stubby fingers were roaming over her body, under her nightdress, stirring her unwillingly into a pleasurable wakefulness. Still she kept her eyes closed, mimicking sleep, or at least inertia.

Even when Patrick pushed his way into her, with the unmistakable enthusiasm of the early-morning fuck, she managed to keep her face impassive. She focused her attention on what she was going to wear that day, then forced herself to wonder whether she ought to pluck her eyebrows, until suddenly, with an involuntary cry, her concentration was overcome and she surrendered to pleasure.

When Patrick had exhausted himself he collapsed beside her. 'You enjoyed that,' he said in an accusing tone. Caroline ignored him. 'Didn't you?' he persisted. She shrugged.

'I suppose so.'

'So why did you pretend you didn't?' He raised himself on one elbow and looked at her. Caroline smiled lazily. Her fingers were tingling and she felt benevolent.

'I don't know,' she said. 'Probably to piss you off.'

They lay in silence for a few minutes, then Patrick heaved himself up, avoiding Caroline's eye. He wrapped an unnecessary towel around himself and disappeared reproachfully into the *en suite* bathroom. Caroline, staring after him, couldn't quite summon the energy to call after him. Once upon a time she would have followed him into the shower; kissed and made up under the powerful blast.

But this morning she felt indolent and heavy limbed. She could barely bring herself to scrabble for her cigarette case, let alone leap up for a repeat session. She stared up at the white ceiling, at the white muslin curtains, translucent with morning sunshine, and wondered vaguely why she could no longer bring herself to respond to Patrick's lovemaking. She certainly wasn't frigid, and he certainly hadn't lost his touch. Perhaps it was just that she didn't want him to feel pleased with himself.

She sighed, reached for her lighter and, without moving from the pile of broderie anglaise pillows, lit up a menthol cigarette, inhaling deeply and blowing clouds of smoke up into the canopy of their dark, oak four-poster. She could hear the shower going; it wouldn't be long before he came back in, probably still with that wounded look. Well, today he would just have to remain wounded. He would soon cheer up. And he should count himself bloody lucky that they still occupied—even if not always in perfect harmony—the same bed. She could think of couples who had experimented with single beds and separate rooms—never to return to the cosy familiarity of a shared duvet.

But when Patrick came in again, hair slicked back and chest gleaming with droplets of water, he was actually whistling. Caroline peered at him suspiciously through the haze of smoke and waited for him to say that smoking in bed was a fire hazard, but he briskly threw open his wardrobe, pulled out pristine white socks, shirt and shorts, and began to get dressed.

'Why are you so bloody cheerful?' she demanded, as he tucked in his shirt. He ignored her, and began to comb his damp hair. Then he pulled open the curtains and thrust open the window. A breeze billowed the curtains, and Caroline, warmly cocooned in the duvet, scowled as the cool air hit her face.

'You should get up,' he said. 'It's going to be another scorcher.'

'What time is it?'

'Nine o'clock. We should get cracking. They'll probably all get here around ten-thirty, eleven. The Mobyns are leaving at ten.' He looked at himself in the mirror and made a few imaginary shots.

Those bloody Mobyns again, thought Caroline, and gave Patrick a distrustful look.

Stephen and Annie arrived in Bindon at exactly ten-thirty. The roads out of Silchester had, contrary to Stephen's predictions, proved remarkably clear, and even the children had chosen their ice-lollies at the service station with a brisk efficiency.

'I hope we're not too early,' said Annie, as the car pulled into the Tarmac drive of The White House. 'Are there any other cars here yet?' They all peered out of the windows. A sprinkler was playing on the semicircular lawn in front of the house, swinging round to douse the immaculate shrubs bordering the drive; then swinging back to play on the central flowerbed. As it changed direction, a spray of drops landed on the car, and the children shrieked with laughter.

'There's a car,' said Nicola, pointing to the very shiny navy-blue Mercedes which was parked at a skewed angle in front of the house.

'That's Caroline's,' said Annie. 'We must be the first. Well, they did say to arrive between ten and eleven.'

'Can we go under the sprinklers?' said Nicola. Annie glanced at Stephen.

'I'm not really sure . . .'

'Why shouldn't they?' he said, in a slightly defensive voice. 'They won't do any harm.'

'OK then, but make sure . . .' Annie tailed off as Nicola and Toby slithered out of the car. Toby ran cleanly towards the lawn, a little brown body in blue shorts and T-shirt. Nicola hurried along beside him, her right foot trailing slightly with an expedi-

with this one.' As they rounded the corner of the house, Annie gave a backward glance to the Mercedes, gleaming expensively in the sunshine.

'You must be doing well,' she said. Patrick shrugged.

'It hasn't been a bad couple of years. I've been keeping my end up somehow. Just going with the flow. You know how it is.'

'Not really,' said Annie, honestly. 'There isn't much of a flow in Seymour Road.' Patrick laughed.

'Don't knock Seymour Road! I have fond memories of that street.'

'Do you?'

'Don't look so surprised. In fact, Georgina was saying only yesterday how much she wished we still lived there.' He gave Annie a rueful look and she laughed.

'Typical children! Never grateful!'

'That's what I said.'

They came out at the back of the house, and Caroline looked up from the terrace, where she was pouring out drinks for two people Annie didn't recognize. She was looking very brown, thought Annie, looking down at her own pale legs with a slight twinge.

'Annie!' shouted Caroline. 'Just in time for some Pimm's!' She sploshed a rather dark amber liquid into a long glass held by the strange woman, who giggled affectedly.

'Now, now,' said the man. 'Can't have you getting tipsy before you play, Valerie.'

'Why the hell not?' enquired Caroline, filling the man's glass. Valerie giggled again.

'Hello all,' said Patrick. 'Annie, meet Don Roper and his daughter Valerie.'

'How do you do?' said Don, winking at Annie. He was a stocky, cheerful-looking man, with a rather large face and eager eyes.

'Hello!' carolled Valerie. She seemed slightly younger than Annie—perhaps around thirty—and had the same large face as her father, but to less pleasant effect. Her skin was pale and dead-looking and her hazel eyes had a rather flat sheen.

'What can I get you?' said Patrick, gesturing expansively to the glass drinks trolley.

'Pimm's would be lovely,' said Annie. 'But if I could have it a little weaker than that . . .' Caroline poured out nearly a glass-ful of the dark liquid and added a splash of lemonade.

'Have some mint,' she said, poking about in the top of the jug. 'And a couple of strawberries.'

Annie sat down on a steamer chair, took a sip of Pimm's and waited for the kick of alcohol to hit her stomach. The sun was hot on her face and she wished she had brought some sunglasses. Looking surreptitiously at the others' clothes, she realized she was certainly going to have to avail herself of Caroline's offer of an outfit. Valerie was nattily attired in Slazenger, while Don's shorts looked so crisp as to be almost uncomfortable. And Caroline was looking her usual glamorous self, in a pale-pink sleeveless tennis top and matching pleated skirt. Her thick, blond, highlighted hair was in a bouncy pony-tail and she was wearing a white towelling wristband on each arm.

Stephen came striding around the corner of the house, carrying Toby on his shoulders.

'Hi, everyone,' he said.

'What a sweet little boy!' cried Valerie.

'Have some Pimm's,' said Patrick. 'Have you met Don and Valerie?'

'How do you do?' said Stephen. 'I'm Stephen Fairweather.'

'And who's this?' said Valerie archly at Toby. Toby buried his face in his father's neck.

'Our son, Toby,' said Annie.

'What a gorgeous creature,' said Valerie. 'I do love children.'

Nicola followed round the corner, with a drenched T-shirt and gleaming spectacles. Her right leg dragged slightly as she went, and she was panting.

'The sprinkler's *brilliant!*' she said. 'It's better than going swimming.'

'You look as if you have been swimming!' said Caroline, smiling warmly at Nicola. 'Does Georgina know you're here? She can't wait to see you.' Nicola flushed slightly with pleasure.

'I haven't seen her,' she said.

'She must be in her room,' said Caroline. 'Do you want to go and find her? Or do you want to cool down and have a Coke?'

'I think I'll go and find her,' said Nicola, looking with alarm at the smart chairs and strangers on the terrace.

'You know where her room is. Take Toby, too, if you like.'

'Yes, go on, Tobes,' said Stephen. 'Go and annoy the big ones.' He grinned at Nicola.

As Nicola hurried off, Toby in tow, Valerie turned to Annie with a mixture of horror and sympathy on her face.

'Oh dear, poor little girl,' she said. She had a high, rather flutey voice. 'It must be so difficult for you.'

'Not really,' said Annie.

'She must be a very loving creature,' continued Valerie. 'I read in an article that children with disabilities are often the most rewarding.'

Annie and Stephen glanced at each other.

'But your little boy,' she continued, 'he's quite normal, is he? I must say, he looks a charming child.'

Nicola proceeded timidly along the long, cool corridors of The White House, trying to remember which door was Georgina's. She kept a firm grip on Toby; Georgina's house was full of things, balanced on pedestals and shelves, which she recognized as both expensive and easily broken. She vaguely supposed that was why Caroline and Patrick hadn't had any more children after Georgina. Everyone knew Georgina was neat and tidy and never dropped things or ran into them; but if they'd had someone clumsy like her, or Toby, who never kept still . . . They passed a little table laden with Lladro china ornaments and she shuddered to think of them all lying broken on the floor; knocked off by a sweeping arm movement or one of Toby's tennis balls.

Eventually she thought she'd found the right door and knocked timidly.

'Come in!'

Georgina was sitting at her desk by the window, and she looked up, her face bright, as they entered.

'Brilliant! You're here!' she said. 'Why are you all wet?'

'We went under the sprinklers,' said Nicola, a little shamefacedly.

'I do that sometimes,' said Georgina, kindly. 'Do you want a drink of water?'

'Yes please,' said Nicola, watching mesmerized as Georgina went to a large transparent water dispenser in the corner of her room.

'Isn't it brilliant?' said Georgina. 'Mummy got it for me because I'm always coming out for drinks of water at night. The water in my bathroom is yuck.'

She returned to her desk and lifted up a sheet of paper covered with writing.

'I've got a plan sorted out for what we're going to do!'

'Can't we go and see Arabia?' said Nicola.

'Of course,' said Georgina. 'But we need something for this afternoon.' Nicola took a sip of water. It was cool, clean and delicious. She looked at Georgina and waited.

'I've decided we're going to do a play,' said Georgina. 'We can make one up. Isn't it a brilliant idea? We can rehearse today and do the performance tomorrow. We can have costumes and everything. What do you think?' Her bright blue eyes fixed on Nicola determinedly, and Nicola stared back with respect.

'All right,' she said. 'That sounds brilliant.'

Annie and Caroline, passing Georgina's door on the way to Caroline's bedroom, heard her issuing instructions in clear tones.

'Bossy little cow,' said Caroline, rolling her eyes. 'Thinks she's in some bloody Angela Brazil novel.'

'It's a shame they aren't outside, it's such nice weather,' said Annie.

'You're right!' exclaimed Caroline. 'I never think of things like that.' She pushed open Georgina's door. All three children looked up.

'You should all go outside,' said Caroline. 'You'll never get brown in here.'

Caroline's walk-in wardrobe was nearly the size of the boxroom at 18 Seymour Road. Annie watched, trying unsuccessfully to remain nonchalant as Caroline tossed tennis shirts, skirts, T-shirts and shorts onto the bed in a heap of sugary pastels. Some were plain, some discreetly trimmed, others a riot of abstract pattern. She surreptitiously eyed the logos, despising her heart for beating faster as she recognized not only well-known sporting labels— Ellesse, Tacchini, Lacoste—but also the more universally coveted insignias that no one could be unaware of these days. Gucci. Yves Saint Laurent. Chanel. Her gaze fixed on a plain white T-shirt with two interlocking Cs. How much must that have cost?

'I don't know what kind of thing you like,' Caroline was saying. 'Try them all on, if you like.'

'I don't know where to start,' said Annie. 'I didn't know you were so keen on tennis.' Caroline looked surprised.

'I'm not, really. We go to the country club over at Henchley— and you need proper tennis stuff for that. Not only whites, thank

God. I mean, you need a really good tan to be able to wear white.'

Annie, who had been about to pick out a white sleeveless tennis top, changed her mind.

'What do you think?' she said helplessly. Caroline looked at her consideringly, and Annie involuntarily glanced down at her legs—pale and short, though not flabby. Rather like the rest of her. She had the sort of English complexion which veered from deathly white to embarrassingly pink, and she tended to leave the rest of her body to its own devices.

'Apricot,' said Caroline decisively.

Stephen was onto his second glass of Pimm's. He stretched out his legs in the sunshine and wondered how he would ever summon up the energy to play tennis. Patrick had appeared with a large chart labelled 'The White House Tennis Tournament' and was busy explaining it to Don. Valerie was awkwardly picking out pieces of fruit from her drink and popping them into her mouth. Her hazel eyes met Stephen's and she giggled.

'Ooh!' she said. 'I really think . . .' She petered off, and gazed down into her drink again. There was a pause, during which Stephen gave an inward sigh. It would be too rude to ignore her.

'Do you live in the village?' he said conversationally. Valerie started, and looked up at him. Her forehead was moist, and a few strands of her shaggy brown hair had stuck to it.

'Ooh no!' she laughed, as though he had said something preposterous. 'No, I live in London. But Dad lives here, just along the road, and Patrick phoned him up and asked whether I'd be home this weekend.'

'Lucky that you were,' said Stephen.

'Not really lucky,' said Valerie. 'When Dad told me about the party, I took Friday off work to come down. I did a bit of shopping, too, spending all my salary at once!' She giggled loudly.

'So you came down specially?' Stephen was surprised.

'Well, I do enjoy the tennis, and meeting new people. I play at a club in London, which is very good, and there are social events every so often, you know, discos and parties, karaoke evenings sometimes . . .' Stephen nodded in slight bemusement. 'But then, no one talks very much at a disco,' she carried on, 'and I'm never quite sure what to wear.' She abruptly stopped speaking, and Stephen found himself quite floored for an answer.

Annie couldn't believe how attractive she felt wearing Caroline's apricot-coloured polo shirt and pleated skirt. She stared at her reflection in the mirror, and smelt the deliciously flowery scent which Caroline had insisted she try.

'And you must have a go with this moisturizer,' said Caroline. 'It stops wrinkles and helps you go brown quicker.' She brandished a silver pot at Annie. 'Put it on all over.'

'I should say no,' said Annie. 'That looks extremely expensive.'

'Forty quid,' said Caroline. 'But it's worth it. And Patrick earns enough.'

'He must be doing really well,' said Annie, temporarily closing off her conscience in order to smear forty-pound cream all over her legs.

'I think they all are at his company,' said Caroline. 'People are buying investment plans like there's no tomorrow. God knows how they can afford them. Especially at the moment. But his bonuses have been incredible.'

'What does he get bonuses for?' said Annie. 'Sorry, I'm incredibly ignorant.'

'They give him a target and if he reaches it he gets a sodding great bonus. All of this'—Caroline gestured vaguely out of the window—'is from bonuses.' Annie began to apply the cream to her face.

'It's not fair!' she said. 'They should give teachers bonuses for getting kids through exams! Or give Stephen a bonus for finishing his thesis.'

'They should bloody well give me a bonus for putting up with Patrick's moods,' retorted Caroline. 'If he thinks he's going to miss a target he gets really edgy. Drives me crackers.' She sighed, and picked up a tennis skirt still in its embossed cellophane wrapper. It was pale blue and white striped, with a gold logo in the corner.

'I'd forgotten all about this one,' she said, in surprise. 'I must wear it some time.'

When Annie and Caroline got outside again, they found Patrick anxiously looking at his watch.

'I wanted to kick off at eleven,' he complained, 'but the Mobyns aren't here yet.'

'So what?' said Caroline. 'You only need two couples at a time. We can easily start now.'

'But Charles and Cressida are supposed to be on first,' said Patrick. 'And besides, I wanted to explain the chart to everyone first.'

'For Christ's sake!' exclaimed Caroline. She picked up the chart and surveyed it. 'Here we are,' she said. 'Second match: us against Don and Valerie.' She rolled her eyes at Annie, who giggled. Patrick was staring at the chart.

'I suppose that would work,' he said grudgingly.

'Come on then!' said Don. 'Chop, chop, Valerie.' Valerie scrambled to her feet, grabbed for her racquet, and in doing so knocked over the open bottle of Pimm's.

'Ooh!' she shrieked. 'I'm so clumsy! Caroline, I'm so sorry. Oh, I've cut my hand! What a stupid thing to do!'

When the Pimm's had been mopped up and Valerie had disappeared upstairs with Caroline for a plaster, Stephen sidled over to Annie, who was surreptitiously admiring her reflection in the glass terrace doors.

'You look great!' he said. 'That's a wonderful colour on you.' Annie looked down to savour her new shiny self. Even her socks were little pieces of luxury—fluffy white towelling with apricot-coloured pompoms bobbing gaily over the backs of her plimsolls.

'It's quite nice, isn't it?' she said, trying unsuccessfully to affect nonchalance.

'You should ask Caroline where she buys that kind of thing,' said Stephen. 'Perhaps you could get some new tennis clothes for yourself.'

'At these prices? I don't think so!' Annie's eyes crinkled with amusement. 'If you only knew what this little crocodile costs!'

'Even so,' said Stephen robustly. 'You deserve a few nice things.'

'I've got plenty of nice things,' she retorted. 'A particularly lovely brown coat, for example.' Stephen's mouth twisted into a smile in spite of himself. The brown coat had been donated to Annie by his mother, a well-meaning lady who had spied it at a church bazaar and thought it just the thing for her busy daughter-in-law. It had orange stitching around the lapels, a virulent green lining, and, as Annie often observed, about twenty-five years' life still in it. It hung on the kitchen peg, so that Mrs Fairweather could see it when she came to babysit, and it never ventured out of the house.

'Perhaps we should sew a little green crocodile onto that,' said Stephen.

Caroline and Valerie came out onto the terrace, Valerie's left hand decorated with a plaster.

'Good thing it wasn't your right hand,' said Annie, watching her pick up her racquet.

'I don't know,' said Valerie doubtfully. 'The thing is, I've got a double-handed backhand.'

'It wasn't a deep cut,' said Caroline dismissively. 'Just a scratch. You'll be fine.'

Valerie made a few cautious swings with her racquet and winced slightly. 'I'll be OK,' she said.

'Perhaps we should be given a handicap,' said Don in a semi-jovial tone. 'A couple of points per set or something.' Patrick looked up and gave an uncertain laugh.

'That's getting a bit technical for me,' he said.

'It's not important,' said Don. 'It's just that if Valerie's at a disadvantage because of her hand . . .' The two men stared at each other, and Annie suddenly realized that Don was serious. She stared at Valerie's hand. The plaster was about an inch long. She couldn't possibly have hurt herself badly.

'Valerie,' she said, 'do you really think your tennis is going to be affected?' Valerie looked up with a pained expression.

'Oh no, I shouldn't think it'll really matter. I mean, if I try to avoid playing on my backhand . . .'

'Good,' said Caroline loudly, lighting a cigarette. 'Then you won't need a handicap, will you? Right, let's get started.' She swept Valerie off the terrace and down the grassy path to the tennis court, giving Don a contemptuous glance as she did so. The others followed meekly behind in silence. The path led down a slight incline to the tennis court, surrounded by hedges and with a lawned area for viewing. It was a grass court, in immaculate condition, and Annie stared with pleasure at the inviting soft greenness.

'Lovely!' she said. Patrick turned and smiled at her.

'Looking good, isn't it?'

'I've always said this is a fine court,' said Don surprisingly. 'You've heard about the American at Wimbledon? He asked the groundsman how to get a court into that condition. "It's very simple," said the groundsman. "You just roll it and water it, roll it and water it . . . for a hundred years."' Don looked around with a pleased look. 'Nothing finer than a good English grass court. Although, of course, it's not a surface I'm used to. Too fast, you see.'

'We both usually play on all-weather courts,' put in Valerie. 'Grass is quite different.'

'So you'll have to excuse us while we accustomize,' said Don cheerfully to Caroline. 'You'll probably wipe the floor with us to begin with.'

'I expect we will,' agreed Caroline in a bored voice. Patrick shot her a look and gave a little laugh.

'I shouldn't think that's very likely,' he said. 'You sound very professional. I'm afraid we hardly ever get to play.'

'Aha!' said Don, with a knowing expression. 'It's always the ones who say they never play! Don't believe a word of it, Val!'

As he and Valerie went onto the court, and Annie and Stephen sat down on the bank to watch, Caroline beckoned to Patrick.

'Out of interest,' she said sweetly, 'why the fuck did we invite Don?' Patrick looked uncomfortable.

'He's not so bad really,' he said. 'I didn't realize he'd take it all so seriously. Besides,' he added defensively, 'Don's quite a good client of mine. It doesn't hurt to show a bit of goodwill.'

'Oh, for Christ's sake! I should have known it was something like that.' She looked sideways at Patrick. 'I suppose that's why you invited the Mobyns, wasn't it? Because they're good clients?' Patrick shrugged and looked away. 'This is supposed to be a party, Patrick. For our friends. Not some bloody corporate hospitality event.' She took a furious drag on her cigarette. Patrick glared at her.

'Just remember,' he hissed, 'that it's people like Don who pay for all of this, for your new tennis racquet and your new hairdo and those poncey cigarettes. Not to mention the house, and the car, and the pony . . .' He broke off as Don came to the side of the court.

'Discussing tactics, are you?' he said in a jovial voice. 'Now remember, no playing on Valerie's injured hand.'

'Oh for Christ's sake,' muttered Caroline.

'Of course we won't,' said Patrick loudly. He avoided Caroline's gaze. 'Right, come on, darling. Let's give them hell.' He grinned at Don who chuckled appreciatively. Caroline rolled her eyes and stubbed out her cigarette.

As the four began to knock up, it was soon obvious that Don and Valerie were serious players. Valerie was slogging the ball determinedly at Patrick, while Don was hitting cunningly sliced shots to Caroline. She swiped wildly at each spinning ball, then stared in distaste as it swerved away beyond her reach.

'These balls aren't bouncing properly,' she announced eventually. 'I'm sure that's not allowed.'

'It's called a spin shot,' said Patrick. 'It's perfectly legal.' Caroline gazed at him crossly.

'Well, it's fucking annoying.'

'It's the action of the racquet, you see,' put in Don. 'It's very simple.'

'Well, could you not do it, please?' said Caroline firmly. 'It really puts me off.'

Don and Valerie stared at her in amazement. Patrick smiled hastily at them.

'Caroline's sense of humour on court is something else,' he said. 'You mustn't take her seriously.'

Don and Valerie won the toss and chose to serve. Patrick waited, eyes narrowed, as Don bounced the ball twice, drew back his racquet with a contorted, looped action, and hit the ball smartly over the net. Patrick lunged for it and promptly sent it out.

'Bad luck, Patrick, good serve, Dad,' hooted Valerie. She was standing right up at the net, jumping up and down, clearly ready to blast to oblivion any shots that came her way.

'Patrick, that was complete crap,' said Caroline loudly. Annie, sitting on the bank, began to giggle.

'Look at Valerie's face,' she whispered to Stephen.

Valerie gazed in bemused horror at Caroline as she sauntered to the back of the court. She turned to exchange looks with Don, but he hadn't heard Caroline's comment and was preparing to serve again. He bounced the ball twice, tossed it up, and hit it elaborately to Caroline's forehand. Caroline drew back her racquet and slammed the ball straight at Valerie.

'Ouch!' cried Valerie, clutching her shoulder.

'Sorry, Valerie,' drawled Caroline. 'I was trying to pass you. Fifteen-all, I think that is.'

Stephen caught Annie's eye and snorted with laughter. 'This is priceless.' He got up, and took her empty glass. 'I'll get some more drinks. Tell me what happens while I'm away.' Annie nodded, then leant back on the grass, feeling pleasurably the cool blades of grass against her bare arms; closing her eyes and listening to the irregular sound of ball against racquet. Thwack, thwack, thwack. 'Out!' 'Fucking hell!' 'Thirty-fifteen.' Then silence, then thwack, thwack, thwack, again.

Annie felt calm, happy, slightly numbed from the alcohol, and almost perfectly content. She was suddenly reminded of summer afternoons at school, lying by the tennis courts, listening dreamily to the sound of the players, with nothing to worry about but prep and choir practice and what would be for supper. Although of course, she reminded herself sternly, some of those things had been far more worrying at the time than they sounded now. Double biology had blighted her week far more than any of the duties she had to carry out nowadays. But still, in retrospect, she thought, her life was easy then. It had order, proportion and a definite framework constructed by others. What would the school timetablers make of her life as it was at the moment? Inefficient, rushed and ill-proportioned? Or maybe hers didn't count any more. As a mother, perhaps her function was simply to make sure her children's lives were as ordered as her own had been.

As the thought of the children passed through her head, she experienced the customary irrational stab of fear that she always had when they weren't in front of her—that they were in danger, injured, killed, through her own irresponsible fault. But the dart of pain as her heart jumped was muffled; the sensation of fear slight. They were with Georgina, a sensible girl; Stephen was up at the house and would hear any screams of distress; she was feeling too indolent to get worked up. She felt her mind drift further and further away from consciousness. Should she make an effort to watch the game? Or should she allow herself to fall asleep?

She was woken what seemed like a moment later by Stephen placing an ice-cube on her forehead.

'Aah!' she screamed, and opened her eyes to see his upside-down laughing face above her. 'You rotter!'

'I think Valerie should be allowed to take that serve again,' came a voice from the court. She swivelled her head, to see Don gazing disapprovingly at her.

'This is quite an important point,' he added meaningfully.

'What's the score?' called Stephen cheerily.

'Three-all in the tie-break,' said Don, and turned back. 'Take two, Val.'

'I told you to watch and tell me what happened,' complained Stephen quietly as he sat down beside Annie. 'I've obviously missed all the excitement.'

'Well, what took you so long?' retorted Annie.

'It took me half an hour to find the kitchen,' said Stephen. 'And another half-hour to find the ice-cube dispenser. But I knew madam wouldn't like her Pimm's warm.'

'You were right there,' agreed Annie. She took several long gulps of the amber liquid.

'Mmm, lovely.'

'Good stuff, isn't it?' agreed Stephen. 'Now, tell me how a tie-break works.'

'Three-six,' called Don.

'Don and Valerie need one more point to win,' said Annie. 'Look, we must watch.'

Patrick was preparing to serve. The first went slamming into the net.

'Fault,' said Don and Valerie in unison.

Patrick threw up the second ball and sent it gently curving over the net, landing neatly in the service box.

'Foot-fault,' came Don's voice. Valerie, who had been running for the shot, stopped in her tracks.

'Was it?' she said breathlessly.

'Foot-fault?' said Caroline incredulously.

'I'm afraid so,' said Don. 'I saw it quite clearly. Your foot was over the line. If you're not happy about it, we could play the point again . . .' He raised his eyebrows at Valerie.

'No, no,' said Patrick, attempting a genial voice. 'I'm sure you're right. So that must be . . .'

'Our set,' said Valerie promptly. 'And match.'

'Well, what a thrilling end,' said Caroline, in sarcastic tones. Patrick glanced at her sharply.

'Was that really a foot-fault?' Annie asked Stephen quietly. He shrugged.

'Christ knows. I can't see from here.'

'I shouldn't think Don can see very clearly, either,' she said, catching his eye meaningfully. They both turned and looked at Don, shaking hands with a beaming face. He looked utterly satisfied with himself.

'Oh well,' said Stephen. 'If it's that important to him . . .'

'I suppose so,' said Annie. 'But it doesn't seem fair, somehow. You shouldn't just get things because they're important to you.'

'Shouldn't you?' said Stephen. 'I don't see why not.'

Annie thought for a moment, and opened her mouth to reply,

but was stopped by the approach of Don and Patrick, striding up the grass bank.

'Well done,' she said in a hearty voice. 'What a close match.'

'Wasn't it just,' said Don. 'There were some good rallies there.'

'Especially the last one,' came Caroline's voice from behind. 'That was a corker.'

Annie looked down, and tried not to giggle.

'Who's on next?' she said hurriedly. 'Is it us?'

'You against Charles and Cressida,' said Patrick. 'When they arrive.'

'Tell you what,' said Annie to Stephen, 'let's go and get some practice in.'

She led Stephen down to the court and they began to knock up. The others watched for a few shots. Annie clearly played competent schoolgirl tennis—but Stephen could barely get the ball over the net.

'Sorry,' he kept saying. 'Damn. Sorry, could you get that?'

Caroline watched as Don's face relaxed at the sight. Nothing to worry about there, he was clearly thinking; he and Valerie would soon have that two off the court. Suddenly, Caroline detested him intensely.

'Darling, I'm going to go up to the house,' said Patrick softly, coming over to her. 'I've got a bit of business to look at—and I'll be there if the Mobyns arrive. All right?'

'I suppose so,' said Caroline, morosely lighting a cigarette. She couldn't think why she had looked forward to this fucking party.

'You played really well,' said Patrick, even more quietly.

'Tell that to your friend Don,' said Caroline, blowing smoke into Patrick's face. Patrick shrugged resignedly.

'I know,' he said. 'You don't have to tell me.'

Caroline watched his stumpy form disappear up the path with a mixture of dislike and resignation. She then turned her gaze to the tennis court. Stephen was preparing to serve. He threw the ball far too high, took back his old wooden racquet in an inexpert swing, and whacked it over the hedge.

'Blast,' he said. 'I'd better go and get that.'

Caroline closed her eyes. What a crew of men. Bloody Patrick, odious Don, and Stephen, who, with his old shorts and stringy legs, was clearly a complete incompetent. She'd always thought he was a bit odd—and now, look at him, couldn't even play a decent game of tennis, let alone earn enough to buy his wife some proper clothes. She couldn't think how Annie managed to stay so happy, with that wimp around her the whole time. Then a picture of Patrick came into her mind—and she couldn't think how she stayed so fucking cheerful herself.

CHAPTER THREE

Patrick was in his study when the Mobyns' Bentley pulled into the drive. He glanced out of the window when he heard the low, discreet hum of the engine, and gazed at the distinguished curves of the car with a mixture of envy, resentment and a thudding excitement. He saw the car pause, and glimpsed a blond head looking about as if uncertain of where to park. The natural reaction would have been for him to bang on the study window, shout a greeting and then hurry outside to welcome the family. But Patrick sat where he was. He wasn't ready yet to see Charles.

Caroline appeared around the corner of the house, carrying a tray of drinks. She shouted something to Charles, who promptly stopped the engine. The car door opened, and he got out, stretching his legs and looking about him appraisingly. Then the nanny, a dumpy girl of about nineteen, got out of the back. She heaved a large, squashy hold-all out onto the ground, and delved back inside the car for the twins—identical blond toddlers, who began walking off in different directions as soon as she put them down. Last to appear was Cressida. Long legs, immaculately clad in beige trousers; smooth, bobbed, pale-blond hair; a calm, unlined face. She greeted Caroline with a blank smile and kissed her dispassionately on each cheek.

Patrick couldn't help comparing the two women as they stood together talking. Both blue-eyed blondes, both in good shape, both wearing expensive clothes. But Caroline was just a bit browner than Cressida; her hair was a bit brighter, her make-up a bit stronger, her voice quite a lot louder. Next to Cressida's understated elegance, her blue eyeliner and gold bracelets seemed a bit much. She suddenly burst into loud laughter, and Patrick saw Cressida smile politely at her, a look of slight incomprehension on her face. Charles was looking up at her in amusement. What on earth had Caroline been saying? Suddenly Patrick felt a wave of fierce affection for his wife. They were made of the same stuff as each other—something stronger, coarser, more highly flavoured than the Cressidas of this world.

He looked down at the papers on his desk. His year's performance figures stared back up at him. He had done well by any standards. For Christ's sake, he had sold those bloody investment plans to practically anything that moved. His total was twenty per cent higher than last year. But, of course, that wasn't good enough for the bastards. He'd hit all his targets last year—so this year they'd moved the targets up. He pulled out the firm's bonus chart. The highest bonus figure—one hundred thousand pounds—glowed enticingly at the top of the sheet. But to get that he still had to do a lot of business. His year ended in a week's time and he was still eighty thousand pounds short. It was almost worth putting the eighty thousand into a plan himself, to make sure he reached his hundred thousand bonus. Except that he didn't have that kind of capital. And he would never buy any of the investment plans he sold.

What he needed was for somebody to make a quick lump-sum investment of eighty thousand within the next week. He glanced out of the window again. Charles was carrying one of the twins over to be kissed by Caroline. He was laughing and looked relaxed—as well he might be, thought Patrick. It was all a far cry now from the days in Seymour Road, when Charles and Ella had cooked spaghetti every night and gone backpacking round Europe when they could afford it. Then, it had been Patrick who had helped Charles out, with a loan—admittedly relatively small—when Charles' print gallery had seemed about to fold. It had been Charles who had teased Patrick about money; had told him to relax, chill out, come round and smoke some grass with him and Ella.

And now he was driving a Bentley and wearing a navy-blue blazer. He didn't need anyone's help any more, least of all Patrick's. Cressida had paid the loan back in full as soon as she married Charles. Or perhaps it had even been before. She had clearly hated the idea of Charles being in debt to anyone. But as favours went, Patrick reckoned Charles still owed him one.

As Caroline led the way to the main guest room, Charles looked around, impressed by what he saw. Patrick had, of course, told them about his new house—but somehow Charles hadn't imagined anything so sumptuous. The whole place reminded him of early seventies James Bond films. Not at all in his or Cressida's style, of course—he could see her recoiling as they passed a fitted cocktail bar—but certainly luxurious and, he was sure, very expensive.

Although, of course, property out here was bound to be cheap compared to central Silchester, where they lived. And for a location like that of the house in which he and Cressida lived—right in the Cathedral Close, with a garden—well, anyone would have to pay a lot. Nevertheless, Charles began to feel a strange sensation of resentment as he passed along the cool corridors, glimpsing out of the window what looked suspiciously like a stable block in the distance. Since marrying Cressida, he had become accustomed to thinking of himself as the one who had made good; the one who was to be envied—and he had consciously avoided parading his luck in front of his old friends.

If he had ever given any thought to Patrick and his career, it was to marvel that he, Charles Mobyn, actually numbered a financial salesman among his friends; friends that now included the most accomplished, prominent and socially important people in the county. He knew Patrick made a lot of money—of course he did—but he never thought of this, this *salesman's* money as ever being transformed into anything that he, Charles, might covet. And yet, taking in the obvious comfort of Patrick's and

Caroline's life here, Charles couldn't resist making a brief, disloyal comparison with the house in the Cathedral Close—Georgian and listed, undoubtedly, but also rather gloomy, drafty and expensive to keep up.

The principal guest bedroom suite was a symphony of pink, from the headboard of the bed—shaped like a shell—to the tissues on the dressing table.

'I hope you've got everything you need,' said Caroline. 'If you want a Jacuzzi, just press the controls on the wall.'

'Very kind,' murmured Cressida chillingly.

'Right,' said Caroline. 'Well, see you downstairs.' The door closed, and Charles and Cressida looked at each other. Cressida touched the bedcover gingerly.

'Satin,' she said. She felt underneath. 'Satin sheets, too. Ghastly. I shan't be able to sleep.'

'I don't know,' said Charles. 'Satin sheets might be rather fun. And a Jacuzzi!'

Cressida sighed and dropped her bag on the floor with an air of forbearance. 'I'd better check that the children are all right.'

'I'm sure they're fine,' began Charles, but she disappeared out of the room. He dumped his bag on the bed and began to change swiftly into his tennis clothes.

By the time Cressida returned he was ready.

'They've got cotton sheets, thank God,' she said. 'Decorated with My Little Pony, needless to say.'

'Priceless!' said Charles. 'I must go and have a look. Is Martina all right?'

'She thinks it's all lovely,' said Cressida. 'She's got a blue, shiny quilt edged with polyester lace.' Charles grinned. Martina, their nanny, had spent her childhood in a cosy little box outside Bonn, and had not taken well to life in the Mobyns' house. She had trailed around miserably all winter clad in leg warmers and fingerless gloves, and there had been a memorable scene once when she had got unsuspectingly into a bath full of icy cold water. It had transpired that in Germany—or at least Martina's Germany—the plumbing never went wrong.

'Oh yes,' Cressida added, brandishing a sheaf of letters at Charles. 'She picked up the post on the way out and forgot to give it to us.' Charles grimaced.

'I thought the idea of going away for the weekend was to get away from all of that.'

'This is hardly "away for the weekend,"' said Cressida crushingly. 'It's not exactly like going down to the Blakes', is it?'

The Blakes lived in a mansion in Devon and were having a house party that weekend. Cressida had tried to persuade Charles to agree to chucking the tennis party and going to Devon instead, but he had proved immovable. They had almost had a serious row about it. Now he looked at her wearily.

'For God's sake, Cressida, we've been to the Blakes' house a million times. But we've never come here. These are my friends, you know.'

'I know they are,' said Cressida.

'It would be nice,' continued Charles, 'if I could feel they were your friends too.'

'Well, I don't think that's very likely somehow,' said Cressida. He looked at her furiously.

'Why not? Why can't you at least try?'

'Oh Charles, honestly! What on earth have we got in common?'

'You've got me in common,' said Charles. 'Shouldn't that be enough?' He picked up his racquet. 'I'm going outside. It's too hot in here.'

Outside, in the corridor, he saw Martina and the twins emerging from their bedroom.

'Hello there!' he said cheerfully. 'Everything all right?'

'Everything is fine,' said Martina. 'This is a very nice house. So big, so beautiful . . .' She gestured admiringly.

'Well, yes, I suppose it is in its own way,' said Charles. 'All right, boys?' He looked down at the twins. 'Oh no!' They had sidled over to an alcove by the window. Ben was about to put a glass elephant in his mouth and James was tugging at a pale curtain with chocolate-covered fingers.

'Mrs Chance, she gave the boys chocolate biscuits,' said Martina apologetically, pulling James' hands away and wiping them with a tissue. 'I tried to tell her that Mrs Mobyn did not like it, but she wouldn't listen.'

'Don't worry,' said Charles, removing the elephant from Ben's grasp. Ben's face crumpled, and he held his hands up entreatingly to his father. 'No, Ben. It's dangerous. Let's get these horrors outside.'

'Mrs Chance said we should go and look at the horse,' said Martina doubtfully.

'Grand idea,' said Charles. 'Do you want to see a horse, Ben?' Ben made a grab for the elephant again.

'See the horsey?' said Charles encouragingly, putting the elephant carefully back on its display table and carrying Ben off down the corridor. 'See the horsey?'

'Horsey,' echoed Martina, picking up James. 'We go to see the horsey.'

'She's not a horsey,' said Georgina cuttingly. 'She's a pony.'

'Of course she is,' agreed Charles hurriedly. They had arrived at the paddock to find Georgina leading Arabia round the perimeter while Nicola sat astride, clutching the reins awkwardly and beaming with pleasure. Toby sat peacefully on the fence watching, a placid little boy with a sunny smile. When she saw them, Georgina turned round and brought Arabia up to the fence.

'Isn't she gorgeous!' she said proudly. She buried her face in the pony's mane. 'You're so beautiful!' she murmured.

'Georgina's teaching me to ride,' said Nicola. 'I can walk.'

'Very good!' applauded Charles. He held Ben up to see.

'Look, Ben! Look at the lovely hor . . . er pony!'

Martina was cowering behind, staring distrustfully at Arabia.

'Bring James nearer so he can see,' said Charles. He turned round. 'What's wrong, Martina? Don't you like horses?' Martina stepped forward nervously a pace or two, then retreated as Arabia threw up her head and whinnied. Ben looked up at Charles, his eyes huge with astonishment.

'Come on,' said Georgina impatiently. 'Let's go round again, and trot this time. You'd better put a hat on.'

Charles watched compassionately as Nicola fumbled with the chin strap of the hard hat. Her poor right hand struggled to keep up with the left, and she grunted several times in frustration as the webbing slipped out of its buckle. Georgina watched without expression, neither hurrying Nicola nor offering assistance. Martina gave an initial exclamation as she saw Nicola's jerky hand moving uncertainly up to her chin—but, after a look from Charles, kept quiet.

'Right,' said Georgina, when Nicola had eventually succeeded. 'Let's go.' She pulled gently on Arabia's reins, turned round, and began to walk around the paddock, gradually increasing her pace to a run.

'Hold on!' she shouted at Nicola. 'Go up and down when she starts trotting!'

It was an unexpectedly moving sight. Georgina's hair streamed behind her in the sunlight as she jogged round the paddock; meanwhile, Nicola bounced up and down with a mixture of delight and terror on her face. Charles stole a look at the faces of the twins. They were both staring enraptured at the scene.

Eventually Georgina led Arabia back up to the fence.

'Do you want a go, Toby? You can't go on your own, but you could sit in front of me,' she said. Toby giggled and shook his head.

'I suppose these two are too small,' said Charles, gesturing to the twins.

'Yes, they are a bit,' said Georgina. 'They probably couldn't even sit on a pony without falling off.'

'I'd love them to learn to ride,' said Charles. 'Perhaps when they're a bit older.'

'You wouldn't need to buy two ponies,' said Georgina. 'If they stay the same size they could always share one.'

'Maybe,' said Charles. 'Ponies are very expensive creatures.'

'So what?' said Georgina disconcertingly. 'You must be able to afford it now you're so rich.'

As Cressida unpacked her clothes, carefully shaking out the creases as she had been taught at school, a frown furrowed her brow. Charles was angry with her for being rude about his friends—and perhaps she had been a bit blunt—but what was she supposed to say? Surely he could see that she could never become friendly with that jumped-up salesman and his tarty wife?

It did not occur to Cressida that her own father had been, in his own way, a salesman himself. Owners of large factories were not, in her mind, at all the same thing as vulgar men like Patrick, who, she noticed, hadn't even bothered to come and greet his guests. Besides, it was her mother, the aristocratic Antonia Astley, with whom Cressida identified most strongly. Her mother had always avoided becoming friendly with the wives of her husband's colleagues. 'Think of yourself as a precious present,' she had once said to Cressida, 'not to be squandered on whoever happens across you first.' She had, of course, been talking about sex, Cressida now realized—but it was actually a useful principle for friendships in general.

The trouble was, people like the Chances had no idea of graduating slowly towards friendship—they seemed to treat every chance acquaintance as familiarly as they did each other. Cressida shrank from the kisses, jokes, references and banter which surrounded this kind of event. Caroline, in particular, was the kind of woman who would soon assume an intimacy which Cressida was far from sharing; who would quiz her on intimate subjects and then perhaps even refer to them in front of strangers. It was safer, Cressida thought, to keep one's distance right from the start, before things got out of hand.

She recalled a woman whom she'd met once on holiday staying in a friend's apartment at Menton. The woman had been amiable enough as a beach companion; they had lent each other sun cream, magazines and books. But her conversation had gradually turned to areas which Cressida rarely discussed with anybody, let alone a stranger. She had become more and more persistent, first laughing at Cressida, then becoming offended, and calling Cressida a stuck-up cow. It had been even worse when it transpired that the woman was quite a friend of George Wallace, whose apartment Cressida was staying in.

She frowned uncomfortably at the memory and began to change into her tennis dress. She felt upset by Charles' determined affection for the Chances, and not just because they were not her sort of people. It was also because the Chances—together with just about everyone else here, probably—belonged to that time of Charles' life which Cressida preferred not to think about; the period before he had met her, when he had been living in Seymour Road with that woman (Cressida never articulated Ella's name, even in her thoughts). Of course, everyone could see now that she would have been all wrong for him. But Cressida still felt sometimes that the Seymour Road crowd thought it a shame that he'd left her. There had certainly been a bad atmosphere among them at the wedding.

They'd managed to avoid seeing any of them since then, apart from the odd chance meeting in Silchester—and Cressida had thought that would be the end of it. But then, after months of silence, the invitation had appeared from Patrick and Caroline, warmly pressing them to come and play tennis.

She finished buttoning up her tennis dress, carefully brushed her hair with her Mason Pearson brush and looked in the mirror. Her legs were carefully waxed, her hair well cut and her face discreetly made up. But it did not occur to Cressida to stare at herself gloatingly or try to imagine the appearance she would make on the court. She turned round briefly to check that her dress was straight at the back. Then she turned her attention to the letters still lying on the bed. Perhaps she should go through them. That would please Charles. He always complained that she never opened a letter unless she recognized the handwriting on the envelope.

But a shout from outside distracted her. She went to the window and saw Charles looking up. He was grinning broadly and looked as though he'd been running.

'Come on, Cress!' he shouted. 'It's lovely out here!' Cressida smiled in slight relief. He wasn't angry any more.

'All right!' she called. 'I'm coming!' And without giving the letters another thought, she hurried out of the room.

When they arrived at the tennis court, they found Annie and Stephen knocking up. Caroline was lying in a deck chair, smoking a cigarette and applauding; Patrick was nowhere to be seen.

'We're a bit out of condition, I'm afraid,' said Stephen.

'Speak for yourself,' retorted Annie as they came off court. She kissed Charles. 'It's super to see you!' she said.

'Hello, Cressida,' said Stephen. 'How are you?'

'What a lovely name!' piped up Valerie. 'I don't think I've heard that one before. Is it from a book?' Cressida gave her a look of astonishment.

'Charles, Cressida,' said Stephen, hiding a smile, 'meet Don and Valerie Roper.'

'How do you do?' said Cressida.

'Don lives in our village,' called Caroline from the deck chair, her voice husky with cigarette smoke. The thought seemed to tickle her, and she started laughing rather drunkenly.

'Pleased to meet you,' said Don, nodding at Charles.

'Don and Valerie have just thrashed us,' said Caroline. 'It was a thrilling match, ending on a foot-fault.'

'Ooh!' said Valerie, then blushed as everyone looked at her.

Caroline had swivelled round in her chair to look at Cressida.

'I love your dress,' she announced. 'Where did you get it?' Cressida forced herself to smile at Caroline.

'I had it made for me,' she said.

'I might have known,' said Caroline, in slightly mocking tones. 'There you are, Annie, you think I've got a good wardrobe, but I've never had anything made for me. I bet that cost a packet, didn't it?' Cressida's hand tightened round her racquet, and she laughed lightly.

'Go on, how much? Two hundred? Three hundred?'

'Really?' said Annie. 'Would it be that much?'

'Might be more,' said Caroline. 'Or might be less. Depends if a designer makes it or your granny makes it!' she cackled with laughter again. 'Actually,' she added, 'I don't think I'd like to have my things made for me. I mean, the whole point of buying clothes is going and trying them on in the shop.' She smiled reminiscently. 'When I was young,' she said, 'I used to spend my entire Saturday going round Biba and Mary Quant, trying on clothes. It was great. You just stripped off what you were wearing and tried everything on in the shop. Once I walked right out of Biba wearing a brand-new outfit!'

'But that's shop lifting!' said Valerie, in a shocked voice.

'No it isn't,' said Caroline scathingly. 'I didn't mean to do it. I just forgot what I was wearing when I went in.'

Charles had turned to Annie. 'I've just seen Nicola trotting round the paddock on Georgina's pony. She was doing very well.'

'She's talked about nothing else for the last few days,' said Annie, smiling. 'She simply adores coming here. And Georgina's very good with her.'

'So I noticed,' said Charles. 'There's a lot to that young lady.'

'Are they still in the paddock?' asked Annie. 'I might go and have a look.'

Charles shook his head.

'They were just finishing,' he said. 'Georgina was beginning to organize them all into some game or other. Including our two,' he added to Cressida, 'and Martina, believe it or not. That's our nanny,' he explained. 'Georgina seems to have her well under control.'

'What on earth are they all doing?' said Annie. 'They're a bit of a mixed bag to be playing together.' Charles shrugged.

'I don't want to know. Let them get on with it.' He looked up and gave a smile of surprise. 'At last! Patrick, where have you been?' He went forward and grasped Patrick warmly by the hand.

'I'm sorry I wasn't around when you arrived,' said Patrick. 'Ah, Cressida, there you are.' As he went to kiss her, his eyes fell on Caroline's grinning face and he looked away. 'Right, who's on next?'

'Annie and Stephen,' said Don. 'Against Charles and Cressida, as a matter of fact.'

'Splendid,' said Charles. 'Come on, Cress, let's go and warm up.'

The Mobyns made an elegant couple on court, both well-schooled in the strokes, agile and deft. Cressida began hitting some practice serves, and Don turned to Valerie.

'I can see we've some competition here,' he said. 'Look at the way her serve spins away from the forehand. You'll have to be careful with that.' Valerie was staring, awe-struck, at Cressida.

'She's really good,' she said.

'His serve is harder, but probably easier to return. More straightforward,' continued Don.

'She looks a bit like Princess Diana,' said Valerie. Stephen raised his eyebrows at Annie.

'Well, you never know,' he said conversationally. 'She might be related to her.'

'Ooh! Really?' Valerie swung round.

'I don't think so,' said Annie firmly, glaring at Stephen. But he was not to be put off.

'Her mother was the Honourable something,' he said thoughtfully. 'Or was it Lady something? Very smart, anyway, I know that much. And I'm sure I've heard something about a royal connection.' He nodded wisely at Valerie, who was staring at him, agog.

'Well,' she said, 'I must say . . .'

'Valerie,' interrupted Don, 'watch the way Cressida guards the net. She'll be difficult to pass. Look, her eye never leaves the ball.'

Annie and Stephen joined the court and began to knock up with Charles and Cressida. Both Charles and Cressida considerately modified their games slightly as they realized the standard of the Fairweathers. But even so, every second ball Stephen hit seemed to go in the net. Annie was slightly better, but as Charles gave her a few practice volleys, she turned and looked at Stephen in dismay.

'He hits it so hard!' she wailed. 'I'll never get any of these!'

'Don't worry,' said Stephen. 'It's the playing that counts.'

'Yes, but what if you can't play?'

Caroline was watching Cressida critically.

'She thinks she's in bloody Wimbledon or something,' she said disparagingly.

'Who, Annie?' said Patrick in mock surprise. 'I wouldn't have said so.'

'Very funny,' said Caroline. 'Just look at her,' she persisted, watching as Cressida neatly put away a backhand volley. 'Thinks she's a bloody pro.'

'She's got a nice technique,' said Patrick. 'We could all learn from her.' He looked around. 'Where's Georgina? She should watch a bit of this.'

'Christ knows,' said Caroline. 'She said she'd be ballgirl. That didn't last long.'

'The play's *The Three Little Pigs*,' said Georgina firmly. 'The reason is, we all know the story, and the little ones can be the pigs.' She looked at the twins. 'Can you be pigs?'

'The pigs are the most important people,' objected Nicola.

'No they're not,' said Georgina. 'The wolf is more important than the pigs.'

'Who's the wolf?'

'I am.'

Nicola felt a familiar crushing sense of disappointment come over her. It was to be the same here as it was everywhere. She looked down, nursing her bad hand, and remembered countless nativity plays, school concerts, speech days; endless conversations held over her head by people who thought she couldn't understand: *'That little Fairweather girl—we're going to have to put her at the back'; 'Poor little thing, we'll have to take her out of the dancing'; 'She really can't manage—can we find her something else to do?'*

'But the most important of all,' continued Georgina, 'is the man who sells the straw and the twigs and the bricks to the three little pigs.'

'What?' Nicola was confused. She didn't even remember that there was a man. 'Is he in the Ladybird book?'

'I can't remember,' admitted Georgina. 'But he must have been there. They didn't just find the straw and things on the road, did they? And if they hadn't bought such stupid stuff to build their houses with, the wolf wouldn't have got them. Would he?' She looked impressively at Nicola.

'Except the bricks,' said Nicola, who had a logical mind.

'Except the bricks,' agreed Georgina.

Nicola was beginning to feel a faint ray of hope. But such rays were deceptive, she knew from experience. She put her head down again.

'Aren't you going to ask who's the man who sells the straw and twigs to the little pigs?' demanded Georgina.

'Who's the man who sells the straw?' mumbled Nicola. There was a silence, and she cautiously looked up. Georgina was grinning at her.

'You, stupid! It's you, of course!' Nicola started to smile, and instead broke into laughter; loud laughter, that emptied her lungs of breath and filled her face with colour. Instinctively, Georgina leaned over and gave her a hug. Martina, who had sat silently watching all of this, suddenly appeared overcome by emotion and looked away.

'Look at her,' said Georgina. 'She's crying. Soppy.' She began to giggle, and Nicola, strung up, began to join in almost hysterically. Toby, who had wandered off, came back and started laughing companionably with them, whereupon Martina harumphed crossly and got up.

'You can't go!' said Georgina. 'You've got to look after the twins.'

'Perhaps she should be in the play,' said Nicola reasonably. 'She could be mother pig.'

'All right,' said Georgina. 'Martina!' she called. 'Will you be a mother pig?'

Martina glared at Georgina, muttered something in German, picked up the twins and stalked off towards the house.

'I don't think she understood,' said Georgina, beginning to laugh. 'I think she thought I was *calling* her a mother pig.' The three children fell on their backs in the sun in fits of giggles.

'Mother pig!' gasped Nicola, fuelling fresh paroxysms of mirth.

When she couldn't laugh any more, she lay still, giving the odd gurgle, staring up at the sky and smelling the mixture of grass, earth, and the scent of Arabia on her clothes.

'I'm really glad we're staying the night,' she said lazily. 'I wish we lived here all the time.' Then she wished she hadn't said it. Georgina would think she was soppy. She stole a look at her. Georgina was lying flat on her back, staring straight up at the sky. Slowly she turned and looked at Nicola with fierce blue eyes.

'So do I,' she said.

CHAPTER FOUR

Lunch was served on the terrace. Mrs Finch, Caroline's daily, had appeared towards the end of the match and called uncompromisingly from the top of the path, 'Mrs Chance, I'm here.'

'Oh hello, Mrs Finch,' shouted Caroline, turning towards her and causing Cressida to lose concentration and hit her first serve in the net. 'Can you dole out the lunch? You know where it all is. And then perhaps tidy up a bit.' Cressida was waiting patiently to serve. 'Sorry about this,' called Caroline cheerfully. 'All right, Mrs Finch?'

'Yes, Mrs Chance.'

So this was Mrs Finch, thought Annie, glancing up from the court. Not the apple-cheeked retainer that Annie had imagined whenever Caroline had referred to her, but a thin, determined-looking woman in her mid-thirties, with dyed-red, curly hair. She had the local accent, but her voice was sharp and strident; she and Caroline had obviously failed to get a cosy employer-employee relationship going.

Annie watched Mrs Finch survey with disapproval the dishevelled scene of tennis racquets, bottles, ashtrays and glasses, then pick up her shopping bag and disappear up the path. Perhaps her family once owned the village, thought Annie romantically. Perhaps she can't bear to come back and clean the house where her grandfather was once lord. Then it occurred to her that The White House was only about ten years old. But maybe this had been the site of the manor.

'Annie!' Annie started as the ball went whizzing past her.

'Gosh, sorry,' she said, and giggled guiltily. 'I wasn't concentrating.'

'Game, set and match,' said Stephen.

'Oh no! Did I just lose us the match? How awful.'

'Six-one,' said Charles, approaching the net, hand outstretched. 'Thanks very much. Good game.'

'You are kind, Charles,' said Annie. 'I should think you were bored rigid.'

As she came off court, her mind returned to Mrs Finch.

'Valerie,' she said. 'Is there a manor house in the village? Or was there ever?'

'Ooh!' said Valerie. 'Didn't you know? Dad bought the old manor house. He's going to turn it into a hotel. It's ever so pretty.'

'Oh,' said Annie, disappointed.

'Are we changing for lunch?' asked Cressida.

'Christ, no,' said Caroline. 'Unless it's into a bikini. I wouldn't mind doing a bit of sunbathing.'

The players collapsed on the grass and Patrick began dispensing the drinks.

'I might have a go at the Pimm's,' said Valerie. 'This fruit cocktail's really delicious,' she added to Caroline. 'I can't think what you put in it.'

'Most refreshing,' agreed Don, who was reclining on the grass. 'And a very interesting flavour to it.' He smiled beatifically. Annie gave Valerie another glance. Her cheeks were pink and she seemed in very good spirits.

'Let me try it,' she said casually, taking a sip from Valerie's glass. 'Ahh, I see what you mean,' she said, catching Caroline's eye. Caroline snorted into her glass of Pimm's. 'Maybe you should stay with it if you're going to play again later.'

'Nonsense,' said Don jovially. 'This is a party, is it not? I always say, it's a mistake to take the sporting side of these events too seriously.'

'I hear you're going to open a hotel,' said Stephen conversationally to Don.

'That's right! I've found a super location here in Bindon. The old manor house, no less. Bound to be a winner. Although it still needs a lot of work done to it.' His face clouded over slightly. 'It's been an expensive business.'

'Were you in the hotel trade before?'

'Me? No! I trained as an accountant. Worked in the City for twenty years, then thought, Sod this, I'm going to do something

I enjoy. Fine wines, good food, company all the year round—
and a beautiful house. What could be better?'

'It sounds wonderful,' said Annie. 'When do you open?' Don
drew in breath sharply.

'We were scheduled to open this autumn,' he said. 'Now it
looks as though it'll be Christmas. There's still some building
and decorating work to be done, and getting the brochures
ready. Valerie's going to take care of that. Then all I need to do
is find a good cook and a housekeeper—someone with a bit of
class. You know what I mean.' He looked at Annie thoughtfully.
'In fact, if you hear of anyone—or any kind of hotel staff, come
to that—I'd be grateful if you'd send 'em my way. Can't run the
place all on my own!' Annie looked surprised, and glanced at
Don's wedding-ringed hand.

'So Valerie's mother . . .'

'Passed away three years ago,' said Don abruptly. 'Breast can-
cer. Fifty-three, she was. She went to the doctor as soon as she
found the lump, but it was already too late.'

'How terrible,' said Annie. 'I'm truly sorry.'

Don looked sharply at her. 'I hope you go for your scan every
year, do you?'

'Well,' said Annie hesitantly.

'Could have saved Irene, a scan could. If she'd only gone for a
check-up.'

'I'm not sure I qualify yet,' said Annie soothingly. 'But I will
find out.'

'Pay for one if you have to,' insisted Don. 'That's what I say to
all the ladies I meet now. Get yourself scanned. You never know.

I pay for Valerie to be scanned every year. I see it as a tribute, almost, to Irene.'

'How lovely,' said Annie awkwardly—then, aware that this didn't sound quite right, added, 'I mean, what a thoughtful gesture.'

They were interrupted by Caroline.

'Lunch is ready,' she said. 'And before you start saying how wonderful it is,' she added to Annie, 'I didn't cook it. The caterers did.'

Annie struggled to her feet, feeling the effect of a morning's drinking. The backs of her legs were covered in grass stains and the apricot tennis ensemble was looking rather rumpled. But I won't have to wash it, Mrs Finch will, she thought, and was amazed to discover how elated that made her feel.

The children were already on the terrace, piling their plates high with potato salad and crisps.

'What about some of this lovely vegetable terrine?' said Annie to Toby encouragingly. He wrinkled his nose and shook his head. 'Or some mushroom quiche?'

'Don't bother,' said Stephen idly. 'Let him eat what he wants. Potato salad and potato crisps. Obvious, really.'

Valerie was first to start filling her plate. She approached each dish with an exclamation of delight, and then loudly wondered what it was.

'Ooh! This looks like a swiss roll! But it must be savoury. How imaginative. I wonder what's in it. Is the green spinach?'

'Full of iron, spinach is,' observed Don. 'Ah, spring onions in the salad, I see. You know, they apparently reduce cholesterol.

Worth knowing, that is. Worth repeating, too.' He chortled merrily. 'Get it? Worth repeating. Spring onions.'

Valerie suddenly hooted with laughter. 'Ooh Dad, really!' She glanced at Cressida, standing at the other side of the terrace. 'What will people think?'

Cressida was not thinking of Don and his joke. She was wondering how early they could leave the next day without appearing rude. They would, presumably, attend church in the morning—and no doubt a large Sunday lunch would have been planned—but she didn't see why they shouldn't leave as soon as that was over. She would, however, have to broach the subject delicately with Charles. He seemed to be enjoying himself immensely, heaping food onto his plate in indiscriminate piles, and cheerily waving his glass in the air as he chatted to Caroline. She rarely saw him so abandoned. It was as if he was on holiday. But did that mean that everyday life with her was the equivalent of work? For a moment her mind teetered uneasily on the edge of the question, subconsciously aware that to answer it might be to come to some alarming, unwelcome conclusion. But even as she began to feel disturbed, her mind fluttered and lost grip of the problem, and her thoughts slid easily onto the more mundane reflection that Charles really should put a hat on in this sun.

Valerie came up to her, munching in an unattractive manner.

'You should have some lunch,' she said, 'it's delicious.'

'I will in a minute.'

'I suppose you're used to lovely food like this all the time,' continued Valerie. She gazed at Cressida admiringly. 'But you've got such a good figure. I expect you always just eat a little of everything, to be polite.' There was a pause, while Cressida tried to work out what this woman was talking about.

'I attend a lot of charity events,' she said eventually.

'Yes, you must do,' said Valerie. 'I suppose you've got loads of lovely ballgowns?' Cressida looked around for escape.

'If you'll excuse me, I think I'll go and get myself some lunch,' she said, giving Valerie a taut smile.

'That's all right,' said Valerie brightly. 'I could do with some seconds myself.'

After lunch, no one seemed inclined to move. Everyone lolled on chairs or on the grass, except for Cressida, who was sitting bolt upright, unable to escape Valerie's fawning commentary. Patrick looked around. Now may be the moment. He sauntered casually across to Charles, who was lying back with his eyes closed.

'Remember that collection of prints I started,' he remarked. 'Well, I've been adding to it.' Charles opened one eye.

'Really? What have you bought?' Patrick laughed.

'Now you've caught me. I can't even remember who they're by. They're both modern, though. Cost me a fair bit, too.'

'Where did you get them?' Charles' attention was now fully engaged. 'You could have come to us.'

'I know,' said Patrick. 'But these were impulse buys. In London.' Charles scowled.

'I expect you were robbed.'

'Probably. In fact, I was hoping you'd come and give them a look. Tell me just how much I was ripped off.'

'Now?'

'Why not? While everyone's asleep.' He surveyed the dozy

scene. 'I don't know how we're going to get anyone back on the tennis court this afternoon.'

Charles reluctantly got to his feet.

'OK, let's come and see the damage. Although I really wish you'd contain your impulses until you're in the Print Centre. Then you can be as impulsive as you like.'

'I'll remember that,' said Patrick, 'next time I'm feeling in the mood.'

Patrick's study was cool and tranquil, and for a few minutes the men blinked, trying to focus in the dim light. Charles sank into a leather sofa.

'This is a nice room,' he said. He looked around. 'I bet you haven't read all those books.'

'No, but I'm intending to,' said Patrick. 'Actually, Caroline bought a lot of these. Because they look nice, I think.' Charles shrugged.

'And why not? The book as a visual art form. I think it has potential. Why should we bother to read what's inside?' He reclined further into the squashy leather. 'So, show me these prints.'

'Here you are.' Patrick placed two small, unframed prints on his lap. Charles sat up and, with a practised eye, looked carefully at each, turning them over, scrutinizing the signature, examining the texture of the paper.

'Actually,' he said eventually, 'I think these are rather nice. Where did you get them?'

'Mocasins. Bond Street.' Charles sighed.

'Of course. My word, Patrick, you must be doing all right for yourself if you can afford to impulse buy there.'

Patrick shrugged. 'It's the right time to be investing. I realize it, my clients realize it. I mean, if I'm doing well, you should see how they're doing. If I had the money to invest properly in some of the ventures I know about . . . Well, let's just say I wouldn't be buying little prints; I'd be onto the big stuff by now.'

Charles was still examining the prints, and Patrick judged it best not to interrupt him.

'One of my clients,' he said, 'invested ten thousand pounds five years ago. Emerging markets, he went into. Now he's sitting on a hundred thousand.'

'Really?' murmured Charles absently.

'He said to me, "If I'd known that would happen, I would have invested ten times as much. I'd be a millionaire!"' Patrick laughed reminiscently. 'I said to him, "How do you think I feel? I did know that would happen—but I hadn't got anything to invest!"' He paused. 'And it's true. Those of us who know what's a sure winner can't take advantage of it—meanwhile, all the people who could afford to put their money in don't know about it!' He laughed gently. 'It's a crazy world.' Charles raised an eyebrow.

'Come on, Patrick, you must have a few thou lying around to invest.'

'I wish,' said Patrick. 'Look around. House, cars, pony. None of it comes cheap. But I can tell you, if I had the cash, I know exactly where I'd put it.' He stopped. 'Cigar?'

'Thanks.'

Patrick took his time snipping the cigars, picking up the onyx lighter, taking a few puffs, before continuing.

'There's an investment fund,' he said confidingly, 'which is going to blow all the others out of the water. No one knows about it yet. I'm not even telling all my clients. We've had a policy decision only to tell a few. Our most loyal customers. We're telling them now, while they can get in at a low price. It's a bit like a reward for staying with us over the years. And I can tell you, every single person we've told has snapped it up. We're almost oversubscribed.' Again he laughed gently. 'One man took all his money out of every single investment he held with us and put it all straight into the new fund. It caused a real headache, I can tell you! The administration was a nightmare.' He took a puff on his cigar. 'Not bad, these, are they?' Charles eyed him thoughtfully.

'I take it,' he said, 'that you're going to tell me why this fund is so marvellous. It would seem a bit cruel to lead me on so far, and then shut the door in my face.'

'Well,' Patrick seemed doubtful, 'I'm not really supposed to be telling anybody except our existing clients. But, since you were so good as to tell me I wasn't ripped off with those prints,' he laughed, 'I owe you one.' He took a breath. 'Where do I start? I suppose you're familiar with the idea of investing in international equities?'

'Stocks and shares,' said Charles.

'Right,' said Patrick. 'And are you familiar with the idea of investing in futures and options? That's to say, promising to buy shares in the future, at a certain price?' Charles shrugged.

'I dimly remember being told something about it once. What's that got to do with it?'

'Well,' said Patrick, 'this fund invests half in stocks, calculates which way the price is going to go, and then uses the other half to work the market with futures and options.' Charles shook his head.

'You've lost me. I was never any good at maths.'

'That's a shame. If you knew a bit more about it, you'd see the potential. If you're interested, I've got some graphs somewhere that explain how it works.'

Charles looked alarmed. 'I don't think so.' He looked at his watch. 'Shouldn't we be getting back?'

'Of course, that's not our only fund,' interrupted Patrick smoothly, 'although it's the most exciting. We've got some that are safe as houses—boring as bricks, we call them. It really depends what kind of attitude the investor has got to risk. I mean, take yourself. What kind of approach have you got to risk?'

'I don't really know,' said Charles, diverted briefly. 'It's quite an interesting question, isn't it? What is one's attitude to risk?' He puffed on his cigar. 'I mean, I suppose leaving Ella and marrying Cressida was quite a risk. But at the time it seemed the obvious thing to do.'

'Exactly,' said Patrick. 'That's the kind of problem our fund managers deal with all the time. Investing in a certain stock may seem the obvious thing to do—but sometimes you'll get far better results by doing the unobvious.'

Charles wasn't listening.

'I sometimes wonder what it was about Cressida that attracted me,' he said slowly. 'And I think it was that she was so different from Ella.' He pushed his hands through his hair, and stared ahead with a sudden bleak expression. 'Ella and I had been having problems—well, you know that. Most of it was over the gallery. I mean, it was so stupid, things we used to fight about. She used to get completely irrational in arguments, and that would drive me mad.' He winced at the memory. 'She's so passionate, Ella, and she believes in things so strongly, that she can't understand anyone who doesn't agree with her—or, even worse, doesn't really care. She used to accuse me of being too apathetic, of sitting on the fence. She really used to lay into me. And then one day, during all of that, I met Cressida. She was like an antidote to all the shouting and screaming. I mean, Cressida never even raises her voice.'

'She's a very elegant lady,' agreed Patrick. He left a decent interval of silence before saying, 'Now, I wonder what her attitude to risk is? In investment, I mean. Because—'

'Look, Patrick,' interrupted Charles in an exasperated voice, 'can't you see? I'm not interested. I'm sure you've got wonderful investment plans and there are all sorts of opportunities just dying to be exploited. But, if you don't mind, could you find someone else to do the exploiting? Our portfolio is managed by a very reputable company in London, and I'm afraid we haven't got any spare capital to put into any of your plans.' He looked at Patrick kindly. 'It's nothing personal. No hard feelings.'

Patrick stared at Charles through a haze of black and red. It wasn't possible that he had completely failed; that he hadn't even mustered ten or twenty thousand's worth of business. He thought of the hundreds of thousands that Charles must, *must* have under his control now, and his heart began to thump hard at the thought of his failing to garner any of it. The blind anger he felt towards Charles, still sitting there smiling at him, was tempered by the pragmatic realization that he must keep things on a pleasant basis. If it had been anyone else he would have launched into a more aggressive selling routine. But Charles wouldn't react well to that. And there was always the chance he might be interested in the future.

But underneath it all, Patrick knew that he had muffed it, probably for ever. Charles regarded him with an air of superiority that was hard to cut through; probably later he and Cressida would laugh about the way their oikish host had tried to flog them a dodgy investment plan. The thought drove out all pragmatism from Patrick's mind. Charles was looking fidgety; soon he would get up and go and the chance would be lost for ever.

'So who is it that manages your investments?' Patrick found himself saying. (What was he doing? Rule one: never refer to your opponents.) Charles gave him an amused look.

'As a matter of fact, it's Fountains. You know, the private bank.' Patrick summoned up a casually concerned look.

'Really? They're still taking on clients for portfolio management? I'm surprised.' (Rule two: never *ever* be derogatory about your opponents.) 'I heard they'd been going through a rough patch.'

'Really?' Charles regarded him with slight amusement. 'Well, I can assure you, Patrick, they've served us very well, and Cressida's family for the last fifty years. And that family certainly knows how to look after its money.' He made as if to get up. Patrick stared at him desperately, unable to stop him, but knowing that once he was outside the study door, all would be lost.

Suddenly his attention was caught by a small figure crossing the lawn outside the study window. It was Georgina, looking flushed and happy and hot, clutching a pile of straw and laughing something to Nicola, who followed. The sight of his beautiful daughter, who was the reason behind his efforts and yet was so entirely oblivious of them, sent waves of panic coursing through Patrick's body, as he observed Charles drawing his feet up, getting ready to make his departure.

'Just listen to what I've got to say,' he blurted out. 'It won't take long. Then you can talk to Cressida and make up your minds together. No pressure.' Charles' smile faded, to be replaced by a look of distaste.

'Look, Patrick, I don't think I can put it more plainly. I'm not interested in buying anything from you. Our money is doing quite nicely where it is.' He hesitated, and then added, 'And to be frank, I think it's a bit much trying to do business with one of your guests. This is supposed to be a party, isn't it? Keep your charts for the office.'

Patrick felt burning humiliation cover his face and his chest heaved.

'You weren't so picky when it was you who needed money, were you?' he shouted. His voice came out much more loudly than he had intended, and Charles, who had been getting up, sat down again in surprise. 'You weren't so picky,' said Patrick more quietly, 'when you needed that loan for your precious gallery, were you? Quite happy to come and talk business in my kitchen, you were then.'

'I know I was,' said Charles. 'I was very grateful and I still am. But that was entirely different.'

'No it wasn't,' said Patrick. 'One neighbour doing another a good turn. I had the money then and you needed it. Now you've got it, and I need it. I'm not even asking you to lend it to me. Just have a look at some of the investment plans I've got to offer.'

Charles sighed. 'Look, Patrick, I didn't realize you really needed the money. I mean,' he gestured around him, 'you hardly give the air of someone who's hard-up.' Patrick said nothing. 'If I did put some money into one of your funds,' said Charles, 'how much are we talking?'

Patrick didn't move for a second. His cigar had gone out; he carefully relit it. When it was going properly again he looked up at Charles.

'I would think around a hundred thousand? Perhaps eighty?'

'What?' Charles looked genuinely shocked. 'You must be mad, man. If that's the kind of money you need, you've got the wrong guy.' He paused, and thought. 'I could put around five thousand into a plan if that was any use to you. Perhaps seven or eight at a pinch.'

Patrick's face felt numb. Seven or eight thousand. And he was eighty thousand short of his target. It was hardly worth the ink. With an effort, he looked up at Charles and gave him a professional smile.

'I'll have a look through my fund details and put together a package which I think might suit you. How's that?'

'Fine.' Charles seemed relieved. He got to his feet. 'Coming back outside?'

Patrick shook his head. 'No, I'll just sort out a few things in here. See you later.'

They smiled at each other again and Charles left the room. Patrick went over to his desk and sat down heavily in his leather-bound swivel chair. The folder marked 'Charles' was still lying to hand in his top drawer. With a scowl he took it out and ripped it in two. Then, suddenly feeling drained, he slumped down on his desk and buried his head in his hands.

CHAPTER FIVE

Stephen, sitting alone on the grass with the remains of his raspberry pavlova, felt as if he had had too much. Too much food, too much drink, too much envy. As the day wore on, he was becoming more and more aware of how rich and successful everyone here was compared to him and Annie. Patrick and Caroline, Charles and Cressida; even Don, with his manor house hotel. They all had the air of comfort, if not wealth; they all had reached their goals. Whereas he hadn't even worked out what his goal was.

He abruptly stood up and shook the crumbs of meringue off his legs. Annie looked up drowsily.

'Just going for a little stroll,' he said. 'I won't be long.' She smiled and closed her eyes again. Caroline and Don seemed to be asleep; Valerie was chatting animatedly to Cressida. She paused and glanced up at him, and he hurried off before she asked him where he was going—or, even worse, suggested accompanying him. He was in no mood for talking.

He walked briskly and mindlessly to the far end of Patrick's grounds, beyond the tennis court, past the paddock, till he was at the fence which bordered the garden with a field full of sheep. Then he turned and surveyed the scene behind him. The White House was almost invisible behind the trees. There was no sign of anyone else. He was on his own.

Stephen sighed, and sank down onto the grass. He didn't want to see any of them, not even Annie. They all seemed to be mocking him; his failure to reach the same goals as them; his dusty old car, his scruffy old clothes, his indeterminate career path. Annie, too, though she didn't mean to, had slipped into the clothes of Caroline with consummate ease; over lunch they had giggled together like schoolgirls, and his last ally in this glossy, alien world seemed to have slipped away to the other side.

Where had he gone wrong? Until he left Cambridge, he had seemed one of the chosen ones—a bright, popular scholar who gained his first in history, took part in the university musical scene, acted, debated, even rowed for a term. 'A brilliant all-rounder' was how his final reference from his tutor described him, 'destined to go far.' He had left intending to become an academic. His M.Phil. had gone well, and he had begun research for a doctorate. In those days, he had still been the bright, intellectual success among his peers, who themselves were pursuing careers in advertising, accountancy, even retail management. Stephen, left behind in Cambridge, had felt sorry for them, having to settle for such tedious jobs. And that had been the sentiment among everyone at Cambridge. He could still remember his tutor gently mocking one of his friends, who had joined a well-known firm which made cooked meat.

But what the hell was wrong with cooked meat? That friend now figured frequently in the business pages of newspapers, as his company mounted takeover after takeover. The contemporary who had 'wasted himself' in advertising now had his own agency. He had recently been quoted in the paper as saying that he thought graduates weren't worth the space. 'Give me a sixteen year old any day,' he had said. 'I'm tired of these graduates who think they're God's gift because they can quote a bit of Plato.'

After four years of making notes, attending seminars, and tutoring the odd undergraduate, Stephen's doctorate had not taken shape. He was disillusioned, lonely and poor. And then he had met Annie. The burning desire to achieve knowledge, to be published, to make his mark in the academic world, had been succeeded by more mundane requirements. A house, a car, an income. The decision to take a teaching post in the comfortable city of Silchester had seemed an obvious one.

And for a while, he had seemed to be swimming with the rest of them. His income from teaching wasn't bad, a legacy from his father had bought them a house, they were able to afford a comfortable life. He had befriended a local history expert; had joined a local choir; all his needs had seemed to be fulfilled. It was only in the last couple of years that the canker had started. Seeing contemporaries' names in the lists of university appointments as well as on the finance pages. Realizing that he was destined to have neither the prestige of an academic career nor the financial rewards of a commercial one. For a few months he had been severely depressed. Was this mediocre, suburban life all he, who had been one of the brightest stars at Cambridge, was to aspire to?

It had been Annie who had proposed, then insisted, that he should go back to studying. He had carried on, sporadically, with his research since abandoning the doctorate; his notes still sat in their folders; his original ideas still had backbone to them. If he took a year's sabbatical, perhaps two, she suggested, they would be able to manage with their savings and her part-time work. It wasn't too late for him to achieve his ambition of becoming Dr Fairweather. Her enthusiasm had given him the impetus to submit a fresh proposal, find himself some funding, negotiate a sabbatical with his school, and begin his research all over again.

Stephen hunched his back over his knees. The familiar sinking feeling which he had whenever he thought of his thesis had gripped his stomach again. He couldn't, couldn't admit to Annie that his thesis wasn't going, let alone going well, that he was terrified of failure, that he had no one to confide in. He gazed miserably at the ground. Had he made yet another mistake? Should he have stayed in teaching? Should he have decided to move into a more lucrative area? Taken accountancy exams? Don, bloody smug Don, with his moron daughter, seemed to have done all right out of accountancy. Why had everybody derided it at Cambridge? Patrick, who hadn't even been to university, was making a fortune; Charles might have been in financial straits once, but he was doing all right now. They were all moving onwards and upwards, to bigger and better things, while he and Annie were left behind.

His legs were beginning to feel stiff, and Stephen stood up. He would have to rejoin the party before people began wondering where he was. He began walking reluctantly back towards the house. His hair felt rumpled and he was sure his shirt must be covered in hay.

He walked past the tennis court, avoiding the terrace, and went round to the front of the house. He would go and tidy up before facing the others. As he entered the cool house, he saw Charles disappearing out of a side door at the end of the hall. He paused, and looked at himself in the hall mirror.

'Stephen! Didn't hear you come in!' Stephen turned in surprise. Patrick was standing at the door of his study.

'Thought I'd have a quick wash and brush up,' said Stephen. 'I'm sure I need it.' Patrick waved his hand dismissively.

'Come in and have a cigar. I'm not sure I had this brand last time you were here. I'd appreciate your judgement.'

'I'm hardly in a position to help you, since the only time I ever have a cigar is when I'm here,' said Stephen, more harshly than he had intended. Patrick gave him a surprised look.

'Come in anyway.'

'Sorry,' said Stephen, stepping into the long, dim room. 'I guess I've had too much sun.' Patrick clapped a hand on his shoulder.

'Come on, Stephen. We're friends. If you can't sound off to me, who can you sound off to?'

Stephen sank on to the leather sofa. The ashtray on the table to the side of the sofa was full.

'Have you been soliciting Charles' advice, too?'

'What?' Patrick looked taken aback as he sat down. Stephen gestured to the ashtray.

'About your new cigars. I saw him going outside just now.' Patrick paused.

'Oh. Yes, I did ask him what he thought. But actually, I'm afraid to say we were talking business.'

'The gallery again? I would have thought he was OK for money by now.' Patrick smiled as if at a nice memory.

'No, not the gallery. Just a bit of an opportunity I was able to put his way. He should do quite nicely out of it.'

'Oh.' Stephen held up his cigar to the lighter. 'He's become quite a capitalist, old Charles, hasn't he? All a bit different from the Charles we used to know and love.'

Patrick shrugged. 'It's not really a question of being a capitalist. Anyone would take advantage of this opportunity if they knew about it. Did you see Charles' face?'

Stephen shook his head.

'Pity. I was wondering how wide his grin was.'

'Why?' said Stephen curiously. 'What's this fantastic opportunity?'

Patrick grimaced. 'It's very boring. And quite technical. You don't really want to hear it.'

'Why not?' Stephen looked up, nettled. 'How do you know I don't have a stash of cash, just waiting to invest?'

'I don't. Do you?'

'No.'

'Well then.' Patrick took a puff of his cigar and looked thought-ful. 'Although, of course, that's not quite true,' he said. 'You do have a stash of cash.'

'What?'

'It's not an obvious one, but it's there, if ever you need it.'

'What are you talking about?'

'Your house.'

'What, eighteen Seymour Road?'

'Must be worth a fair bit now.'

'I'm sure it is,' said Stephen. 'But you forget, we live there. If we sold it, we'd only have to buy another one.' He began to laugh. 'We're simple folk, Patrick. We don't have spare property hanging around to sell.'

'I know that. But you don't have to sell your house to get all its potential from it.' He looked directly at Stephen. 'You don't have a mortgage, do you?'

'Well, no,' said Stephen. 'We just about had enough from my father's legacy to buy it outright.'

'And that was, what, ten years ago? It'll have held its value since then, I'm sure.'

Stephen was silent, listening.

'My point is only this,' said Patrick. 'That, if you wanted to, say, if you needed the money, you could always take out a mortgage on your house.'

'That's a bit extreme,' said Stephen. 'I mean, it's one of the things I'm continually grateful for, that we don't have mortgage payments to worry about.'

only one who could do business with Patrick. He watched pleasurably as Patrick poured out two generous glasses of brandy, and
then sat up intelligently as he approached, bearing a series of
colourful-looking graphs. Stephen took a sip of brandy.

'Fire away,' he said. 'I'm all ears.'

Cressida was clutching her glass harder and harder as Valerie's
hooting, fluting voice poured a mixture of inane observations
and sycophantic questions into her ears. Caroline and Annie were
chatting quietly to each other with a cosy intimacy that was
impossible to join; Stephen had gone for a walk; Charles had disappeared off somewhere with Patrick; and Don had popped
home to feed the dog. There was no escape.

'I do love your ring,' said Valerie. 'Is it a real diamond?' Cressida nodded, feeling a sudden, alien desire to shout, 'No, it's out
of a cracker!'

'I thought it must be,' said Valerie. She glanced down at her
own pudgy, white hands. 'I've never bothered with rings,' she
said.

I'm not surprised, thought Cressida, eyeing Valerie's slug-like
fingers with distaste.

'I don't suppose . . . would you mind if I tried it on?' continued Valerie in a rush, looking at Cressida with suddenly eager
eyes. She thrust a finger out and Cressida shuddered.

'Actually,' she said, 'I must go and find Charles.' She got up,
stiff from the morning's tennis.

Valerie looked down disappointedly. Caroline, glancing up,

saw Cressida making her escape and called, 'What do you want to see Charles for? You must see him enough every day!' She smirked at Cressida, who gazed at her in cold fury.

'There was something I wanted to mention to him,' she said offputtingly. 'If you'll excuse me.'

As she passed through the terrace doors into the house, she heard Caroline sniggering, and then Valerie's voice calling, 'Cressida! Charles is out here! He's walking towards the paddock! Cressida!'

Cressida ignored them. She went quickly through the hall, suddenly desperate to get up to their bedroom for some peace. Voices were coming from behind one of the doors; she recognized them as Patrick's and Stephen's. But her tennis shoes were silent on the carpet and she was soon safely behind the door of the spare room. She sank onto the bed, grimacing as her skin slipped against the satin.

She looked at her watch. It was only three o'clock. Another twenty-four hours to go at least. It was simply too much. But she had promised Charles she would try to make an effort. He wouldn't be very impressed if he heard how she'd skulked away inside, ignoring his friends. She would have to say she had come inside for a reason. To finish unpacking—her eyes fell on Charles' half-empty suitcase—and deal with the letters. Of course.

She went into the bathroom—rather nicely done, she grudgingly admitted to herself—and splashed her face with cold water. Then, feeling restored, she went back into the bedroom to tackle the rest of the unpacking. She left the letters until last, until she'd put away every one of Charles' shirts, socks, pieces of shaving equipment and cuff-links. Then, with a sigh, she sat down at the pink-frilled, kidney-shaped dressing table in the corner of the room and began to slit open the envelopes.

She left the crisp, white, London-postmarked one till last, even though it was addressed to her rather than to Charles or both of them. It was bound to be some boring notice to shareholders, or a statement of account that she would immediately pass on to Charles. As she opened it, her mind was still on the dress bill that the last envelope had contained (was it for the cream suit or the cocktail dress? Charles would be bound to ask her), and for a few moments she didn't register the words before her.

Then, gradually, they began to impinge upon her consciousness; one by one arresting her attention; bouncing off her brain and mixing themselves up in her mind so that, with a sudden exclamation, half of impatience, half of panic, she closed her eyes, opened them, and forced herself to read the letter, slowly from the beginning.

When she had finished reading it for the first time she thought she might be sick. With customary self-control, she folded the letter, slid it carefully back into its envelope, and put it with the others. She sat completely still for a moment, staring blankly at her reflection in the mirror, reminding herself that she was a complete ignoramus when it came to financial affairs. No doubt it was all a mistake.

But before she could even finish articulating the thought, her hands had grabbed the envelope again and ripped it open, and she was gazing at the sheet of paper once more, her hands unable to hold it still, her heart thumping, her eyes flickering from the heading at the top of the paper down to the signature and up again, focusing first with disbelief, then with terror, at the figure, in pounds sterling, glaring in black and white in the middle of the page.

She closed her eyes for a moment, swaying in her chair, and emptied her mind. Then she opened her eyes again. The letter was still in her hand; the figure in the centre of the page still glared blackly at her, seeming to increase in size until it filled the whole of her view and she could see nothing else. With a sudden smart of humiliation, she clutched her stomach and rushed into the bathroom.

When she emerged again, her legs felt shaky. She looked at herself in the mirror and was shocked to see that her face was white, her lips were dry, her whole face seemed to have crumpled. She longed to lie down, curl up and bury her head in her knees. She sank to the floor of the bedroom and sat still for a few seconds. But she was self-conscious and could not relax. This was a stranger's house—what if someone came in and saw her behaving oddly? Then a more alarming thought occurred to her. The letter still lay on the dressing table, for anyone to see. With a sudden dart of panic, she looked around for somewhere to store it until she could show it to Charles. At the thought of Charles, another spasm hit her stomach, and she half-crawled, half-ran into the bathroom.

Coming out again, her first priority was to remove the letter from the dressing table. She looked feebly around the room for somewhere to put it. Was Caroline the sort to employ a maid to turn down the beds? One could never be sure of the limit to the excesses of that sort of parvenue. Eventually, she slipped it into the lining of her beauty case. Then, paranoically, she immediately imagined Caroline coming in to borrow some make-up, fiddling with the case, saying loudly, 'You've got something stuck in here,' pulling it out, reading it, gazing up in horror . . .

But that really was a foolish, hysterical way to think. With the letter safely out of sight, Cressida began to feel better. She slapped her cheeks, combed her hair, and sprayed some scent behind her ears. She rubbed some lipsalve vigorously into her lips and took a few deep breaths, as she had been taught in elocution lessons when she was eleven.

But when she went to the door of the room, she found that her nerve was failing her. Twice she reached for the door handle, paused with her hand on the knob, physically unable to leave the safety of her temporary haven. On the other side of the door were people, reality, Charles, the children. This side of the door there was only herself, the pink satin bed and the letter— which, stuffed into her vanity case, didn't really exist yet. Not while she hadn't told anyone about it.

She looked at her watch. Half-past three. Earlier she had been desperate for time to move on; now she wished it could stay still. She would have to tell Charles tonight, in bed, where there was no chance of anyone hearing. Until then, for a few hours, perhaps she could pretend nothing had happened. But she would have to display her usual confidence. She would have to put on a good show. Summoning up unknown reserves of determination, Cressida grasped the door handle firmly and strode out into the corridor and, staring ahead blankly, unthinkingly, her mind deliberately dead, she made her way out into the garden.

CHAPTER SIX

Caroline and Annie had taken a jug of Pimm's down to the tennis court. There Georgina was teaching Nicola to play tennis while Toby sat happily in the umpire's chair. Nicola grasped the lightweight racquet awkwardly, and swung ineffectually at each ball that Georgina threw, only occasionally making contact. But Georgina continued patiently to make cheerful, encouraging comments.

'She's incredible, your daughter,' said Annie quietly.

'I could say the same thing to you,' said Caroline. 'Nicola's made so much progress. You must be thrilled to bits. I mean, did you ever think she'd be able to play tennis?'

'Well,' said Annie, 'we never gave up hope. But I have to admit, there were times when I couldn't see her leading a normal life.' She gazed silently ahead for a moment. 'She's got so much willpower,' she continued, 'she's so absolutely determined to succeed, it makes one feel quite weak in comparison. She's got more tenacity than both of us put together.'

'And she's bright, too, isn't she?' said Caroline.

'Oh yes.' Annie flushed with pleasure. 'I think in other circumstances she might have been labelled gifted. But it would seem a bit ironic, under the circumstances.'

They both involuntarily looked at Nicola's skewed foot, her clenching, uncoordinated arm, her glowing face.

'Poor little sod,' said Caroline. 'How does the school treat her?'

'Oh, very well, considering,' said Annie slightly defensively. 'It must be difficult for them. She's so bright, and so enthusiastic to learn, but then when she has to write it all down, of course, she's much slower than all the others. She gets very frustrated with herself. And then,' she added, slightly bitterly, 'some of the teachers seem to think that nothing can be any good unless it's written out neatly.'

'Doesn't sound great to me,' said Caroline. 'No offence.' Annie shrugged.

'What can you do? They're overstretched, they're busy, they haven't got time for a child who doesn't conform. I do all I can to help Nicola at home, but . . . How's Georgina getting on?' she added abruptly.

'Oh, great guns,' said Caroline. 'Reckons she's going to be head of junior house next term, whatever the hell that means. I think she's getting in a bit of practice on poor old Nicola. She's getting far too bossy.'

'Oh, I wouldn't worry about Nicola,' said Annie laughing. 'She loves it. She simply gobbles up all those boarding school books—pretty trashy stuff, really. And to meet someone who actually does all those things—you know, trunks and tuck boxes and dormitories—is utter bliss.'

'Well, tell her she can come and pack Georgina's trunk any time,' said Caroline, 'since I'm the one who always ends up doing it.'

'Oh, but that's the mother's job,' said Annie, grinning at Caroline, 'and she's supposed to hide a little surprise under one's nightie. That's what my mother always did.'

'Then she was a mug,' said Caroline. 'As soon as Georgina's in the senior school she's doing her own trunk, or it doesn't get done. Anyway, she's much better than me at that kind of thing. I can't understand how she turned out so bloody efficient.' They both looked at Georgina, busily picking up tennis balls.

'So she's going to stay on at St Catherine's?' said Annie.

Caroline shrugged. 'We had a bit of a look round other senior schools, but there didn't seem any point moving her. It's a lovely school, she can take her pony there, the staff seem OK—a bit snotty maybe, but, you know, all right basically. And she knows the place.'

'It is a lovely school,' agreed Annie. 'I remember visiting it once, when Nicola was tiny.'

'Really?' Caroline looked surprised.

'We always meant to send her to a private school,' said Annie, 'when she was eight or so. We thought that would give us time to get the fees together. Toby, too.' She shrugged. 'Things didn't work out quite as we planned. First the stroke—then Stephen going back to his doctorate.'

'How much longer does he have with that thing? He's been doing it for bloody ages.' Annie shrugged.

'Depends how it goes. Another year, perhaps two.'

'Christ, I don't know how you put up with it. I couldn't. I mean, no job, no money—I'd go crazy.'

'Well, he still teaches a bit,' said Annie, 'and I do proofreading when I have the time. It's not so bad, really. And with no mortgage on the house and no school fees—you know, we can keep our outgoings quite low.' Caroline shuddered.

'Rather you than me. Can't you persuade Stephen to get a job again, give up this degree?'

'It's what he wants to do,' said Annie firmly.

There was a noise behind them and they both looked round. Cressida had come down the path to the tennis court and stood, watching the girls playing tennis. As they turned, she seemed to wobble slightly. Her face was drained of blood and her smile appeared artificial.

'Hello, Cressida,' said Annie cautiously. She hesitated, and then added, 'Are you all right? I mean, do you feel OK?'

'You look terrible,' said Caroline, bluntly. 'Must be too much sun. Here, sit down.' She drew up a chair and patted it invitingly. 'Have some Pimm's. Or do you want something stronger?'

'If you've had too much sun, perhaps you shouldn't have any alcohol,' said Annie.

'Is it the sun?' Caroline peered closely at Cressida's face. 'Hang on a minute. Do you feel sick? Is there any chance you could be . . . ?' Cressida gazed at her uncomprehendingly. 'You know, pregnant,' said Caroline impatiently. 'Are you? Tell me quick before I pour out all this lovely booze and you say you can't drink it.' Cressida exhaled sharply.

'Don't worry,' she said slowly, 'I can drink all I like.'

'Attagirl,' said Caroline approvingly. She gave Cressida an appraising look as she poured out the drink. 'There, now you relax and take it easy,' she said. 'I always thought playing tennis was a bad idea. Why not just have people round for the weekend? That's what I wanted to know. But Patrick insisted on this stupid tournament and now the whole thing seems to have turned into bloody Wimbledon.'

'That's hardly fair,' protested Annie. 'We've only had two matches. And I like playing tennis. What about you, Cressida?' she said, turning to Cressida in a friendly manner. 'You're really good. You must enjoy it.'

'What?' said Cressida, looking up distractedly. 'Sorry, I didn't hear you.'

'It doesn't matter,' said Annie, glancing at Caroline.

'Hello, you lot, all sitting around doing nothing?' It was Patrick, beaming and jovial and smelling of cigars. Behind him was Stephen, looking defiantly pleased with himself.

'Have you two been gorging yourselves on cigars?' asked Annie, shooting a teasing look at Stephen.

'Cigars and brandy,' said Patrick, briskly rubbing his hands. 'Just the job before a game of tennis.'

'I don't know how you can!' exclaimed Annie. 'I feel zonked enough as it is.'

'Ah well, you women don't have the stamina, that's what it is,' said Patrick. 'Isn't that right, Stephen?'

'I wouldn't like to say,' said Stephen, grinning back at Patrick. He seemed in buoyant spirits, thought Annie. Perhaps she should stock up on brandy and cigars at home.

'Now, we must get back to business,' said Patrick. 'Where's the chart?'

Caroline groaned loudly.

'Here we are,' he said. 'It's Cressida and Charles against Don and Valerie.'

'Well, we haven't got Don, we haven't got Valerie and we haven't got Charles,' said Caroline. 'We're doing well.'

'Who hasn't got Charles?' Charles emerged around the corner, carrying one of the twins. Behind him followed Martina, carrying the other twin, and Valerie.

'We've just been to look at your lovely horse,' began Valerie. 'I must say, he's a beautiful creature.'

'It's a she,' said Caroline. 'Where's your dad? You're supposed to be playing.' Valerie looked worried.

'I think he went home to feed the dog. Perhaps he got held up.'

'The thing is,' said Caroline, glancing wickedly at Annie, 'if he doesn't make it back we'll have to treat the match as if you lost, by default. We'll have to score you both nil. Unless you want to play Charles and Cressida on your own?'

Valerie's eyes darted nervously up the path. 'I'm sure he won't be long. Shall I give him a ring?'

'Why not?' said Caroline kindly. 'You know where the phone is.' Valerie disappeared up the path and Annie erupted into giggles.

'What did you say that for?' said Patrick. 'There's no hurry.'

'So what? Serve Don right for being such a git.'

Charles went over to Cressida, kissed her lightly and perched on the arm of her chair.

'I heard you were trying to find me,' he said. 'Was it something important?'

'Oh, no,' stammered Cressida.

'You know,' he continued, 'I really think it would be a good idea to get the boys a pony when they're old enough. We could move to a bigger place with a bit of land, perhaps. Have you seen Georgina's pony?'

Cressida shook her head numbly. Charles' eyes shone with enthusiasm.

'It's a very nice animal,' he said. 'And Georgina's not at all a bad rider. I can see her eventing in a few years' time. I'd really love the boys to be able to do the same one day.'

'Eventers are expensive,' said Cressida in a dry, scratchy voice. She stared at her hands, and forced her thoughts away from the bedroom with the pink satin cover and the vanity case and the letter.

'Well, yes,' said Charles, surprised, 'but then so are a lot of things. Anyway, it's just a thought.' He leapt up and picked up his racquet.

'Right!' he shouted at Georgina and Nicola, still on the tennis court. 'Who's going to give me a game?'

'Hello, beautiful.' Stephen came over and wrapped his arms round Annie from behind. 'Doesn't she look fantastic in that gear?' he said to Caroline.

'Marvellous,' said Caroline.

'I've been telling her to ask you where you bought it,' said Stephen. 'I think my wife deserves a new tennis outfit or two, don't you?' Annie turned round to face Stephen.

'You've been drinking too much brandy,' she said, laughing, but slightly puzzled. She peered at his eyes. They were very bright and didn't meet hers properly but darted quickly about. If he had been one of the children, she would probably have called him overexcited and told him to go to bed. But why was Stephen suddenly in this manic mood?

Stephen was aware of Annie looking puzzledly at him, but he ignored her gaze. He was feeling confident, alive and invigorated. He watched Charles racing about the tennis court, clowning with the children—and didn't feel the customary stab of envy. He looked genially around at his expensively clad friends, noting their gold watches and smart racquets, for once without a pang of jealousy. He was now up among them. He was as able as Charles, Don or any of them, to make high-powered deals over fat cigars; to talk of his investments, to wink knowingly at Patrick when he talked of stocks, shares and portfolios.

Signing that piece of paper had given Stephen the biggest rush of adrenalin he could remember having since discovering he'd got a first at Cambridge. Patrick had produced a beautiful Cross fountain pen and invited him to sit at his desk. He'd watched benignly as Stephen ran his eyes down the small print—looking for what? Stephen hadn't really been sure—and suggested Stephen took it away with him to think about. But Stephen had made a dismissive, rather debonair gesture.

'Think about what, Patrick?' he'd said. 'Whether I want to be rich or poor? I reckon I've thought about that enough already.' Patrick had chuckled appreciatively and poured out yet another brandy. Stephen had taken one, final look at the paperwork and then signed briskly, coolly, matter-of-factly; as though he were used to making that kind of transaction on a regular basis.

Stephen tightened his grasp around Annie as his mind skated over the exact figure he'd signed away to Patrick. Patrick had assured him that it would all be covered easily by a part-mortgage on their house, and that he would be able to fix it up as soon as he got to the office on Monday. And of course, as Patrick had explained, there was no point thinking about it in the context of everyday amounts of money. Making a serious investment was quite a different business from, say, paying the gas bill, or even buying a car. Patrick had certainly looked unconcerned at the amount Stephen was entrusting to him. He was obviously used to sums as big as, if not bigger than, this one.

The feeling of power which Stephen had suddenly felt, dealing in such a large amount of money, was irresistible. He was suddenly reminded of a stag party to which he had once been invited by a Cambridge friend whose father was in the hotel business. They'd stayed, six of them, all expenses paid, at a big London five-star hotel over the weekend. By the end of the stay, the delight of signing large bar bills, choosing steak à la carte and drinking the mini bar dry had gone to Stephen's head. He'd lingered in the hotel shop after they'd all checked out, fingering cashmere jerseys and silver-plated tankards appraisingly, desperate to prolong his role in the world of the rich. The exorbitant prices had begun to appear reasonable to him, detached as they were from the reality of his student grant and weekly budget. He'd even eventually gone so far as to buy a ridiculously expensive leather wallet, embossed with the name of the hotel, signing the cheque without flinching; even wondering aloud whether he ought not to have the key fob as well. And now he was experiencing the same heady sensation. He caught Patrick's eye and grinned.

'That's a fine brandy you keep,' he said jovially. Patrick's eyes twinkled.

'Well now, you'll have to sample my other favourite after dinner,' he replied in a genial tone.

'Looking forward to it!'

Patrick smiled again at Stephen, and then turned away. His sensation of sheer delight at having snared his last, his most crucial deal, was proving difficult to control. He stared down at his hands, unable to stop a beam creeping over his face. One hundred thousand pounds bonus. One hundred thousand pounds! He clenched the back of the chair in front of him, and took a deep breath. It had been almost impossible to stay calm as he had slowly manoeuvred Stephen into signing away exactly the right sum of money. It had been pure artistry, the way he had paced his pitch, balancing nonchalance with enthusiasm, keeping the warmth in his voice, the credibility in his smile, not pushing, but inviting. When it had come to the actual signature, he had almost lost his cool. Seeing Stephen poised, pen in hand, over the documents, scanning the page, looking as if he might hesitate, the desire to force his pen down onto the page and *make* him sign had grown frighteningly strong. But somehow he had managed to remain outwardly sanguine, resting his fingers lightly on the back of Stephen's chair with a tense patience, keeping his voice smooth.

And finally it had happened. Stephen had signed away eighty thousand pounds of his money. Patrick didn't allow himself to consider whether this was a safe move for Stephen. He had explained what the fund was; he had allowed Stephen to make up his own mind—it was Stephen's decision, not his. And eighty thousand wasn't so much, really. Not compared with the amount of business Patrick had already done that year. He remembered with a quiver of delight his performance charts, waiting in his desk drawer for the final figures. He would be top salesman again that year. And would be well rewarded. Patrick gazed at Georgina, playing tennis beautifully and giggling hysterically as Charles pretended to miss all her shots, and he felt a surge of triumph. Now they could afford a new house, a new pony—anything his daughter wanted, she could have.

His eye fell on Charles and he felt a twinge of anger that he had not been able to close the deal with him. Fucking tight git. But then, Charles was always there for the future. Whereas Stephen . . . Patrick shook his head. Stephen was about the least likely person he could imagine having as a client. It had never even occurred to him to pitch at Stephen. But a good salesman should be able to sell to anyone. And he had excelled himself that afternoon. It had been a model exercise in salesmanship. Suddenly he felt too keyed up to stand still, and he wandered over to Caroline. He ran his hands over her hips, and nuzzled her neck.

'You're gorgeous, you know that?' he whispered. 'Fucking gorgeous.'

Caroline eyed Patrick suspiciously. First this morning's good mood, now this. What was he up to? She had not failed to notice him invite Charles into his study. What had been his reason? To look at those prints he'd bought a couple of weeks ago. She'd been surprised when he'd shown them to her. Weird, modern efforts—not his kind of thing at all. It really wouldn't surprise her to learn that he'd bought the prints especially to have an excuse to ask Charles into his study. And Charles had gone along trustingly. But it didn't fool her. Had Patrick tried to sell some sort of plan to Charles? And had he succeeded? She glanced up at Patrick's face. He had an expression of suppressed glee; his mouth was twitching into a smile and his eyes were bright. He must have sold Charles something. No wonder he was in such a good mood. No wonder he had plied poor old Stephen with brandy so generously. It must have been a big deal. Caroline looked consideringly at Charles, romping on the tennis court. He seemed in a good mood as well. She inwardly shrugged. Good luck to them. And now Patrick had achieved his aim of extracting money out of Charles, perhaps they wouldn't have to invite them over again. She could certainly do without Cressida's bloody miserable face about the place.

Eventually Don turned up, rather flustered, and was ushered onto the tennis court by a smirking Caroline. Valerie followed him, looking rather anxious, and finally Cressida got up and made her way silently onto the court. Her face was still pale, and she fingered her racquet in a desultory way. But Don's face lit up as he saw her and realized that he and Valerie were to play against Charles and Cressida.

'Here's a real challenge, Val!' he exclaimed. He turned and grinned perkily at Annie and Stephen. 'This'll be a nightmare! Wake me up when it's all over!'

Annie smiled back encouragingly.

'Fucking prat,' murmured Stephen.

Georgina and Nicola, usurped from the tennis court, flopped down, panting, on the grass.

'You're very good at tennis,' said Annie to Georgina.

'I'm all right,' she replied conversationally. 'I'm in special coaching at school. But I'm not in the house team. You see, about ten people in each house have special coaching if they're good enough, but only six are in the team. And a reserve.' Patrick raised his eyebrows at Caroline.

'You didn't tell me Georgina was having special coaching for tennis.'

'That's because I didn't know,' said Caroline unconcernedly.

'Sweetie,' Patrick addressed Georgina, 'why don't you tell us things?' Georgina shrugged.

'I do tell you things.'

'You didn't tell us about that.'

'I forgot.' Georgina abruptly leapt up. 'Time for another rehearsal. Martina, bring the twins.' She looked around and called in a stentorian voice, 'Toby! Come on!'

'What are you rehearsing?' said Annie.

'A play,' said Georgina, discouragingly. 'You'll see it tomorrow. Toby!'

'He's stuck in the umpire's chair,' said Nicola. 'Someone'll have to get him out.' But already Martina had put down the twin she was carrying and hurried over to release Toby from his perch.

'She's certainly got them all organized,' said Stephen admiringly, as the troop of children left the tennis court. 'Even the nanny.'

'She'll overdo it one of these days,' said Caroline. 'Not everyone likes being bossed about.'

'She doesn't boss people,' objected Patrick at once. 'She just gets what she wants. That's the way you've got to be.' Caroline rolled her eyes at Annie and said nothing. She turned her gaze to the tennis court.

'Bloody hell,' she said after a few moments. 'What the fuck's wrong with Cressida?'

The four on court had begun to knock up. Don was sending a series of swift, low balls to Cressida, who seemed barely able to return them.

'Sorry,' she kept saying, as another went into the net.

'Saving it till the match,' quipped Don. 'I know that trick!' He beamed at Cressida, who returned a weak smile. They tossed for sides; Don and Valerie won. As they walked to the back of the court, Don began to mutter to Valerie an audible series of instructions and warnings about Cressida's and Charles' play.

'Guard the net; she's got a nasty sliced forehand, might take you on the hop; don't try to lob him unless it's over the backhand. Is he steady at the net?' he suddenly demanded.

'Well, quite steady,' stammered Valerie.

'Mmm. Well, don't play to either of them at the net. Off you go, now. It's me to serve, remember?'

Valerie scuttled to the net and Don prepared to serve to Cressida. She stood, apathetically watching his mannered action, and lunged dispiritedly when the ball came spinning into her service box.

'Bad luck, darling,' said Charles. Don shook his head and clicked his tongue.

'You had that one,' he said to Cressida. 'Don't know what happened there.'

Charles returned the next serve straight to Valerie, who put it away with a vicious volley.

'Good girl,' said Don. 'Nice approach, that was, well away from the body.' He prepared to serve to Cressida again. The first serve went out, and he stood stock still for a minute or two, as though meditating on the horror of such a mistake. Then, shaking his head slowly, he took a second ball from his pocket and served again. His second serve was a looped shot which landed just the other side of the net and bounced surprisingly high. Cressida, who had begun to run forward, was taken unawares, and hit the ball wide. It veered towards Valerie, who made an exaggerated jump aside to avoid it, and landed well outside the tramlines.

'Forty-love,' called Valerie.

'Sorry,' said Cressida to Charles. 'I can't think what's wrong with me.'

'Watch the ball,' piped up Don. 'That's always the answer. If things are going badly, don't think about anything but the ball.'

'Yes,' said Cressida shortly. Don served again, Charles returned the ball to him, and he sent an easy shot to Cressida. She volleyed it straight into the net.

'You're just not watching the ball,' said Don complacently. 'That's all it is. Isn't that right, Valerie?'

'Well,' said Valerie uncertainly. She looked at Cressida's face, drawn and tense. 'Maybe.'

Cressida's misery seemed to be getting deeper and deeper. Sitting quietly by the side of the tennis court, watching Charles clowning with the children, it had abated slightly, and she had, for a few blissful minutes, forgotten about the letter. But now she could think of nothing else. And everyone seemed to be watching her. Don, with his comments; Valerie, with her cow eyes; even Charles, thinking he was encouraging her by turning round and making faces behind Don's back. Caroline and Annie, too, were probably staring at her, wondering why she was playing so poorly.

She stared blindly at the tennis net, trying to rationalize her feelings. The letter could be a mistake—was probably a mistake. Charles would soon sort it out. He would sort it out. She repeated it to herself, trying to sooth herself into a state of calm. But a pounding background worry would not let her spirits rest. What if it wasn't a mistake? What if they had to pay? Where would they find the money? Cressida had successfully managed to close her ears to most of the financial information that had passed her way during the last ten or so years since her mother had died. She had only a hazy idea of her fortune; an even hazier one of where it had been invested. But she knew that most of it had dwindled away since her marriage. Was there still enough there? She screwed up her mind, trying to remember what her last account from the portfolio managers had said.

'Darling?' Charles was looking quizzically at her. 'We're changing ends.'

Cressida flushed and her head jerked up. Everyone was staring at her. Of course. They had lost the first game. Charles was already on the other side of the court; Don and Valerie were hovering at the net, looking at her in polite surprise. They were all waiting for her. Any minute now, someone would ask her if she was feeling all right. Caroline was so insensitive, she would probably shout out something awful, like, was it Cressida's period and did she want some Feminax. Or they might guess that something was wrong, and show a horrible, over-familiar sympathy.

The thought of exposing herself—her vulnerabilities—to these awful people, stiffened Cressida's resolve. She simply had to pull herself together. She gave a chilly smile, and quickly walked round to the other side of the court.

'Sorry,' she murmured to Charles. 'I was miles away.' She narrowed her eyes. She would just have to concentrate. Turning towards the net, she focused her attention on a particular corner of netting. 'Concentrate,' she muttered to herself. 'Concentrate.' She tried to blank everything else out of her mind.

'One-love down,' said Charles cheerfully. 'Looks like I'm going to have to pull something pretty special out of the bag. Eh,

Cress?' He served to Don; a straightforward unpretentious shot. Don returned the ball straight to Cressida, obviously expecting her to miss. But she stuck her racquet out, almost in a reflex action, and whipped the ball away.

'Great shot!' shouted Charles in delight.

'Well played,' said Don tetchily.

'Wow!' said Annie. 'That's more like it.'

The next game passed quickly. Cressida's mind, black with misery, had blocked out everything but returning the ball. She was unaware of the score; unaware of the looks of amazement as she sent one after another top-spin forehand rocketing into the far corner of the court.

'Cressida, darling, your serve.' She looked up, startled, to see Charles smiling affectionately at her. 'You're playing incredibly.'

Cressida felt as though she might burst into uncontrollable sobs. Instead, she picked up two balls and prepared to serve. She threw the first ball high, far too high, and hit a serve which ballooned right out of the court.

'Mummy!'

Cressida ignored Georgina's high-pitched cry and threw the ball up again. It went behind her.

'Have another,' said Charles.

'Mummy, look who's here!'

This time Georgina's excited shriek was too compelling to ignore. Cressida, Charles, Caroline, everyone, looked round.

Standing next to Georgina, barely taller than her, was a smiling girl with a glowing, tanned face. She was dressed in an Indian-cotton dress of bright turquoise, and her golden-brown hair was tied up in a scarf of the same colour. The dress, sleeveless and low cut, showed off a pair of full breasts, tanned as far as the eye could see to the same colour as her face, and the rest of her body was similarly voluptuous—rounded shoulders, dimpled arms, a slightly curved belly visible through the thin cotton of her dress. A gold chain round her neck glinted in the afternoon sunlight; her feet were shod in brown leather sandals and she carried a large leather bag. Her deep-brown eyes quickly surveyed the scene, and she murmured something to Georgina, who laughed slightly and then looked nervously at her mother. The entire party stood looking at the girl for a minute or two in silence. Then Stephen spoke.

'Jesus Christ,' he said. 'It's Ella.'

CHAPTER SEVEN

'I'm so terribly sorry,' said Ella. She and Caroline had gone inside and were walking up the stairs. 'I just assumed Georgina was, well, you know . . .'

'Telling the truth?' supplied Caroline. 'Fair enough, why shouldn't you?'

'She was very convincing,' said Ella. 'I really thought she'd asked you. I mean, otherwise I'd never have come. Maybe she'd forgotten about the party?' she added suddenly.

'No chance,' said Caroline. 'She's known about it for weeks. When did you say you phoned?'

'Oh, four or five weeks ago,' said Ella. 'I was still in Italy. I asked her if it was OK to come over, and she said she'd go and ask you. She was away from the phone for a few minutes, then she came back and said you were in the bath but you'd said it was fine. I mean, I didn't see any reason not to believe her. I suppose I should have called again, to check it was still all right to come, but you know what it's like . . .' She grinned guiltily. 'Have I ruined the delicate balance of your gathering?'

'I'd say you've ruined Charles' delicate balance all right,' said Caroline, smirking. 'Not to mention his charming wife's. Did you see her face?' Ella shook her head.

'I have to say, I avoided looking at either of them.' Caroline glanced swiftly at her.

'Are you OK about it? I mean, seeing them?'

'Yes, I am,' Ella said slowly. 'I'm fine. It's been long enough now, and there have been others since Charles. I don't want him back or anything. But even so . . . I look at her, and I think . . .'

'You think, You rich cow,' said Caroline. Ella laughed.

'Something like that.'

'That's what we all think.'

Caroline halted in front of a door. 'Since it was Georgina's idea to tell you it was all right to come,' she said, 'I think the least she can do is donate you her room.'

'Oh no,' protested Ella. 'I can go anywhere. I've got a sleep-ing bag . . .'

'Rubbish,' said Caroline. She opened the door. Georgina's bedroom was large, light and spotlessly tidy. The window, the dressing-table mirror and the water dispenser all glinted in the late afternoon sun; the books and pencils on the desk were neatly arranged; a single china horse and a lamp stood on the white bed-side cabinet.

'Very nice,' said Ella. Caroline shrugged.

'I'm sorry we can't come up with another spare room. You would have thought this house was big enough.'

'How many bedrooms has it got?' said Ella, dumping her bag on the sheepskin rug in the middle of the floor.

'Six, altogether. But they're all taken.' Ella was peering round the bathroom door.

'Lucky Georgina. This is really nice.' She sat on the bed. 'Makes a change from sleeping mats and mice running up and down my legs all night.' Caroline gave her a horrified look.

'Is that what it was like?'

'Not all the time.' Ella laughed at Caroline's expression. 'It was pretty sordid in India and bits of South America—but I've been back in Europe for the last four months. Still, nothing as luxurious as this.' Caroline shook her head.

'I don't know how you did it,' she said. 'Three weeks is enough for me, however nice the place is. Didn't you get homesick?'

'A little. After the first two months I got really miserable and I thought about chucking it in and flying home. But I got through that pretty quickly. It was really basic things that were getting me down—like no hot water and the food. I got quite ill at one point. But, you know, I got used to it. And the whole experience was so wonderful . . .' Her eyes were shining.

'Mad woman,' said Caroline. 'Well look, welcome back.'

'Thank you,' said Ella. 'And apologies again.'

'It's my bloody daughter who should be apologizing to you,' said Caroline. 'I honestly don't think it ever occurred to her that you might not *want* to see Charles.'

'Oh, I don't know,' said Ella. 'I'm actually quite looking forward to talking to him now. He looked so completely amazed.' She looked down at herself. 'Is it all right if I have a bath straight away?'

'Oh, sure, go ahead,' said Caroline. She pushed open the door of the bathroom. 'We have the water hot all the time, so use as much as you want. I'll go and get you a towel.'

When she returned, Ella was standing unselfconsciously naked, brushing out her honey-brown hair while hot water thundered into the bath. Her creamy-brown body was curved and dimpled, and with each stroke of the hairbrush her full breasts rose and fell.

'Here you are,' said Caroline, holding out a pair of huge white towels. 'What a wonderful tan.'

'Actually I got this on the beach in Greece,' said Ella, who was engrossed in teasing out a knot in her hair. 'I was with a bunch of nudists—or, at least, nude sunbathers. It was very eye opening.' She looked up seriously, caught Caroline's lascivious eye, and they both dissolved into giggles.

'That's not what I meant!' protested Ella eventually, still snorting with laughter.

'Then it was a Freudian what's-it,' said Caroline. 'You can't be getting enough sex.'

'Well, actually,' said Ella mysteriously, 'that's where you're wrong.' She winked at Caroline and took the towels.

'Why? Who? What's been happening?' demanded Caroline.

'I'll tell you later,' said Ella, 'maybe.' And she disappeared into the bathroom.

Outside, the tennis match was nearing its conclusion. Cressida, gripping her racquet tightly, was not allowing her concentration to slip. She didn't dare think about where she was, or with whom she was playing. Her eyes were fixed on the ball; her shots had sharpened up; and she was playing to win. The harder she concentrated on the game, the less easy it was to think about the disconcerting arrival of Ella; or about the letter waiting for Charles upstairs; or even about the grim prospect of a whole evening with these awful people. She skimmed a winning forehand past Valerie at the net, collected up the balls, and walked swiftly to the other end of the court to serve.

Charles paused at the net to exchange a pleasantry or two with Don. But Don was looking ruffled.

'She's playing well, your wife,' he said.

'Isn't she?' Charles shot a puzzled glance at Cressida, who was bouncing the ball up and down and staring fixedly at the ground.

'Wonderful concentration,' said Don. 'You see, Val,' he addressed his daughter, 'if you concentrated a bit harder, you wouldn't keep making all those mistakes.' Val looked down, and scuffed her shoe with her racquet.

'Well,' said Charles quickly. 'I make that five-four.'

'Now come on, Val,' said Don sharply, as they walked off. 'We really need to win this game.'

'Georgina,' interrupted Caroline, 'go and get your stuff out of your room and take it to Nicola's room. You'll be sleeping there tonight.'

'Brill!' said Georgina, deflected from her speech. 'In a sleeping bag?'

'Yes,' said Caroline.

'Wicked!' said Georgina, slithering down the tree. 'Come on, Nick.'

'Don't just go charging in,' warned Caroline. 'Ella's having a bath.'

'Is Ella having my room?'

'Yes,' said Caroline. 'I think it's the least you can do, don't you?' Georgina blushed slightly under Caroline's piercing look.

'I suppose so,' she said, shifting from one foot to the other.

'Well, go on then,' said Caroline. 'And knock first.'

'It's all right,' said Georgina. 'I've seen Ella without any clothes on before. She won't mind.'

There was a short silence as she and Nicola ran off, during which the image of Ella without any clothes on hung unavoidably in everyone's minds.

'Right,' said Caroline briskly. 'I think I'm going to get changed. We'll be having dinner around eight, with drinks beforehand.'

'Very civilized,' said Stephen. 'What about the kids?'

'I've sorted that out. They'll have theirs earlier on, in the kitchen. Mrs Finch is organizing it.'

'Bliss,' said Annie. 'I think I'll just lie here for a few months or so.'

'I'm afraid not,' said Patrick. 'You're on again, against us.'

'No!' groaned Annie.

'Patrick!' said Caroline. 'I've got to get changed! Can't we leave it till tomorrow?'

'Hear, hear!' said Stephen.

'Well, I suppose so,' said Patrick grudgingly. 'But we must play it. Otherwise we won't know who's in the final.'

'We will,' said Annie. 'Promise.'

'We'll be off home then, to change,' said Don. 'Drinks around seven-thirty, Caroline?'

'Whatever you like,' said Caroline dismissively.

'Yes, seven-thirty,' said Patrick, smiling at Don.

Caroline wandered slowly up to her bedroom. Passing the room where Georgina had moved to, she heard sounds of rumpus, and wondered briefly whether to intervene. But she really couldn't be bothered. And she had more important things to think about. The first was the sudden appearance of Ella. Although, of course, she disapproved of Georgina's lying, a part of her, she realized, rejoiced at the discomfort of Charles and Cressida. This was a meeting which probably would not have happened otherwise. And it would serve Charles right to see what he had turned down.

Ella was looking utterly radiant—and had obviously had an incredible trip. So glamorous, thought Caroline, to go whizzing off round the world like that. Although perhaps it sounded better than it really was. Caroline's own idea of a holiday was being shipped, with no effort on her own part, from front door to airport to hotel to beach. But Charles had always liked those hippy, studenty holidays with backpacks and no tour rep—and would probably love to go round the world like that. Caroline made a note to herself to ask Ella loudly about her travels at dinner—and watch Charles' face. She smiled to herself as she turned on the taps and watched the water gushing into her bathtub.

'Having a bath?' It was Patrick, bustling cheerfully into the room. 'Going to be long?'

'Yes,' said Caroline uncompromisingly.

'OK then. I'll read the paper. Give me a shout when you've finished.' He opened the balcony door and went to sit outside. Caroline watched him distrustfully, then quickly stripped, leaving her clothes on the floor, and got into the hot, scented, foamy water. She opened her mouth to call to him, and then realized that she would be overheard.

'Patrick, come here,' she shouted. 'Patrick!'

'What?' He appeared at the bathroom door.

'I want to talk to you. Close the door.'

'What about?' He stood and let his eyes run over her body in the foamy bath water. She ignored him.

'About Charles. No,' she held up a hand, 'let me finish. I know what you were up to today. You tank him up, disappear off to the study on some pathetic pretext and then all of a sudden, I can just see it, you haul out the brochures and sell him some completely unsuitable product just for your bloody commission.'

'Now wait a moment,' said Patrick, raising his voice.

'Sssh!' hissed Caroline. 'Do you want everyone to hear?'

'Now wait a moment,' he repeated more quietly. 'You can

stop talking about *my* bloody commission. It pays for your food, your clothes . . .'

'OK, OK,' she said impatiently, 'but I'm not completely hung up about it like you are. Anyway,' she held up her hand again before he could interrupt, 'the point is, why do you have to do business in the house? It's bad enough entertaining people like Don because they're *good clients*,' her voice mocked the phrase, 'but when you invite Charles Mobyn here just in order to sell him some crappy policy . . . it's really naff.' Her blue eyes regarded him with disdain.

'And how,' he said, 'do you know I sold anything to Charles?'

'Oh, it's obvious,' snapped Caroline. 'You disappear off with him; the next thing you're in a really good mood, doling out brandy and cigars like there's no tomorrow. Either you sold some whacking great plan to Charles or else you've got a coke habit I don't know about.' Patrick gave a small smile. He peered into the steamy mirror, licked his finger and smoothed his eyebrows.

'Or else,' he said casually, 'I sold some whacking great plan to someone else.'

'What?' Caroline stared at him in surprise. 'Who? Cressida?' Patrick continued smiling pleasurably at his reflection. 'Don?' she said.

'I sold the plan,' he said slowly, 'which will take my bonus this year up to . . . go on, have a guess how much.'

'Don. It must have been Don. He didn't go off to feed his dog at all, did he? He went off to be conned by you.'

'One hundred thousand pounds,' said Patrick, relishing the

sound of the words. 'That's not salary, that's bonus. One hundred thousand pounds of lovely bonus.'

'But Don's strapped for cash. He's in real trouble, Valerie told me. He can't have invested that much.' Patrick broke off from his pleasant reverie and looked at her in surprise.

'It wasn't Don. What made you think it was him?'

'Well who the fuck was it then?' Patrick smiled at her.

'Stephen, of course.'

Annie was trying to make conversation with Mrs Finch in the kitchen. The children, including a resentful Martina, were assembled round the table, munching fish cakes, cheesy baked potatoes and salad. Georgina had insisted on grinding piles of fresh black pepper on to everyone's potato, with the result that Toby had found his too hot to eat and had had to have the topping scraped off. Annie suspected that Nicola was finding hers a bit too hot as well, but was valiantly refusing to say anything in front of Georgina. She was breathing rather heavily as she put each forkful in her mouth, and was gulping lots of water. The Mobyn twins, meanwhile, had each been given a mound of grated cheese, which was now all over the table, the floor, their hair and stuck between their fingers. Martina gave each of them a perfunctory wipe every so often, but otherwise seemed content to leave them to their own devices and stare moodily into space.

Mrs Finch was sitting on a kitchen stool, smoking a cigarette. Having discovered that Annie was willing to give a hand with

administering the children's supper, she had relinquished all re-
sponsibility, and was now comfortably regaling Annie with the
failings of the village shop.

'Went in there the other day, when I'd forgotten to get a
sweet for our evening meal. There wasn't nothing I could buy! I
just had to walk straight out again.'

'What were you looking for?' said Annie absently, as she
poured out glasses of Ribena.

'Well . . . I don't know,' said Mrs Finch consideringly. 'A
nice chocolate mousse, maybe. Or crème caramel. Those ones
that come in little glass pots, they're nice, now. Or a frozen gâ-
teau. But you have to go to Safeway for those.'

'Are we having chocolate mousse?' said Georgina suddenly.

'You're having ice cream,' said Mrs Finch. 'Raspberry rip-
ple.'

'Yummy!' said Nicola. Mrs Finch regarded her fondly.

'Poor little pet,' she said. 'It's a shame.'

'We were thinking of taking the children to church tomorrow,' said Annie hurriedly. 'Do you know what time the service
is?' Mrs Finch wrinkled her nose.

'Can't say I do. I see them walking up there sometimes on a
Sunday, you know, but I can't say I've ever noticed what time it
was.'

'So the congregation isn't very big?'

'Oh, I don't know about that. It's a pretty church; people
come to it from other villages. I'd say they get a fair crowd. I was
married in that church, you know,' she added surprisingly.

'How lovely,' said Annie enthusiastically. Mrs Finch stubbed out her lipstick-stained cigarette end, and nodded.

'Fifteen years ago, that was. Reception at the Horse and Groom in Moreton St Mary. We went on a package to Ibiza for the honeymoon. First time I'd been abroad. You wouldn't believe it now, would you?'

'Well, no,' said Annie.

'We've been abroad every year since then. Spain, Portugal, the Canaries, you name it. This year, we went to the Gambia. Took the kids, you know, proper family holiday. They loved it, of course. Lee, that's our eldest, learnt how to water-ski. He's got a real knack. We're thinking about Florida next year. Disney-world.'

'Gosh,' said Annie.

'You fond of holidays abroad?'

'Well,' said Annie honestly, 'I do love going abroad, but we haven't been away for a while. It's a bit difficult.' Mrs Finch nodded wisely.

'I suppose what with the kiddy and all . . .' Her eyes fell on Nicola, awkwardly spreading butter onto a piece of bread.

'It's not that,' said Annie hastily. 'More the money, really.' She laughed.

'Finished!' announced Georgina. 'Shall I get the ice cream?' Mrs Finch nodded, and lit another cigarette. Georgina disappeared out of the kitchen and Annie put her dirty plate in the dishwasher. Mrs Finch didn't move.

'Can't decide between Florida and California,' she said musingly, as Annie returned to her seat. She took a long drag on her cigarette. 'Maybe we should do both.'

Patrick couldn't understand why Caroline was so angry.

'Oh very funny,' she had said, lifting up a foamy leg to admire it. 'Come on, who? It's Charles, isn't it?'

'No it's not. I told you. Stephen.'

'Oh right, yes, Stephen's really got that kind of money.' Her tone was confidently sarcastic, and Patrick, who usually glossed over the details of his business transactions when he talked to Caroline, felt nettled.

'He has if he takes a mortgage out on his house.' He gave her a triumphant look. 'Which he has done, more or less.'

'What?' Caroline's leg stopped moving and she turned disbelieving eyes on him.

'It's very easy to set up,' said Patrick. 'I mean, if you think about it, he's underborrowed at the moment. Not using his potential.'

'You've conned him into taking out a mortgage?' Patrick looked uncomfortable.

'There's no need to put it like that.'

'How much?'

'Does it matter? It's well within his means.'

'What means? He hasn't got a job, or had you forgotten? How much?'

'I think he'd probably want that information to remain confidential,' said Patrick smoothly.

'Fucking hell, Patrick!' Caroline got out of the bath with a great swoosh of water and stood in front of him, dripping and furious. 'How much?'

'Only eighty thousand, for Christ's sake! Stop getting so worked up. His house must be worth at least three times that.'

'He's borrowing eighty thousand to invest?' Caroline put her hand to her head. 'And what's he putting it in?'

'Is it really relevant? You wouldn't understand even if I told you.'

'Like hell I wouldn't! It's not that Sigma fund, is it?' Patrick started.

'How do you know about that?'

'I'm not completely stupid,' she said scathingly. 'I know what you're up to. I know all about the fucking Sigma fund and your fucking bonuses. Jesus Christ! How could you do it?'

'I really don't see what the problem is.'

'Yes you fucking do. Don't pretend you don't. It's obvious. Annie and Stephen can't possibly afford to pay that kind of mortgage. They'll struggle for a bit and then they'll come to you in about a year's time and ask for their money back. And how much will you give them? Or rather, how much will you cream off in fees? Ten thousand? Twenty thousand?'

'There won't be any question of that,' said Patrick huffily. 'Annie and Stephen can well afford a small mortgage like that. And the fund should do extremely well over the long term.'

'Patrick, they haven't got any fucking income.' Caroline's eyes blazed at Patrick. 'What good is the long term?' Patrick looked at her for a second.

'Calm down,' he said irritatingly, and walked into the bedroom, out onto the balcony.

Caroline stared after him in rage for a minute or two. Then she roused herself to action. She dried herself briskly and slapped on body moisturizer, thinking furiously. Patrick really had sunk to new depths. He'd always been an unprincipled salesman— that had been something that had attracted her to him in the first place. He and his friends, in their flashy suits, with their over-smooth voices and eager darting eyes, had tickled her fancy, had made her laugh. And at the beginning, Patrick had treated her a bit like a favoured client—deferential murmurs, respectful remarks, but all the time that tacit undercurrent: *we both know what we're here for, don't we?* Except that she wasn't there to buy financial services.

She gazed at herself in the mirror, remembering herself, the busty promo girl with the blond hair and the big smile. No wonder Patrick had fallen for her. In fact, he'd been incredibly cool about the whole thing, considering how desperate he was to have her—although she'd only found that out later. Half the time it had been her worrying that he'd gone off her. Incredible, really.

And what a bastard he'd turned out to be.

'You bastard,' she said to the mirror. She smiled. Despite her protestations, the thought of Patrick once again as an unprincipled salesman faintly excited her.

She conjured up an image of Patrick fifteen years ago: determined, pugnacious, cocky. Young and virile; forthright and thrusting. They'd met when they were both working at a personal finance show in London. She'd been on some other firm's stand, handing out leaflets for a champagne draw. On the fourth day, she rigged the draw so Patrick won the champagne, and they spent the afternoon getting steadily drunk. Then he'd pulled her behind the stand and kissed her. She could still remember the shock waves that had gone through her drunken mind. Was she really kissing this short, ugly person? And becoming excited by it? He'd pulled up her company promotional T-shirt, groaned at the sight of her breasts, pushed aside the lace of her bra and fastened his lips to her nipple. She'd almost cried out in ecstasy. Then he'd pulled himself away.

'Gotta go,' he'd said. 'Clients out there. Gotta get them.' And she'd stared after him with swollen, tingling lips that ached to be kissed by him again.

Caroline stared at her lips in the mirror. They were still full, still kissable. Her breasts were still firm; her skin still soft and smooth. And Patrick was still a bastard. They might both be fifteen years older now, but really they were no different from the way they'd been then. This realization cheered her. But at the same time, she was angry with Patrick. Little as she thought of Stephen, he was still a friend, and Annie more so. Caroline was in fact, she realized, very fond of Annie. And Nicola. The idea of them falling into financial trouble, worrying over the bills, quarrelling about money, upset her. An image came into her mind, of Stephen hunched over the kitchen table, sobbing, of Annie comforting him, of Nicola appearing at the door, wide eyed and worried.

Patrick came in from the balcony and caught her eye in the mirror. He looked guarded and suspicious.

'You're a real bastard,' said Caroline. 'A real heel.' Patrick opened his mouth to speak and then closed it again. 'And poor old Annie and Stephen have no idea. They trust you completely, did you know that? They deserve to be put right.' Patrick's frown deepened, and he strode towards the bathroom. But Caroline got up and stood in his way. 'They need a good friend to tell them what you're really like,' she said.

'You're not going to say anything,' said Patrick. 'You know which side your bread is buttered. You lose me clients, I lose money, we both end up poor.'

'Hardly poor,' scoffed Caroline.

'If no one wants to buy financial services from me, then yes, poor,' retorted Patrick. 'It doesn't take much to ruin a reputation. Remember what happened to Graham Witherspoon? Excuse me.'

Caroline stared after him angrily. Half of her wanted to warn Stephen and Annie to cancel the deal, for their own sakes. But Patrick was right. One disillusioned customer—however good a friend—was enough to spread the word and lose customers. In fact, being a friend made it worse. Graham Witherspoon had been a colleague of Patrick's. He'd been a top salesman until once he'd drunkenly told a dinner party full of friends and clients that his products were rip-offs. After that he'd barely sold a thing, and soon after that he'd been fired. Should she risk that happening to Patrick?

Frowning slightly, she walked into her wardrobe. She hadn't yet given a thought to what she was going to wear. Absently, she pulled out cream satin knickers and bra, a buttercup linen shift dress, matching suede pumps from Italy. She put them all down on the bed and took out her jewellery box. Gold knot earrings and her diamond solitaire ring. She wasn't going to have that cow Cressida out-jewelling her. To be on the safe side, she added a diamond bracelet. She sprayed herself all over with scent and then dressed, admiring her brown shoulders against the yellow; pointing her foot and rotating it prettily.

She looked in the mirror. Simple but chic. Too simple? She imagined the impression she would make against the cream leather sofa in the living room, holding a champagne glass, laughing at a joke. Her eyes landed on the gold earrings. Too dull. She ripped them out and searched for her diamond studs. They sparkled in her ears, and she smiled at her reflection. One could never have too many diamonds. Was that a famous saying? Or had she made it up?

She pondered on it as she walked down to the living room, admiring herself in every shiny surface that she passed. She surveyed the empty living room with satisfaction, poured herself a glass of champagne and sat down on the sofa. The plight of the Fairweathers had, for the moment, quite vanished from her mind.

CHAPTER EIGHT

Cressida shifted uncomfortably, took another sip of champagne and gazed out of the window at the sun setting over the glowing fields. She felt marooned and rather miserable. The leather sofa she was sitting on was soft and very squashy, and having sunk into it, she didn't think she would be able to get out of it without an effort. Charles, who had been sitting next to her, had sprung up to examine an antique cricket bat which Patrick was showing to Stephen, and so far no one had taken his place. Caroline and Annie were giggling at the far side of the drawing room, lingering at the built-in bar while Caroline poured out a glass of champagne.

Caroline's raucous laugh rang out through the room, and

Cressida flinched. She couldn't bear Caroline's rowdy spirits at the best of times; least of all now, with the worry of that letter still in her mind, and still unshared. She hadn't been able to find a suitable moment to take it out and show it to Charles; first of all she'd felt too nervous to bring the subject up, and then Martina had appeared with the twins, wanting to know if they could use the Jacuzzi in their bathroom. Charles had suggested this, it transpired, and he spent the rest of the time before dinner romping in the bathroom with the twins, covering the floor in bubbles, and thoroughly over-exciting them.

In the end, Cressida had retreated to a bathroom that she'd found at the end of the corridor, which no one else seemed to be using. She'd gone through her usual routine mechanically, using the same make-up that she'd been taught to apply at the Lucie Clayton grooming school fifteen years ago and had never digressed from since. She had brushed out her hair, sprayed on scent and smiled bravely at herself in the mirror. But now she felt cold inside her dress, and her smile stopped at her lips. Hadn't she once read somewhere that babies learnt to smile as a defence mechanism? That was all her smile was tonight—a defence, to stop people looking too closely, or saying 'Cheer up' in that dreadfully hearty way.

Her mind kept veering between optimism and despair. Of course, the letter must be a mistake. As soon as she told Charles about it, he would reassure her, point out the error, put his arms round her and say fondly, 'You really haven't got a clue about money, have you?' It would be like the time she decided to pay some bills herself for once, and ended up paying them all twice.

That had happened just after they'd been married, and Charles had been so amused. He actually seemed to like it when she made blunders and didn't understand things. And just as she thought she'd got something sorted out in her mind, she would try to make an intelligent comment and he would burst out laughing at her. She was always one step behind. So, of course, this letter must be another mix-up. There would be something she hadn't thought of, or didn't know about, that would explain it all. They would both be laughing about it tomorrow.

So why did the thought of it make her feel sick, and anxiously swirl the drink round in her glass? She recalled the sum of money mentioned and shuddered. She was rich, of course she was. But was she that rich any more? Could she stand such a demand for money? She willed herself to remember what Mr Stanlake, her portfolio manager, had said at their last meeting. She could remember his thin-lipped smile; his clean, cool handshake; the view from his window and even the face of his well-groomed secretary who always brought them coffee. But what had been said? How much was left of her assets? She fingered the fabric of her dress. Perhaps she could find out what her financial situation was before telling Charles about the letter. It would take time, but then, this house didn't seem the right place to tell him. Especially not now. Not now that girl—woman, whatever she was—had arrived.

Right from the start, Charles had always been unwilling to talk about Ella, and Cressida certainly hadn't wanted to rake up his past. She knew hardly anything about Ella, apart from the fact that Charles had lived with her for at least five years in that house in Seymour Road. In fact, before this afternoon, Cressida had never even known what Ella looked like. Somehow she'd been surprised when she saw her. She had imagined her slightly fatter, slightly less . . . she searched for a word in her mind . . . exotic looking.

She was jolted out of her thoughts by a sudden burst of laughter from Caroline and Annie. Caroline was brandishing a bottle of Malibu.

'Annie, you haven't lived if you haven't tried this,' she shrieked. 'It's great stuff!' Annie's cheeks were flushed and her eyes were bright.

'But I've still got some champagne,' she protested, as Caroline began pouring it out.

'So what?' Caroline looked around wickedly and then put the bottle of Malibu to her lips.

'I once did a promotion for Malibu,' she said, wiping her mouth. 'Or was it Piña Colada? We all wore grass skirts and loads of fake tan. Really orangey stuff. I got it all over the sheets when I went to bed that night.' She paused. 'But then, if I remember rightly, they weren't my sheets, so I didn't give a shit.' She broke into bubbling laughter again.

Patrick had gone to fetch more of his cricket memorabilia, and as he entered, his eyes swivelled distrustfully in the direction of Caroline's laughter. Then they fell on Cressida, sitting alone on the sofa. She immediately flashed him a bright, rather desperate smile, and willed him to rejoin the men. She intuitively felt that Patrick was the sort of man who would realize that something was wrong and wheedle it all out of her with no effort at all. He looked at her half-empty glass and called to Caroline.

'Sweetheart, some more champagne over here, I think.' He smiled at Cressida, and she smiled back, even harder.

'Lovely view, isn't it?' she said, gesturing out of the window. Her eyes fell on the fields and she strove for something further to say. 'Lovely colours,' she added eventually. Patrick nodded.

'We do get a superb sunset here,' he said. 'I've taken some marvellous photographs. I'll show you later.'

'That would be lovely,' said Cressida feebly. There was a silence, in which Patrick's eyes seemed to penetrate hers. Her lips trembled; she looked down, and was aware of a pink tinge spreading over her cheeks.

'Cressida,' began Patrick, and moved a step closer. Cressida stared fixedly at her knees, unsure why she was blushing.

Then, to her relief, the door opened, and Don and Valerie came in.

'Hello!' hooted Valerie. 'Are we late?'

'No, no,' said Patrick genially. He moved to kiss her cheek, and she ducked awkwardly towards him, so that they collided with some force. As his head rose, Patrick's eye met Cressida's with the briefest of flickers, and she found herself grinning down into her champagne glass, feeling ridiculously warmed. When she looked up, she saw Patrick shaking Don's hand with a perfectly straight face and Valerie waving at her as though they were separated by several miles.

'Ooh! I do love your dress,' said Valerie. 'It's just like mine!'

This, Cressida realized, gazing at Valerie in slight horror, was not far from the truth. Both of them were in simple, tailored, navy-blue dresses. If Cressida's was in exquisitely cut linen and Valerie's in ill-fitting polyester, Valerie certainly couldn't tell the difference.

'I do love the classic look,' exclaimed Valerie complacently, sitting down beside Cressida. Her white hand shot out and fingered the fabric of Cressida's dress; Cressida suddenly and irrationally felt sick.

'Yours is lovely,' Valerie said. 'Where did you get it?'

'London,' murmured Cressida.

'Me too,' said Valerie. 'In the sales. Actually, it's not quite the right size, but it was such a bargain!'

'Drink, Valerie?' said Patrick genially. 'Champagne?'

'Ooh, lovely!' said Valerie. She settled back next to Cressida. Her legs, dead white apart from a strip of pink sunburn down the front of each, were covered in the minute red dots of skin which has been recently shaved and a plaster was flapping at the heel of her navy-blue patent-leather shoe.

Cressida glanced surreptitiously over at Caroline, who was now opening another bottle of champagne. She was a vision of yellow, with her buttercup dress, golden skin and bright blond hair, shining under the spotlights of the bar. She had too much make-up on, in Cressida's opinion, and was being her usual vulgar, outrageous self, but at least she looked vivacious with it. And Annie, in her richly patterned Indian sarong dress, looked flushed, happy and animated. She had caught the sun on her cheeks, and had twisted her hair up into a knot. Cressida had never seen her look so attractive.

Looking down at her navy-blue lap, and at Valerie's, Cressida suddenly felt as if she were back at school—and she and Valerie were the misfits of the form. Her dress—beautiful and expensive though it was—seemed both dowdy and over-smart at the same time. And she was the only woman in the room wearing tights, she noticed. She took a miserable sip of champagne. Everything about her seemed wrong. Yet she had worn exactly the same outfit a few weeks ago—to drinks with the Marchants— and felt entirely at ease.

Patrick had made his way over to the bar. Caroline was sitting alone on a bar stool, sipping a huge cocktail with her eyes closed.

'Sweetness,' he said, 'people are waiting for drinks.'

'Here you are.' Caroline eyed him balefully and gave him the open bottle. 'You can take this round.' Patrick gave her an annoyed look.

'I meant,' he said, 'you could go round and talk to a few people.'

'I'm talking to Annie,' said Caroline obstinately. 'She's just gone to the loo. She'll be back in a moment.'

'Well, you can't talk to her all evening,' said Patrick, in an attempt at jocularity. 'We do have other friends.'

'Friends!' mocked Caroline. She swivelled round on the bar stool and raised contemptuous blue eyes to Patrick's. 'Are you Annie's friend? Are you Stephen's friend? Well, if you are, Christ help your enemies.'

Patrick shifted uncomfortably. 'I hardly think this is the place,' he whispered.

'Exactly,' replied Caroline in a grudgingly low voice. 'Neither is it the place to rip off people who trust you. Like they do.

Like they did, perhaps I should say.' Patrick peered at her with mounting anxiety.

'Caroline!' he hissed. 'You bloody better not have said anything to Annie.'

'Or what?' Caroline's smile challenged him.

'Hello, Patrick!' Annie's cheerful voice hailed them and Patrick smiled uneasily.

'You're looking lovely tonight,' he said.

'I'm feeling wonderful,' said Annie cheerfully. 'It's been a really super day! I can't tell you how much we've both enjoyed it. And the children have been in heaven.' She turned to Caroline, smiling. 'Nicola worships Georgina even more than she did before. She's insisted on calling their bedroom the dormy. And I think Georgina's going to do her lights-out, go-to-sleep, head-prefect bit for them later on.'

'My God,' said Caroline. 'We really have raised a little Hitler.' Patrick frowned, and opened his mouth to protest, but then changed his mind.

'Dinner soon, do you think, sweetheart?' he said.

'We're still waiting for Ella,' pointed out Caroline. Patrick's frown deepened.

'Oh yes,' he said shortly. 'Well, I'll go and take some more champagne round.'

'I'm sure she won't be long,' said Annie soothingly.

Charles was ignoring Cressida's pleading looks from the sofa. She was stuck next to the dreadful Valerie—and for that he couldn't help feeling sorry for her—but there was something in him tonight that couldn't bear to sit tamely down with his wife.

He felt an unspecified anticipation; a slight exhilaration; a mood of gaiety and energy. It was probably, he thought to himself, the combination of outdoor exercise, sunlight and champagne. He didn't allow himself to wonder why this mood had only over-taken him after the surprise appearance made by Ella. He was used, after four years of marriage, to swiftly diverting his thoughts whenever they turned in the direction of Ella; remembering only the bad times; most of the time blocking her memory completely from his mind.

Stephen seemed in good spirits too, he noticed; more sure of himself than he had been that morning. He and Don were still poring over old photographs, programmes, score sheets, cricket balls, even a couple of old cricket pads. Patrick's collection of cricket memorabilia was clearly fascinating them. Charles found it boring. The cricket bat had been interesting to look at, both aesthetically and as an historical artefact—but endless lists and photographs of bygone players were really not his thing. And yet he still hovered by them, studiously avoiding Cressida's wan face. He was in far too good a mood to have to go and sit beside his miserable-looking wife.

Cressida's spirits had plummeted even further. Her position on the sofa was uncomfortable and she could feel that her dress was rucked up; but to stand up and shake herself out would draw attention to herself—and at that moment, she didn't feel as if she could bear anyone's eyes on her. Her glass was warm from the clutch of her fingers; her stockinged legs were uncomfortably slippery against the leather of the sofa; and Valerie's shrill voice was unending.

She had regaled Cressida for the last fifteen minutes with unsavoury pieces of gossip from the London office where she worked. She related each story in a detached, almost innocent voice, that displayed her complete ignorance of how these affairs might utterly destroy a marriage; ruin a relationship of trust; shatter a family. To Valerie, it was all fair game for entertainment.

'And then you'll never guess what,' she was saying. 'Michelle—that's his secretary—went and called his wife by the wrong name. She nearly died!' Valerie paused, and looked with bright eyes at Cressida, waiting, without much hope, for a response. Cressida was evidently a disappointment as a gossip partner. 'But that wasn't when she guessed,' she continued. 'The wife, I mean. It was about two months later. And it was such a stupid mistake. She saw his expenses list—and one of them was for a double hotel room. He just didn't think on his feet. I mean, he could have come up with a story or something, but he just told her everything. Next thing, he was off sick for a week.'

Cressida was beginning to feel sick herself. She had never heard such a sordid catalogue of misdemeanours. She felt like weeping for the wife's sake. For all the wives' sakes.

'Are you OK?' said Valerie, becoming aware of Cressida's downturned face.

'I'm fine,' said Cressida shakily. 'I'm just a bit tired.'

'I know what, I'll get you a drink of water,' said Valerie, suddenly self-important, casting herself as Cressida's aide. 'I'll get you a nice glass of Perrier, shall I?'

'That would be lovely,' said Cressida. 'And perhaps I'll go outside on the terrace.'

'Get some fresh air, good idea,' said Valerie. She placed her clammy hand on Cressida's arm. 'You probably had too much sun today.' Cressida fought off the desire to retch.

As Valerie made off to the bar, Cressida struggled to her feet. Her dress was, as she had thought, rucked up at the back, and the linen had become rather creased. Not only that, but a spare button or something inside the dress seemed to have been caught on her tights. She fiddled uncomfortably at the spot. The only solution was to go to the bathroom and see what was wrong. She put her drink down and made for the door. But it opened before she could get there. A husky, coppery voice cried, 'Sorry I'm so late!' and Ella made her entrance.

She was wearing a dress made from layers of floating chiffon in palest yellow, cinnamon and burnt orange. Around her neck was a long string of amber beads, on which was strung a large, ornate silver cross. Her cheeks were radiantly glowing and her hair tied up in a silk, coffee-coloured scarf. Her deep-brown eyes surveyed the room, and she smiled first of all at Patrick, who was dispensing champagne to Stephen.

'I'm terrible,' she said apologetically. 'Once I get into a hot bath I just can't get out. Am I shockingly late?'

'No, no, don't be silly,' said Patrick. 'Come in and have a drink.' He led Ella in, until she was suddenly directly in front of Cressida. Cressida hastily stood up straight, stopped fiddling with her frock, and flashed her bright smile.

'Hello,' said Ella. 'We didn't really get a chance to meet this afternoon. I'm Ella Harte.'

'Yes, how do you do,' said Cressida in a colourless voice. She felt like a shadow beside this voluptuous, glowing figure. 'I am Cressida Mobyn.' She saw Ella flinch very slightly before taking her outstretched hand.

'It's funny,' said Ella, looking round at Charles and Stephen, who were watching in uncomfortable fascination. 'I somehow hadn't taken in the fact that you'd be called Mobyn. I associate the name Mobyn, you see, with Charles.'

Her hand was warm, and as she moved closer, Cressida was aware of a pulsing, foreign scent. There was a split second of silence before Cressida spoke.

'Well,' she said brightly. 'It was strange for me just after we were married. Having a different name. But I'm quite used to it now. I sign cheques without thinking.' She smiled again. Ella looked at her for a few moments without speaking, and then smiled slowly herself.

'I should think you do,' she said. 'Cressida Mobyn.' She rolled her tongue round the name. 'Well, I'm glad we've met.' Cressida tried not to look surprised.

'Oh, so am I,' she lied, in complete incomprehension.

Caroline, roused at last to hostess-like behaviour, had hurried over to where Ella and Cressida were standing. Now she chipped in.

'Come and get a drink, Ella,' she said, leading her away from Cressida.

Cressida watched them go with an unfamiliar feeling of resentment. Ella was plainly a member of the favoured group. She wondered whether to go to the bathroom and straighten her dress. It might look as though she was offended by Ella being there. Which naturally, she thought briskly to herself, she wasn't.

'Hello, darling,' said Charles, coming up to her with a rather unnatural smile. 'I see you've been talking to Ella. I'm glad you two have met at last.' Cressida stared at Charles in renewed incomprehension. Why would anyone be glad that she'd met Ella? She couldn't see any benefit in it at all.

As Stephen went in to dinner, he felt agreeably content. He was relaxed and glowing after the day's tennis; his appetite was sharpened by the sight of the plates of delicately arranged smoked salmon on the table, and he still had a lingering sense of exhilaration at the deal he'd done with Patrick. He glanced at the others, following him in to the dining room. They all looked sophisticated and cosmopolitan—even Annie. An image of their usual homely family suppers flashed through his mind. Annie always looked pretty, he thought loyally, even when she was hot and bothered over the stove, or coping with Nicola in a frustrated mood. But tonight her face was alive and excited, and she seemed to be laughing a lot. That was Caroline's influence, of course. He'd forgotten quite how determined that woman was to have a good time.

'Hello.' A voice at his elbow caused him to turn round. It was Ella, her dimpled face creased in a smile. 'I haven't said hello to you properly yet,' she continued. Stephen bent to kiss her cheek, which was smooth, glowing and smelling faintly of coconut.

'You're looking very well,' he said, aware that he was dealing in clichés. But how else was he to talk? 'Travelling certainly agrees with you . . .'

'. . . or something,' she finished, laughing. Her brown eyes searched his face. 'And you? Are you happy?' Stephen shrugged casually. He remembered now that Ella had always stood just a little closer than other people; asked slightly more penetrating questions; had always pursued a difficult line of enquiry where others would meekly have said 'oh, I see' and changed the subject.

'I'm fine,' he said easily. He smiled at her; his new, confident smile.

'I told Caroline I wanted to sit next to you,' said Ella. 'I want to hear all about your thesis. I'm so thrilled that you're doing it at last.' She darted to the table, peering at the name places.

'Here we are,' she called. 'We're over here.' Stephen joined her slowly, his confident air seeming to slip away slightly with every step. He had almost forgotten about his thesis. He had cast himself, this afternoon, as a leisured, moneyed deal-maker en-joying some tennis among friends. He had almost convinced him-self that this comfortable and luxurious house, not the grubby libraries and teaching rooms of the university, was his natural environment. Was he now to be forced to go over in his mind his failed attempt at scholarship; to recall the unwieldy, uncertain mass of dubious information and half-baked arguments that haunted and mocked him in his dreams? He flinched at the mem-ory of it. Look at Patrick over there. He seemed to be doing all right, and he'd never been near a university in his life. Let alone given up a relatively well-paid job late in life in the vain pursuit of some sort of academic recognition. Wasn't this easy, leisured life what he really aspired to? He sank uneasily into a plushy, upholstered dining chair and smiled jovially at Valerie, who was sitting on his other side. But Ella was tugging at his sleeve.

'Now,' she said, shaking out her napkin, squeezing lemon over her salmon and looking seriously at him through her lashes. 'I really want to know. How's your research going?'

As Mrs Finch cleared away the plates from the first course, Charles looked over at Stephen and Ella again. What were they finding so much to talk about? Stephen was gesturing animatedly; Ella was nodding enthusiastically. She was leaning forward towards Stephen, clasping her hands, unwittingly pushing up her breasts until a full, golden-brown cleavage was on show. Or was it unwittingly? Charles looked away, and then looked back again.

'But that's amazing!' Ella's husky voice travelled across the table to him. 'Absolutely fascinating.' Charles could bear it no longer.

'What's fascinating, Ella?' he asked in a hearty voice. The whole table stopped talking and looked at him. He ignored Cressida's pale, questioning face, Caroline's raised eyebrows, Patrick's smirk, and ploughed on. 'Sorry, I couldn't help overhearing that something was fascinating. I was just wondering what it was.'

Ella raised her eyes, slightly contemptuous, slightly amused, to his.

'We were talking about Stephen's thesis,' she said. 'It's so interesting. But you must know all about it, I suppose. I'm hearing it all for the first time.' Charles looked at Stephen. Everyone was waiting for an answer.

'Of course,' he said eventually. 'Your thesis. Terribly interesting.'

'Do you think so, Charles?' said Stephen, grinning at him in mock-surprise, knowing full well that Charles couldn't give a damn about his thesis. Charles forced himself not to glare at Stephen. He suddenly felt an irrational hatred for him, sitting next to Ella, breathing in her scent, touching her bare arms, sharing her jokes. But it was Charles that Ella was now looking at, twisting her amber beads thoughtfully round her fingers. He had to say something.

'Oh yes,' he said. 'Seventeenth-century stuff, wasn't it?'

'Fourteenth,' said Ella. 'You're not telling me they were writing mystery plays in the seventeenth century?'

'Mystery plays?' said Charles in surprise. 'Since when has your thesis been on mystery plays, Stephen?'

'Since my original proposal was turned down,' said Stephen, grinning. 'Only about two years ago.'

'I haven't kept up,' said Charles apologetically. To his surprise he did feel genuinely ashamed. He had a sudden flashback to cosy suppers in the Fairweathers' basement kitchen. He remembered Stephen outlining his latest piece of research; eyes lit up with the thrill of discovery; gesticulating with a piece of garlic bread or a pasta-laden fork; pausing in his rhetoric only to swallow a mouthful of food or wine; then looking up to see Annie and Charles giggling at him. And Ella, of course. She had always been there.

'I think the idea of our own local mystery play is wonderful,' said Ella. 'The Silchester Mystery Play. We should organize for it to be put on. In the Cathedral.'

'We could do it for charity,' said Cressida suddenly. She had been following the exchange with very little enthusiasm. She had no idea what a mystery play was and no interest in Stephen's thesis. She did not trust Ella; she couldn't think why Charles was insisting on talking to her, and she was longing for bed. But an instinctive desire to win back Charles' attention, coupled with her belief that it was one's duty to contribute to general conversation, forced her valiantly to speak. Having spoken, she sank gratefully back into her chair.

But Ella had fixed her attention on Cressida.

'What a wonderful idea,' she said, in an intense voice. 'Could you organize something like that?'

'Well,' said Cressida faintly, 'I'm on several charity committees. In Silchester, you know.'

'It's perfect,' said Ella. 'You can stage a show in the Cathedral. Get professional actors. It'll be a marvellous occasion.' She beamed at Stephen. 'And wouldn't it help your research? To see it actually performed?'

'Well, yes,' said Stephen. 'I suppose it would.'

'Of course it would,' said Ella. 'You must let me know when it happens. I'll come back especially to see it.'

'Back?' said Charles in spite of himself. 'Back from where?' Ella gave him a curious look.

'Oh,' she said. 'Didn't I tell you? I'm starting a job. In Italy.'

'Ooh, how lovely!' exclaimed Valerie. 'Imagine working in Italy!'

'Did it?' said Ella. She paused, fork halfway to mouth. 'Well, you never know,' she said. 'Perhaps she is.'

Coffee had been served, Don and Valerie were making signs of departure, and the others were still sitting in the drawing room. The doors to the terrace were still open, and the sweet smell of night air mingled with the lingering aroma of coffee. Annie dreamily swirled a cognac round in her glass. It had been such a lovely day. Her muscles ached agreeably, her skin was warm with sunburn, and her stomach replete with food. She was also, she realized, quite drunk.

'See you tomorrow!' Don's grinning face interrupted her reverie.

'Sorry? Oh, yes, see you then,' said Annie.

'We'll be along to watch your match,' he said. 'Bright and early.' Annie clutched her head.

'But I'll feel dreadful tomorrow!' she cried.

'Drink a glass of water for each alcoholic drink you've consumed,' advised Don cheerily. 'That's my advice.' Annie felt a sudden, uncharacteristic urge to throw her glass at him. She deliberately took a large gulp of cognac, looked up, and spluttered as she saw Caroline grimacing at Don behind his back.

'I'm such a child!' she wailed, when Don was out of the door. 'I've regressed thirty years.' She looked accusingly at Caroline. 'It's all your fault,' she said. 'I was a sane human being before today.'

'No you weren't,' retorted Caroline. 'Remember apple bobbing at that Hallowe'en party? That got really out of hand.' She and Annie collapsed into giggles at the memory.

'I got completely soaked,' said Annie.

'We all did,' said Caroline.

'And Nicola kept saying, "No, Mummy, like this,"' called out Stephen, who was watching Annie in amusement.

'Poor old Nicola,' said Annie, fondly wiping her eyes. 'I don't think she'd ever seen me drunk before.'

'She was good at apple bobbing,' said Caroline.

'She still is,' said Annie robustly.

'Sweet Nicola,' said Caroline. 'She's a darling child.'

'Oh Nicola!' chimed in Ella, from the sofa. 'I love her to pieces!'

Ella had commandeered two thirds of the sofa and was reclining comfortably, shoes kicked off, head thrown back. The remaining part of the sofa was, as yet, unclaimed. Stephen was sitting nearby on the floor; Annie and Caroline were by the fireplace; Cressida was sitting on her own, on a low leather pouffe. Charles was the only one not sitting down; he paced about the room like a big cat, unable to keep his eyes from swivelling towards Ella every time she spoke or moved.

She was again pursuing the subject of the Silchester Mystery Play.

'Really, Stephen, you must put it on,' she insisted, sitting up and hugging her feet through the gauzy layers of her dress.

'I'll think about it,' said Stephen, smiling at her.

'Don't just think about it! Do it!'

'It may not be as simple as all that,' he said. 'These things take a lot of time, a lot of preparation, a lot of money. A serious amount of money, if you want it done well. Where am I to find that?' Ella shrugged.

'You can always find money if you really want it.'

Charles had been listening to this exchange. Now he came over and, with deliberate casualness, sat down on the bit of the sofa not occupied by Ella. She looked at him silently. There were only inches between them; her feet were almost brushing against his trousers.

'If you wanted some money,' he said, looking not at Stephen but at Ella, 'we could always put some up. The Print Centre. It's just the sort of project we should be involved with.' Ella's eyes held his insolently.

'How much?' she said challengingly. Charles' breathing quickened slightly.

'Five, ten thousand, maybe?' he said. Ella didn't move. 'Fifteen?' his voice cracked.

'Fifteen thousand pounds?' Stephen exclaimed. His voice rang through the room. 'My word, Charles, that's very generous!'

Cressida, who had been staring, unheeding, at the carpet, looked up. Were they talking about money? Was Charles promising fifteen thousand pounds to someone? The memory of the letter flooded into her mind; a pang of alarm shot through her body. She had to speak. 'Sorry, Charles,' she said awkwardly, flinching as everyone turned to look at her, 'what were you saying?'

'It's all right,' said Charles, 'it's just Print Centre business. Nothing for you to worry about.' He turned away. In a slight haze, Cressida took in the fact that he was sitting on the sofa with Ella. And yet when she had been sitting on the sofa earlier on, he had insisted on standing up. It was like a bad dream. And worst of all was the untold secret of the letter.

'What sort of business?' she persisted. Charles gave her an annoyed look.

'A sponsorship deal. We're going to back the Silchester Mystery Play. You can help to organize it.'

'Oh,' said Cressida. Waves of panic went through her. She had to tell Charles. Before he promised any more money. She had to talk to him.

Shakily she stood up, and flashed a smile around the room.

'I think I'll go to bed actually,' she said. She smiled hard at Charles. 'Are you coming, darling?' Charles gave her a surprised, rather irritated look. He glanced at his watch.

'It's not midnight yet,' he said. 'Do you want to go so soon?'

'Yes, I think so,' said Cressida, staring at him with what she hoped was a meaningful expression. 'It's been a long day.'

'Well, I think I'll stay up a while longer,' said Charles. 'See you later.' Cressida stood still for a few seconds, trying not to appear desperate.

'You won't be too long, will you?' she said eventually. She was aware of how awful she must appear to everyone. They would all laugh at her when she was gone but she couldn't bear another hour going by without having told Charles about the letter.

'No, I won't be too long,' replied Charles evenly. 'Good night.' He turned back to Ella, leaving Cressida stranded in the middle of the room. She began to back uncertainly towards the door.

'Good night, Cressida,' said Patrick kindly. 'I hope you sleep well. If you want anything, just shout.'

'Good night,' chorused the others.

'Don't worry,' said Caroline, smirking. 'We won't keep Charles up much longer.' Cressida flashed a smile at her, and hurried out through the door, tears stinging her eyes. They were all laughing at her. And Charles despised her for trying to rush him off to bed.

She went hurriedly through the hall and up the stairs, wondering if it was too late to run herself a hot bath. She walked briskly along the pale corridor, which seemed much longer now than it had been during the day. But when she reached the door of the boys' bedroom she paused. She had been preoccupied that evening, and had said good night to them in a rush. Now she carefully pushed open the door and looked into the moonlit room. Two little blond heads glinted on their pillows; Martina was gently snoring in the corner and the floor was carpeted in toys. She moved in a few steps, longing to pick up her babies and hold them tight against her chest, to feel their puny heartbeats and let their soft breathing soothe her. But a sense of discipline stopped her from doing anything so silly. The boys needed their sleep; she would disturb Martina; what would people think if they saw her? She stood a few seconds more, then reluctantly tiptoed out of the room and made her lonely way to her own bedroom.

There was a general atmosphere of hilarity in the drawing room once Cressida had left. Patrick went round and filled everyone's drinks; Caroline put a compact disc on the hi-fi. Soon, the rhythms of South American dance music were pulsing through the room. Charles leant back on the sofa and let the sound wash over him. Ella was tapping her foot and softly swaying. Then Caroline got up and began to dance. Her trained dancer's limbs were still supple; her sense of rhythm faultless. Her hips gyrated; her hands gently skimmed her pelvis and thighs.

'Very good,' applauded Ella. 'That's just how they do it.'

'Did you learn any dancing when you were in South America?' asked Annie, watching Caroline in admiration. Ella shrugged.

'A little.'

'Oh, go on!' Annie's eyes were bright, like a child. 'Show us.' Ella smiled, and uncoiled herself from the sofa.

'I need a partner. Caroline?' Caroline held out her hands to Ella, as if for ballroom dancing.

'Closer than that,' said Ella. 'Much closer.' She pulled Caroline towards her, grasped her firmly and began to move her feet, gyrating her hips back and forth. Caroline followed her movements hesitantly and Stephen, moving quietly to the hi-fi controls, turned up the volume of the pulsating music. Nobody spoke. The two women's bodies moved around slowly as if joined by the hips; Caroline's face intense with concentration, Ella's stern and distant. Charles wondered with a sudden fierce pang of jealousy whom she was thinking about. He was beginning to feel unbearably aroused by the sight of Ella and Caroline; looking at the faces of the other men, he suspected he was not the only one.

The atmosphere was broken when the song ended, and Caroline collapsed onto a chair in fits of laughter.

'Take me to South America,' she cried dramatically. 'If that's how the men dance, I want to go there!'

'It's how the women dance, too,' said Ella quietly. But everyone was looking at Patrick, who had stood up and begun to sway his hips in imitation.

'I don't think so, Patrick,' said Stephen comically. 'Better leave it to your wife.'

Patrick sat back down, adopting a disgruntled air, and Ella returned to her place on the sofa. The mood of hysteria seemed to have vanished.

'I'll make some more coffee, shall I?' volunteered Annie.

'I'll show you where everything is,' said Caroline.

Out in the kitchen, Caroline sat down on a chair.

'Actually,' she said, 'I'm not sure I know where everything is. Christ knows where Mrs Finch puts the coffee.' Annie giggled.

'You live in a different world,' she said, opening and closing cupboard doors. 'Not knowing where the coffee is in your own kitchen!'

'Well, I usually leave it out on the side,' said Caroline. 'But that silly cow always puts it away. Try that cupboard. No, that one.' Annie put the kettle on, put coffee in the pot, then came and sat down beside Caroline.

'It's been such a lovely day,' she said. 'I can't thank you enough.' Caroline smiled.

'We should get together more often,' she said. 'I really miss all of you, being stuck here in this village.'

'But it's so lovely here!' exclaimed Annie, surprised. 'Especially for the children. Nicola's had such a wonderful day. Well, we all have, really.' She glanced at the door. 'I think it's done Stephen some good, too,' she added in a low voice. 'I didn't actually realize he and Patrick were such good friends. But they've been chatting away all day.' She beamed at Caroline, but Caroline had a slight frown on her face. She seemed to be thinking.

'When does Stephen finish his thesis again?' she said abruptly.

'In a year or two,' said Annie, looking slightly surprised.

'And what happens after that? Jobwise.' Annie shrugged.

'He'd really like to go into higher education. Perhaps a junior teaching post at one of the universities, or a research fellowship.'

'And do those pay well?' Annie grinned.

'No, they don't. But it won't be for ever. He'll move up to better things.'

'And meanwhile . . . ?'

'Meanwhile, we manage.' Annie looked honestly at Caroline. 'We're very lucky, compared to some. No one goes into academia to be rich.' She glanced up. 'Look, the kettle's boiling.'

The drawing room was quiet as Caroline and Annie came back in with the coffee. The music was soft again, no one was talking, and the sound of the terrace door banging in the wind made them all jump. Caroline put down the tray, closed the terrace door and began to pour out the coffee. When everyone had a cup, she took a deep breath.

'We're all old friends here,' she said. 'We all know each other well enough to talk frankly. And now that it's just us six, there's something I want to say.' Everyone's heads rose interestedly. 'There's a . . .' Caroline paused, searching for the word, 'a particular matter I'd like to discuss. It actually only concerns Stephen and Annie—and Patrick and myself—but somehow I'd like everyone to hear it.' She paused, took a sip of coffee, and gave a defiant glance at Patrick. 'It's a financial matter,' she added. Patrick's heart started beating faster. He tried to give Caroline a silencing yet unobtrusive stare, but she was ignoring him. The stupid fucking bitch. What was she going to say? What was she going to tell them? I'm going to kill her, he thought. I'm going to fucking kill her.

Cressida had undressed as slowly as she could. She brushed her hair, removed her make-up, rubbed moisturizer into her face with upwards movements and applied eye cream. Eventually, when she was utterly ready for bed, when there was nothing else she could do, she looked at her watch. Half-past midnight. And Charles was still downstairs. The ominous phrase 'Don't wait up' floated through her mind. But tonight she had to wait up. She had to talk to Charles, urgently. She fingered the letter, which she had retrieved from her vanity case, and unfolded it. Then she folded it up again without reading it. She could remember what it said without looking. And Charles would soon explain it all to her.

She gazed at herself in the mirror. Her skin was taut with worry; her eyes anxious. Suddenly she missed her father. He had been a generous, comforting figure; mostly absent, but larger—and louder—than life when he was there. He had always been a welcome antidote to the peculiarly feminine air of worry that built up in the house when he went away. Her mother, who was prone to particularly feverish panic attacks, would pour out her

woes as soon as he appeared through the door; he would listen
apparently seriously to her worries, point out the flaws in
them—and eventually have her laughing at herself. Cressida
could remember his hearty guffaw; his huge, strong hands; his
down-to-earth air which would cause her mother to cringe even
as she was locked in his embrace.

But now he was dead, and her mother too. Cressida could feel
the tears rising and took a deep breath. She no longer allowed
herself to weep for either of them. She drank half a glass of water, switched off the light in the bathroom and went back into
the bedroom. She paused by the side of the pink satin bed and
made a few, rather inarticulate attempts at prayer. After a while,
unsatisfied with herself, she stopped. She climbed into bed, shivering slightly, and sat up against the pillows, clutching the letter,
waiting for Charles.

Patrick couldn't quite believe his ears. He stared incredulously at
Caroline, who beamed gaily at him.

'We've discussed it fully, haven't we?' she said. 'Darling.' Patrick smiled feebly at Stephen and Annie. Stephen looked shell-
shocked; Annie's eyes were shining.

'We couldn't let you,' said Stephen eventually.

'Rubbish,' said Caroline briskly. 'We've only got Georgina to
pay for. We might easily have six sets of school fees to fork out
every year. One extra won't make any difference. And it makes
us mad to see Nicola's talents wasted at that school. She needs
a better chance in life. Patrick thinks', she added, 'that Nicola

should have riding lessons.' Patrick's head jerked in amazement. 'He thinks St Catherine's would do wonders for her confidence,' she added blithely.

'Didn't you say that, Patrick?' Patrick glared at her.

'Yes, yes,' he said. 'Wonders.' He turned to pour himself another brandy and caught the eye of Ella. She grinned at him, as if she knew exactly what was going through his mind.

'I think it's a lovely gesture,' she said. 'I'm sure Nicola would benefit from private education. It's very generous of you.'

'Very,' said Charles sardonically. 'Six years of boarding school doesn't exactly come cheap.'

'Well, of course, we'd pay as soon as we could,' said Annie eagerly. 'We'd think of it as a loan.' She gave Patrick a wide smile. 'All my instincts and manners tell me we must refuse your offer; but when I think of Nicola, of how much it would mean to her . . . I don't think I can bring myself to.' Her eyes began to moisten. 'Look at me!' she exclaimed. 'I'm pathetic!'

'I don't know.' Stephen was still frowning. 'As Charles says, it is a lot of money.'

'It's all relative,' said Caroline. She flashed a wicked look at Patrick. 'I mean,' she said deliberately, 'think how much money Patrick deals in every day. What's a few years' school fees compared to that?' Watching in impotent fury, Patrick saw this idea taking root in Stephen's mind. Christ, Stephen was so fucking naïve. After today's performance in the study, he probably thought Patrick dealt in sums of eighty thousand every minute. And Caroline knew it.

Stephen raised doubtful eyes to Patrick, and Patrick forced himself to smile.

'Caroline's right,' he said, hardly able to believe he was saying it. 'We can easily afford it.' If we forget any idea of new cars, let alone a new house, he thought. And Caroline can fucking well get rid of her Barbados brochures.

'Good,' said Caroline. 'That's settled. I'm so pleased. We both are, aren't we, sweetheart?'

'Delighted,' said Patrick, and knocked back another brandy.

CHAPTER NINE

Nothing much more was said for a while. Annie, who had drunk more than anyone—including herself—had quite realized, began weeping quiet, unobtrusive tears of gratitude at Caroline's and Patrick's offer. Stephen smiled apologetically round the room and put his arm round her; the others sat blankly as if overcome by sudden torpor; staring silently down into their coffee grounds with numbed, drunk, late-night expressions. After a while, Caroline began to yawn rather ostentatiously. Stephen glanced at his watch and began to shift position; Patrick quietly collected the coffee cups and put them back on the tray.

Charles realized, with alarm, that the party was breaking up. Suddenly the idea of tamely going up to bed filled him with horror. After this evening, he felt alive and invigorated. He felt young again. Hearing about Ella's travels, about her friendship with Maud Vennings, talking about artists, even discussing Stephen's mystery play, had suddenly reminded him of what he used to be like. Christ, how his values, his interests, even his idea of a good time had changed since marriage. Or, really, since Cressida. When was the last time he had stayed up all night, or got stoned? When was the last time he had thrown himself headlong into an argument, debating the point for debating's sake—even if he agreed with his opponent? When was the last time he had spent a whole evening excitedly sketching out some new project for the Print Centre that was doomed to be a commercial failure?

He glanced down at his wrist, expensively cuffed in a Jermyn Street shirt, expensively adorned with a Swiss watch. Of course, his life had changed. No one could expect him to remain a bloody hippy all his life; to live off bread and sex and cheap drugs. And it wasn't just him. The world had changed. It was Stephen who was the oddity these days, still idealistic; still naïve; still poor. Charles' thoughts flickered complacently to the house in the Cathedral Close. It had cost a fucking fortune, that house.

His mind paused, and waited for the customary kick of pleasure that thinking about his new wealth generally brought him. But this time it hadn't worked. The feeling of excitement in his stomach had nothing to do with his wife and her worldly goods. He imagined her face, waiting for him upstairs; pale, insipid, stupid. Going up to bed was unthinkable.

He glanced at Ella, clutching her knees and gazing dreamily at nothing.

'I feel like a bit of a walk,' he said quietly. 'A breath of fresh air. Want to join me?' Ella regarded him consideringly.

'All right,' she said eventually, and smiled her secretive smile. 'You can show me the garden. Caroline,' she said, raising her voice, 'it's not too late to go walking in the garden, is it? We won't get bats in our hair?'

'Oh no,' said Caroline, 'I don't think so.' She looked puzzledly at Patrick, swaying very slightly. 'Bats?' she repeated. 'I don't think so.'

'Go ahead,' said Patrick, smiling at them over Caroline's head. 'Just leave the terrace door open and shut it firmly behind you when you come back.'

'Well, good night,' said Charles hurriedly, not wanting to look at their faces.

'See you all tomorrow,' said Ella. 'Sleep well.'

As Ella opened the terrace door, Charles felt a slight quailing. Perhaps it would be better to announce that he had changed his mind; that he was feeling tired; that he thought he would turn in after all. But before he could make up his mind to do this, he was out into the soft, black, anonymous night. He lingered on the terrace, breathing in the night air, looking at the dark forms of the garden. The fairy lights were still on and he felt as though he were playing a part in some old-fashioned film. Some enchanted evening . . . A tune flickered through his mind.

'I thought you wanted to walk?' Ella was already halfway across the lawn.

'Oh, coming,' said Charles. As he hurried to join her, someone turned off the fairy lights from inside. The garden was plunged into darkness and Charles paused in his stride.

'Where are you?'

'Here.' Her voice travelled, low and husky, through the night air, and he walked blindly towards it, feeling for bumps in the grass with his feet, trying to adjust his eyes to the darkness.

'Here, silly.' He had walked past her. He turned back uncertainly and felt a warm hand seize his.

'You urban creature,' she mocked. 'You've forgotten how to use your eyes properly.' At the touch of her hand, a delicious tingle spread from Charles' neck, up past his ear and over his head. He followed her meekly towards the hedge, through the gate and into the field beyond. As they brushed past the hedge, a bird noisily flapped its way out; further down in the undergrowth there were more animal scufflings.

'In Africa,' said Ella, 'all the animals come together at night to drink. Even those that don't normally mix. It's a wonderful sight.'

'You went to Africa?' ventured Charles. He had never discussed Ella's travels with her, aware that she had gone off, initially, because of him; because of the break-up. At the time, she had not even told him that she was going; he had learned it from Angus, his old business partner, who had sided firmly with Ella.

'Yes, I did,' said Ella. They fell silent for a while. Charles could not think of a single word or phrase that would not sound banal. He woefully tried to remember what he usually talked about. Memories of conversations with Cressida floated into his mind, but were entirely visual. He could not even recall the sound of Cressida's voice, let alone what she ever said, or what he said in return.

'The Ethiopians,' said Ella thoughtfully, 'are the most wonderfully elegant race.' She paused. Charles felt foolish. Should he say something? 'It was one of the things that struck me most about the country,' continued Ella. She was striding forward with a regular pace, not looking at Charles, but talking as though to herself. 'All the people have very fine bones, and aristocratic features. The women are utterly beautiful. They wear these wonderful white robes, which go down to the ground and cover their heads, so they look as if they might be Arabic rather than African. And each robe has an embroidered border. Some are simple and plain, but others are very ornate. I was told they even use thread made from pure gold.'

As Ella talked, Charles listened, enchanted. He had forgotten her husky, dusky, coppery voice; had forgotten her power of telling a simple story so that it captivated her listeners. He walked silently in the dark, willing her to continue for ever. The further they walked from the house, the more he heard her voice, the later it got, the more alive he felt. An unspecified exhilaration ran through him as he considered the empty hours of the night which stretched out before them.

'And then we tried to eat a traditional Ethiopian dish called injera,' Ella was saying. 'It had the exact look, texture and taste of carpet underlay. In fact, maybe it was carpet underlay.' She gave a sudden gurgle of laughter. Charles suddenly felt fiercely jealous. Once, he had been the worldly wise, experienced one.

He had instructed Ella in the vagaries of modern art; had taught her how to eat semolina as a savoury dish; had introduced her to drugs and oral sex. But now she had leap-frogged ahead of him. She had seen, smelt, touched and tasted places he was never likely to see. She had mixed with the kind of people who would despise Charles, his wife, his car, his sailor-suited blond twins. She had met and been invited to live with Maud Vennings. This last, Charles could hardly bear to think about. If it hadn't been for him, Ella would probably never have heard of Maud Vennings.

'When do you go to Italy?' he said abruptly.

'I don't know yet,' said Ella. 'When I get tired of England, I suppose. I've been back a month, and already I'm getting itchy feet.'

'I never thought you were a natural traveller,' said Charles in a rather suspicious voice.

'No, neither did I,' said Ella mildly. 'I surprised myself by how much I enjoyed it. I was expecting to hate it.'

'Then why did you go?' The question was out before Charles could stop himself. Shit, he thought to himself.

There was a short silence. Then Ella spoke.

'Do you want to know why I went?' she said, in a light, toneless voice. 'Do you really want to know?' Charles was silent. 'I decided to go,' she continued, 'when I bumped into you in the street, just after you'd moved out of the house and it was all over between us. It was in Silchester. I was coming out of the wool shop, thinking about something else completely, and there you were.'

'Well, I do live in Silchester,' said Charles, defensively.

'I still remember it so clearly,' said Ella, ignoring him. 'You sort of waved, and smiled, and you kissed me on both cheeks and pretended to be pleased to see me, and said I was looking well. But you didn't look me in the eye. And then you rushed off without saying anything else. That was the first time I'd seen you since we broke up, and the way you acted, I could have been anyone.'

'Rubbish,' said Charles feebly.

'I didn't want you to take me in your arms and say it had all been a mistake. Well, perhaps I did want that. But if I couldn't have that, what I wanted most of all was to talk about it. To you. Not to well-meaning people who didn't understand.' She smiled. 'But you ran away, and pretended I didn't exist. And I couldn't bear that. So I decided to go away.'

They had come to the far side of the field, and she sank to the ground, her voluminous skirts ballooning darkly around her. Charles sat more gingerly, feeling in the blackness for thistles, nettles, suspicious patches of mud. He could see nothing of Ella but the glint of her eyes.

'I didn't mean to run away,' he said. 'I'm sorry.' He struggled for words. 'We should have talked.' He reached impulsively for her hand, brushing against her thigh in the darkness, suddenly wanting to feel her warm flesh against his. But she pulled her hand away.

'I was so alone,' said Ella, in her low, penetrating, merciless voice. 'You had the Print Centre, you had all your friends in Silchester, you had Cressida. I didn't. How do you think I felt?'

Charles desperately cast his mind back, trying to remember what he'd thought; how he'd felt. But it was all a blank. He couldn't even remember why he'd fallen for Cressida in the first place. He began to think he had never had any feelings at all.

'I was a callous bastard,' he murmured.

'Don't glamorize yourself,' said Ella. 'You were a typical male.' She threw her head back and her throat gleamed palely in the moonlight. Charles stared at her, disconcerted. She had grown up on her travels; she had new ideas, new ways of thinking, a new self-assurance. He wondered, with a stab of jealousy, who had put those new ideas into her mind. She moved slightly, and the moonlight shifted onto her breasts, glinting on the exposed curves; highlighting her shoulder where her dress had slipped down. Slowly, cautiously, he stretched out a hand and touched her shoulder. She didn't move. He drew his finger down, over the swell of her breast, then up to her neck and behind her ear. He began to caress her neck.

An owl hooted nearby, and he jumped, startled. Suddenly it came to him that he was alone with Ella in the middle of a field in the middle of the night, and that they were about to make love. Then he wondered why he hadn't realized this sooner.

Patrick and Caroline walked up the stairs with Stephen and Annie in a state of jovial *bonhomie.* They embraced affectionately, then departed to their various rooms. But as soon as they were alone in their bedroom, Patrick rounded on Caroline with coldly furious eyes.

'Just what do you think you're playing at?' he demanded.

'What do you mean?' Caroline walked past him and sank

heavily onto her dressing table stool. She leaned forward and stared at her face in the mirror. Then she groaned.

'Oh God. I'm so fucking *old*.'

'Don't change the subject,' said Patrick sternly. 'You realize how much the fees to that place are?'

'What place?' said Caroline unconvincingly.

'Don't make me laugh,' said Patrick shortly. 'Well, all I can say is, it's your loss. Those fees are coming out of the money I spend on you. No Porsche, no Champneys, no Barbados.'

'I don't care!' hissed Caroline, suddenly swivelling on the stool to face him. 'I'm glad. I don't give a monkeys about Champneys. Or bloody Barbados. You only suggested going there because one of those snotty mothers at Georgina's school said she'd been there.'

She picked up a hairbrush and began to drag it angrily through her hair. 'I can see right through you, you know that, Patrick? You think ladies of leisure spend their whole time going to Champneys and Barbados, so you decide I've got to go, too. Bloody social climber. Well, perhaps I'd rather go on a package to Tenerife!'

'Don't be ridiculous,' said Patrick.

'What's wrong with Tenerife? What's wrong with a bit of real life for a change?'

'You're a fine one to talk about real life,' mocked Patrick. 'The phoniest PR bimbo of the lot, you were. Promoting this, promoting that, never an idea what any of the products were about, whether they were any good, just smile at the customer and take the money!'

'It was a job, Patrick,' said Caroline in a low, furious voice. 'And there's not a lot of those about for an out-of-work, unquali-fied dancer like I was.'

Patrick was silent for a moment, pulling out his cuff-links in abrupt gestures. When he spoke again it was on a different line of attack.

'Anyway,' he said truculently, 'if you don't like Georgina's school, why do you want to send Nicola there?'

'I do like the school,' said Caroline. 'I think it's a great school. I just don't get on with the other mums. Come on, Patrick, I'm not exactly Lady Holmes, am I?' Patrick twitched at the thought of Lady Holmes, the mother of one of Georgina's school friends. A smart, condescending woman who always managed to make him feel grubby and unpatrician. 'And you're not exactly lord of the manor,' continued Caroline brutally. 'Nothing like. So why try to be? Why not just admit you're a rich pleb?' Patrick flinched, and turned away.

'If I want to get on in life a bit,' he said, his voice stiff with embarrassed anger, 'it's for Georgina's sake.'

'Oh yes? Well. I reckon we've got on quite far enough, thank you. I know what you've been thinking. We should make a pile more money, sell up, move on somewhere else, pretend to be smarter than we are, make new friends. Well perhaps I like it here. Perhaps I've got friends here. Perhaps I don't want to be smart, and go hunting, or fishing; or whatever it is that lot do to get their kicks.'

Patrick turned to face Caroline, smiling in contempt.

'You've got friends? What, those scrounger Fairweathers?

You're paying their bloody school fees; what are you going to do next, invite them to live here?'

'If I were you,' said Caroline, her voice quivering with anger, 'I wouldn't say one word about the Fairweathers. Not one word. Otherwise you might just find me popping along to their room and whispering a few things in their ears. Like the fact that their so-called friend has just conned them completely. Like the fact that they'll never be able to afford that mortgage. Like the fact that the Sigma fund has a high-risk rating. Like the fact that they're probably going to lose all their money.' Patrick stared at her in surprise. 'You think I know sod all, don't you, Patrick?' she said. 'Just a bimbo with a big smile? Well, I know more than you think. I know that you're someone who can't be trusted, for a start.' Patrick was silenced, watching her warily like a cornered mouse. Caroline got up and paced about restlessly, suddenly alive, her eyes glittering.

'I can't believe you,' she said, in a sudden outburst. 'You're completely immoral. And you actually have the nerve to complain about my offer to them. Christ, you con Stephen out of eighty grand, and you can't afford a few thousand a year for his kid?'

'It's not as simple as that,' began Patrick.

'What *is* it as simple as, then?' interrupted Caroline. 'As far as I can see, Stephen is still the loser.'

'Stephen will do very well from my advice,' said Patrick.

'Like hell he will. He stands to lose a fucking fortune. In fact, there's something else I want you to do as well as the fees.' She sat down on the bed and gave him a defiant look.

'What?'

'I want you to promise that if Stephen can't keep up his mort-gage payments, you'll help him out. Just temporarily.'

'You're mad,' said Patrick.

'You owe it to them,' said Caroline. 'I want you to promise.'

'Bloody hell, I'll be supporting them for life!'

'Well then, tell Stephen you think you gave him the wrong advice. Cancel the deal.' Patrick looked at her.

'Do you know how much that deal was worth?'

'Do you know how much a friend is worth?' Caroline stared at him with bloodshot blue eyes.

'Oh, for fuck's sake!' shouted Patrick, suddenly losing his temper. 'Where's all this crap coming from? What's a friend worth? I'll tell you. Fuck all. When did any of our friends ever do anything for us? Never.'

'That's because we've never had any fucking friends!' Caroline shouted back. 'Never! Annie's my first proper friend, and I want to keep her!' To her dismay she felt a fat tear rolling down her cheek.

'What do you mean we've never had any proper friends?' said Patrick, incensed. 'We've plenty of friends.'

'What, clients you mean?' cried Caroline. 'They're not friends. And neither are those awful people from your work. I can't stand them.'

'Well, what about the people in the village?'

'They're all horrible. I hate them.' Caroline was weeping bit-terly now, hugging her knees and not bothering to wipe away the mascara that ran down her face. As Patrick watched her he was reminded of the way she'd wept when she discovered she couldn't have any more children after Georgina. It was one of the few times he'd seen her childlike and vulnerable. Most of the time she was either relentlessly cheerful or determinedly bad-tempered. Rarely did she let her guard down. Suddenly he was filled with a strong wave of compassion, mixed up inextricably with sexual desire. Caroline was sniffling now, refusing, as she always did, to blow her nose properly. He moved towards her uncertainly, sat down beside her on the bed and put his arm around her shoulders rather awkwardly.

'Of course I'll help them out,' he murmured. 'I didn't realize it meant so much to you.' Caroline buried her wet face in his poplin shoulder and sobbed with renewed vigour. Patrick rubbed her back gently, muttering the sort of soothing words he hadn't uttered since Georgina was about four. Both his wife and daughter were usually so self-possessed as to make him feel, if not unwanted, then certainly not needed. But here was Caroline, whimpering against his chest, looking to him for comfort, asking him to help her. Gently he brushed strands of golden hair out of her eyes and lifted her red, blotchy face till she was looking at him; silent now, but still shuddering with emotion. She opened her mouth to speak, but Patrick hastily leant forward and kissed her swollen lips. Let the picture continue in his mind; let his vision of Caroline as damsel, himself as saviour, last at least for a while. Let her not come out with some cutting or, even worse, unconcerned comment that would put him back in his place again; shatter the picture he was building up.

He kissed her firmly, kneading the tense muscles in the back of her neck; moving down to caress her breasts; swiftly and determinedly unzipping her yellow dress. She said nothing, but her breaths came quicker and shallower, and she gave one small sigh of pleasure as his lips found her nipple. Then, as though they couldn't stop themselves, her hands came creeping up beneath his shirt; running over his chest; undoing his buttons, one by one. Patrick's incredulity soon turned to exhilaration. Caroline was his again. It was something he'd thought would never happen. And if her price was having to shell out regularly to Annie and Stephen—well, perhaps it was worth it. After all, it was only money.

Charles lay, sated, unwilling to move, ever. His body was exhausted, his sexual urges satisfied, even his mind felt as though it had undergone a rigorous workout. He felt unable to hold a thought in his head or to formulate any kind of purpose, he doubted he could even string a sentence together. Various bits of his body were exposed to the night air, and there was now a faint breeze in the air. But although he could feel himself shivering and goose flesh rising, he lay motionless, unable to summon up the energy to cover himself up.

He had fucked Ella vigorously, brutally almost; pulling up the diaphanous layers of her skirt, pushing her down into the ground, burying his face in her creamy, pillowy, coconut-scented skin. He had roughly pulled off her string of amber beads when they got in his way, and ripped off his own shirt when it began to irritate him; and had swiftly come to an orgasm which tore through his body so intensely that he cried out with a voice he barely recognized.

Even now, little waves and stray sparks of pleasure were still alive in him. His skin was numb to the damp grass, the stones, the bump in the small of his back, in the same way that his mind was numb to the fact that he had just committed adultery. He was almost unaware of anything happening outside his own body, his senses were channelled inwards while his thoughts ran abstractly free.

But gradually, after a while, he became attuned once more to the outside world. He became aware of Ella, lying peacefully a small distance away and, he suddenly realized, humming gently to herself. He became aware of the sight that the two of them must present. He became aware that he was lying nearly naked in the garden of a friend, with a woman who wasn't his wife. And she was humming. For some reason this last disconcerted him most of all.

With a huge effort, he raised himself on one elbow and looked over at her.

'You're humming,' he said.

'Yes,' agreed Ella, still lying flat on her back, staring up at the sky. She began to hum again. Charles didn't recognize the tune. He flopped back down and wondered what was going through her mind. Did she regret what had happened? Did she appreciate this was the first time he'd been unfaithful to his wife? Did she realize he had family responsibilities? Part of him wanted to stay there for ever in companionable silence; part of him wanted to confront her with the situation as it was.

Eventually he roused himself. He sat up, wincing, removed the small stones that had embedded themselves in his back and pulled on his shirt. He scrabbled around in the grass and found Ella's amber beads.

'Here you are.' He reached over and put them into her hand. Her fingers seemed to caress him as they grasped the necklace and suddenly he felt a renewed rush of arousal. His eyes flickered to her breasts, still partially exposed; to her thighs, still gently parted; to her softly curving mouth.

'Oh God,' he moaned. 'I still want you.'

'Do you?' Ella's voice held amused surprise. 'You've become very demanding. No wonder Cressida looks so pale.' Charles scowled.

'It's not a joke.'

'Isn't it?' Her face turned to his invitingly and he met her lips with fervour; relishing her taste and her smell; feeling for the curves of her body. Then he pulled away with a groan.

'It's no good.'

'It is a bit soon, perhaps,' said Ella agreeably.

'It's not that!' he said savagely. 'It's the whole situation. Oh God, how can you just lie there humming? Don't you realize we've just committed adultery?'

'In some cultures,' said Ella, 'what we've just done would be considered normal.'

'Yes, well, we're not in other cultures now, are we?' said Charles tetchily. 'Oh God!' he groaned again. 'What are we going to do?'

'Go back inside,' suggested Ella. 'Or stay outside for a while.'

Charles sat in silence for a while. A blackness descended on him.

'Perhaps we should go inside,' he said eventually. 'We must have been out here for at least an hour.'

'All right.' Ella got nimbly to her feet; Charles struggled up heavily. They walked through the field wordlessly. Charles' steps got slower as they went; as they came in sight of the house, he suddenly stopped.

'What about the future?' he said desperately. 'What are we going to do?'

'The future?' said Ella. 'Well, I'll be in Italy, of course. I haven't an idea what you'll be doing. I think I might go out there quite soon,' she added. 'I have a feeling I'll get bored with England before too long.'

'But what about me?' As soon as he said it, Charles felt like a spoilt, whiny child.

'What about you?' Her eyes met his with a mixture of amusement and pity. It was clearly a dismissal. But he couldn't bear to give up.

'Couldn't we see each other some time?' He was begging. It was pathetic.

'If you happened to be in Italy,' Ella said thoughtfully, 'I don't see why Maud shouldn't invite you to stay at the villa. I'm sure she'd be glad to.'

As he stared at her, a delightful vision sprang into Charles' mind; a picture of a double life, spent between England and Italy; between Cressida and Ella. He saw Maud Vennings' villa in his mind's eye; a large, elegant house on the hillside, populated with artists and musicians; himself a regular part of the coterie. There would be workshops and discussions; long leisurely meals;

nights spent with Ella. Perhaps he would take up painting again. As long as he came back each time with a few prints, Cressida would never suspect anything. He would hire someone to take over the day-to-day running of the shop, releasing him for as many trips a year as he liked. Perhaps profits would suffer a little—but they could afford it.

'I'll come as soon as I can,' he said joyfully.

'As you like,' said Ella. 'There's no rush.'

Before Charles pushed open the door to his bedroom, he looked down at himself and brushed a few blades of grass off his trousers. With any luck, though, Cressida would be in bed already. The thought of joining her there no longer dismayed him. He felt ridiculously good humoured and unreasonably pleased with himself. In his own mind, he was once again someone to be envied, with both a beautiful, rich wife, and an exotic yet undemanding mistress. It would all work out splendidly.

He opened the door cautiously and was surprised to see the light still on. Then he looked over at the bed. Cressida was in bed, asleep, but propped up against the pillows, as though she had been reading and fallen asleep over her book. Except there was no book to be seen. Charles went nearer and saw that a piece of paper had fallen out of her fingers onto the bed cover. Had she been writing letters at that time of night? He wouldn't have been surprised. Cressida corresponded with an incredibly large number of people, from old school friends to distant aunts.

He picked up the sheet of paper and began to skim it casually, kicking off his shoes as he did so. *Dear Mrs Mobyn.* It was from Cressida's portfolio manager, Mr Stanlake. He always refused to call either of them by their first names. Charles grinned to himself. Dry old stick. *You may recall that a while ago I wrote to you, explaining again the meaning of the term 'unlimited liability'.* Charles yawned. Some technical matter. He read the first paragraph without giving it his full attention; his thoughts were still outside, with Ella.

But suddenly, as his eyes moved down the page, he let out a cry.

'What the fuck . . . ?' The noise awoke Cressida, who opened her eyes in a fluttering motion. She focused her gaze on Charles, and then took in the letter with a little cry of alarm.

'Charles,' she said weakly. 'I got that letter today. I've been trying to show it to you . . .'

'Have you read it? Have you seen what it says?'

'Well, yes . . .' said Cressida hesitantly. She gazed at him hopelessly. His eyes met hers for a second, then fell back on the page again. He read the letter urgently from beginning to end, desperate for another meaning, for a conclusion other than the one he'd drawn.

When he'd finished, he looked up, with unseeing eyes. A hot, pounding blackness seemed to be rising up in his head. Stanlake's dry, well-chosen phrases ran relentlessly through his mind. *Next demand . . . one hundred thousand . . . future uncertain . . . particular syndicate . . . one million pounds . . . possibly more . . . staggered payments . . . commitment unlimited . . . will understand . . . thought it fair to warn you . . . unlimited liability . . . unlimited liability . . . unlimited liability . . .*

His hands could barely hold the paper still. He felt sick and shaken. A million pounds. The guy had to be joking. He looked down at the page again. *Your next demand will be, I am told, in the region of one hundred thousand pounds.* Charles' mind distractedly flicked over Cressida's portfolio. They could probably manage that. If that was all it was. But his eyes drew him on. *As I explained at our original meeting regarding this matter, your commitment is unlimited.*

Charles was not usually given to panic. But he could feel his breath coming more quickly; could feel sweat breaking out on his forehead. Cressida was a Lloyd's Name. Christ. Jesus Christ; he'd had no idea. Why the fuck hadn't he known? Why the fuck hadn't she told him? *Unlimited liability.* Unlimited. What, until they didn't have anything left? Until they'd sold the house? Got rid of the car? His eyes fell again on the sentence in the middle of the page. *I am informed that the sum total could be as much as one million pounds, possibly more.* But they weren't millionaires. OK, maybe on paper—but it was the house and the Print Centre that accounted for most of that. *One million pounds, possibly more.* More than that? More? The phrase *bottomless pit* sprang into his mind; he had a sudden vision of a fiery hell; of suitcases, full of money, being thrown down to burn in the flames.

He couldn't think where to place his thoughts; how to anchor his panic. For a moment he just stood, swaying slightly in the silent night, feeling almost heady with terror. Then gradually he became aware that there was something ominously niggling at his thoughts. His eyes focused again on the letter. *At our original meeting regarding this matter.* What meeting? What fucking meeting?

Suddenly he felt Cressida's eyes on him. Her pale face looked tired and anxious. Had she known about this for a long time? Had she known but not told him?

'How long have you known about this?' he snapped.

'Only today,' stammered Cressida. She felt cold inside the bed. Charles had read the letter but he hadn't laughed at it; he hadn't shaken his head and pointed out the foolish mistake made by some clerical member of staff; he hadn't tossed it aside carelessly to deal with tomorrow.

'Well, what meeting is he talking about?'

'I don't know.' Cressida felt a sudden wave of panic, as though she'd forgotten to do a vital piece of homework. Was this something she was supposed to know about? Had she had a meeting with Mr Stanlake? She screwed up her pale face and desperately tried to remember. But all her encounters with Mr Stanlake seemed to have merged into one hazy picture in her brain.

Charles sat down heavily on an armchair and began to read the letter through again from beginning to end. Cressida gazed at him silently, not daring to rub her sleepy eyes or push her fingers through her rumpled hair. Her gaze wandered uncertainly through the room, landing indiscriminately on corners of wallpaper, pieces of furniture, on the top of Charles' head and away again. She wondered what time it was. Far away was the sound of a clock ticking; otherwise there were no sounds in the house. Everyone must have gone to bed.

'Unlimited liability,' Charles suddenly said, in a voice which trembled with suppressed emotion. 'Do you know what that means?' Mutely, Cressida shook her head. She thought she did, but she wouldn't risk saying anything. 'It means they can keep asking you for money for ever. For ever!' Charles' voice rose. 'Do you appreciate what that means? For us? For the twins?' Shakily, Cressida got out of bed, went over to the chair and knelt at his feet. She was shivering, and would have liked a dressing-gown. But if she went to put one on, Charles might react badly.

'Perhaps they've made a mistake,' she said, in a wobbly voice. 'They've never done anything like this before.'

'I don't know.' Charles threw the paper onto the ground ex-asperatedly. 'Fuck knows. Jesus Christ, Cressida, why didn't you tell me you were a Lloyd's Name?'

'I don't know,' said Cressida confusedly. 'I didn't think it was important. And anyway . . .'

She pulled up short and gasped. A sudden recollection suffused her cheeks with pink.

'What? What?'

'I don't know,' she said, flinching from his gaze. 'But I did have a meeting with Mr Stanlake a few years ago. I've just remembered.'

'And?'

'And I think it might have been about being a Lloyd's Name.'

'What? When? Why didn't you tell me?'

'It was just after we got engaged. It was only a very quick meeting.' Cressida paused, and tried desperately to remember. 'I was up in town to look at wedding dresses.'

'Get to the point.' Charles' voice was hard.

'Well,' Cressida swallowed, 'Mr Stanlake said something about paying some extra bills or something out of a separate bit of my money. Another special bank account or something. I can't remember exactly.'

'Extra bills? What extra bills?'

'I don't know.'

'You never fucking know anything. Christ almighty. Was he talking about Lloyd's losses?' Cressida's cheeks turned pinker.

'I'm not sure. I think so,' she said hurriedly. 'Something like that.'

'What? Why are you looking like that?' Charles stared at Cressida's blushing face and blinked as it loomed in and out of his weary vision. 'What aren't you telling me? Why do you think it was Lloyd's?'

Cressida stared back at him miserably. She could hardly bear to tell him what she had just remembered. But the idea of lying to him didn't even enter her thoughts. 'Well,' she began hesitantly, 'I've remembered something else Mr Stanlake said.'

'What? For Christ's sake, what?'

'I'd just told him I was engaged, and shown him the ring.' Automatically, she looked down at her engagement ring. 'And he was saying how nice it was,' she continued. Charles stared at her with incredulity.

'What the fuck's that got to do with anything?'

'Well, it was the thing he said next,' stammered Cressida. 'He asked about you, and about the wedding and everything, and then he said, "You know, I wouldn't advertise the fact that you're a Lloyd's Name if I were you."'

There was a short silence. Charles felt a very slow, frighten-

ingly powerful surge of fury rise through him. For a few moments he couldn't quite think what to do with himself.

'You mean,' he said eventually, in an over-controlled voice
that was barely above a whisper, 'you mean that you deliberately
kept the fact of your being a Name secret from me?'

'No!' Cressida's face was aghast. 'I mean, I didn't know it
meant anything then. I went off to have lunch with Sukey and go
to Liberty's . . .' Her voice tailed away.

'And then?' prompted Charles, his face menacingly polite.
Cressida swallowed.

'And then I forgot all about it.'

'You forgot all about it? You *forgot* you were a Lloyd's Name?'

'Yes. No. I mean, I sort of knew, but I didn't think it was
important . . .' Her voice tailed away again.

For a moment, Charles' astonishment almost abated his anger.

'How could you not think it was important? Haven't you
heard about Lloyd's?'

Cressida hung her head and his impatience with her increased.
'Haven't you heard what's happened to people?' he shouted.
'Didn't you realize what it meant for us? Haven't you got a brain?'

'I know, I know,' exclaimed Cressida, giving a sudden sob. 'I
sort of knew, but I just didn't think any of that would happen to
us. Mr Stanlake said he thought everything would be all right.'

'Well, fuck Mr Stanlake!' shouted Charles. 'And fuck you!
You never bothered to listen to anything, or ask, or find out
what was going on, did you?' He suddenly brought his face close
to hers. 'You never bothered to understand your finances, you

always left it up to your fucking father, or me. Well, you can sort this fucking mess out yourself. I've had enough of it.'

'Charles . . .' She gazed up at him with huge, frightened eyes.

Charles felt as though he'd stumbled into some horrible nightmare; some grotesque fantasy with no way out. Only five minutes ago he'd been so arrogantly pleased with himself; it had all seemed as though it was falling into place. He'd constructed for himself a large-scale plan of life for the future—taking for granted his wife, his income, his life as it was now—and embellishing it with even more delights; adding the little extras which would bring it to perfection. A continued affair with Ella; an acquaintance with the great Maud Vennings; a familiarity with Italy: he had imagined all these—even in the few minutes he'd had since parting from Ella—with an intense, desperate vividness. But suddenly all that seemed laughable; the stuff of schoolboy dreams. He could take nothing for granted. What was life without money? Come to that, what was his wife without her money? Could he still love her if she were not a source of riches, but a drain; a burden? Charles eyed Cressida afresh. Her limbs were lanky under her nightdress; her voice high and irritating. Her face was pale and tired. As he looked at her, a sudden vivid vision of warm, brown, coconut-scented skin appeared in his mind and he experienced a shocking, almost painful desire for Ella.

'I'm sure it'll all get sorted out,' said Cressida uncertainly.

'Are you?' said Charles sarcastically, hating her for not being Ella. 'Good. Well then, perhaps I'll leave you to it.' She gazed at him speechlessly for a moment, then burst into tears. Charles' stomach turned. The sound of Ella's bubbling laugh flickered through his head; her gently mocking eyes sprang up in his mind's eye.

'Shut the fuck up,' he shouted. 'Shut up. I can't bear that noise.' Her sobs increased. 'Shut *up*, I said. *Shut the fuck up!*' He raised his hand and brought it slamming down on the side of her face.

Cressida gasped, and put her hand up to her cheek. The side which Charles had hit was already bright blotchy red, but the rest was drained of colour. Charles didn't change his expression. Then Cressida rose unsteadily to her feet and backed away into the bathroom. The door closed and Charles heard the sound of Cressida vomiting. Then the taps were turned on. She had not locked the bathroom door; perhaps she was hoping he would come in after her. The thought made Charles scowl. He slid to the floor, picked up the letter and crumpled it.

'Fuck you,' he said. 'Fuck the lot of you.'

CHAPTER TEN

Annie was woken at seven-thirty by her electronic alarm clock. Its merry bleeping penetrated her dreams gradually; when she realized what it was, she reached out automatically to the left and was thrown into confusion when she hit Stephen's face. Eventually she found it, sitting on an unfamiliar table to her right. She turned it off, flopped back into bed and stared puzzledly for a while at a strange lampshade hanging from a white, well-painted, uncracked ceiling before it came to her suddenly that they were staying at Caroline's house.

And she had a peculiar feeling inside her, she realized. A bit like the ominous dread that one had on the morning of an appointment with the dentist—but this was positive rather than negative. She felt warm, cosy and encouraged. It wasn't just the bright sunlight visible through the chink between the curtains, and it wasn't just the knowledge that she didn't have to cook breakfast. She searched idly around in the recesses of her mind but whatever it was kept evading her. She looked around the room for clues, squinted at the clock and wondered why she'd set it so early.

Then suddenly it all came back to her in a rush. She'd set the clock early so she could take the children to church. The children. Nicola. School fees. Of course, Caroline and Patrick had offered to pay Nicola's school fees. And they'd accepted. Nicola would be going to St Catherine's. Annie sank back into her pillows pleasurably. Now that she was fully awake, she realized that she also had rather a piercing headache. But nothing could mar her happiness on Nicola's behalf.

She nudged Stephen with her foot. Sleepily, he rolled over until he was facing her.

'Wake up,' she said. 'Time for church.' Stephen screwed up his face in displeasure, opened his eyes a crack and groaned.

'I feel awful,' he croaked. 'Why do we have to go to church? We're on holiday.'

'We talked about it last night, remember?' Annie's spirits were irrepressible. 'It's good for the children. And I like going to country churches.' And I want to say thank you for Nicola's school fees, she added to herself. She heaved herself out of bed, ignoring the coloured spots that immediately appeared before her eyes, and added, 'I'll go and wake them up.'

Stephen groaned again, but it only made his head feel worse.

He rolled onto his back and closed his eyes. Memories of the previous day began to filter slowly into his mind. They were here to play tennis, of course, and that had been fairly pleasant. They had also drunk a lot. Stephen didn't want to think about how much. And then there had been that deal with Patrick. Or was that a dream?

He opened his eyes and looked around. He could vividly remember sitting in Patrick's study, agreeing to take out a mortgage of eighty thousand pounds on his house. It wasn't a dream. It had been a real, big-time deal. He tried to recall the feeling of exhilaration he had experienced; the buzz of confidence which it had given him. But what began to go through his mind instead was suspiciously like alarm.

As Annie came back into the room, Stephen started guiltily, as though she could read his mind.

'How did the children sleep?' he asked hurriedly.

'Not very much,' she said, grimacing, 'I think it's been one long midnight feast. Nicola wasn't at all impressed when I told her to get up.'

'Perhaps we should let her sleep in,' said Stephen weakly.

'Rubbish,' retorted Annie. 'I told her we were going to church. And the walk will wake her up.'

'You seem in a very good mood today,' said Stephen curiously.

'Do I?' said Annie, smiling. 'I suppose I'm still reeling over the school fees.'

Stephen gazed at her blankly for a second—and then remembered. Of course. Caroline's announcement last night.

'Yes, that's wonderful news,' he said, trying to work up some enthusiasm. But he couldn't get out of his mind the deal he'd done with Patrick. He felt he was in out of his depth. This was really business more for high flyers like Charles than people like him. He preferred things simple. And he had a growing sense of unease about taking out a mortgage when he didn't really—despite what Patrick said—have the means to pay it.

He looked at Annie's glowing face and decided not to say anything about it yet. Perhaps he would have a quiet word with Patrick later on and see whether he could reduce the loan, or maybe go into it more gradually. Patrick would be understanding. They were friends, after all.

The church at Bindon was fourteenth century and tiny. As Stephen, Annie, Nicola, Toby and Georgina hurried through the churchyard—with only a minute to go—Stephen said, 'Bets on the congregation in there already. I say six.'

'I say ten,' said Annie, giving him a reproving look.

'I say fifty,' said Nicola, who was used to a full, thriving family service at St Mary Magdalene in Silchester.

'It's not the same here,' said Georgina kindly. 'I say four.'

'Oh dear,' said Stephen.

'I say forty-four,' put in Toby, enunciating carefully. 'I say forty-four.'

'Do you, Tobes? And do you know why you say it?' said Stephen, grinning at him.

'Forty-four,' said Toby obstinately.

Georgina was closest. There were, in fact, three members of

the congregation already present at the service as they all trooped in. Two of these were Don and Valerie, who waved excitedly and gestured at the pew behind. Thankfully Stephen had already led the children into a pew on the other side, so Annie was able to smile and gesture apologetically back.

'Dear God,' said Georgina, sinking to her knees beside Annie, 'please help me do well at the East Silchester gymkhana. Help me learn how to do a French plait. And help Nicola not be too scared to jump Arabia.'

'Dear God,' said Annie clearly, 'please help some of Nicola's friends realize she isn't as old or as experienced at riding as them, and that jumping without a riding teacher there isn't a very good idea.'

'Oh, OK,' said Georgina equably, without moving.

Afterwards, they waited politely in the churchyard until Don and Valerie appeared.

'Smashing to see you,' said Don. 'It's a sweet little place, isn't it?'

'Lovely,' said Annie enthusiastically.

'Yes, it's a pretty village altogether,' said Don. 'Isn't it, Val?'

'Ooh! It's lovely!'

'The spot where we live has very good views,' added Don. 'Why not come back and see for yourself? We could have a bit of coffee and I could show you round the hotel.'

'Well,' said Annie doubtfully. She glanced at Stephen.

'Ooh, do come!' exclaimed Valerie.

'Do we have to get back?' Annie said to Stephen, raising her eyebrows.

'Can't think what for,' said Don jovially. 'Only thing you've got to do today is play Caroline and Patrick. And I doubt they'll start without you!'

There didn't seem any answer to that.

'If you don't mind,' said Georgina suddenly, 'I'll go back. I want to look for costumes for our play.' Stephen looked at her in unwilling admiration. She was smiling politely, yet implacably, at Don.

'Could you take Nicola and Toby back too?' said Annie.

'Of course,' said Georgina. 'I was going to anyway. I need Nicola to help me.'

Nicola flushed with pleasure, and Annie smiled at her. 'Be careful!' she shouted after them as they ran off through the churchyard.

'They'll be all right,' said Don comfortably. 'Cars hardly ever pass through here. It's a lovely spot. You wait till you see the view from the hotel.'

At first, Annie was too busy wondering how on earth Don was going to turn this wreck of a house into a hotel to notice the view. They had toiled for ten minutes up a steep, private track, which Don assured them at intervals of thirty seconds he was intending to modernize.

'It stands to reason,' he said, each time. 'You've got to have good access to a place like this.'

Finally they reached the house. Don swung open the door, then told them to stand in the porch and look out over the hills.

'Whenever I have my doubts,' he told them, 'I just stand here and look at that view. This is what it's all about.' The others dutifully turned and followed his gaze. But Annie was staring, aghast, at the dark, dank corridor that gave off the front door.

'Lovely, isn't it?' said Don, smiling down at her.

'Oh, yes,' she said, faintly.

'Over there,' he said, pointing, 'is where the new generator's going to go.'

'You aren't wired up to the mains?' said Stephen in surprise.

'Well, no,' said Don, his face dropping slightly. 'Actually, it's been a bit more of a problem than I thought it would.' They all gazed silently at the patch of land for a few seconds. Then Valerie clapped her hand to her mouth.

'Ooh I know!' she said brightly. 'What about that coffee?'

Annie followed Valerie into the kitchen.

'It's quite a big project, this hotel,' she said conversationally. 'But I expect it's quite fun, getting it all going.'

'I expect so,' said Valerie, putting on the kettle. 'I don't really see much of it, being in London all the time.'

'Don't you come down here at weekends?'

'Sometimes. But it's a long way away. And I often have to work at weekends.'

'What do you do?' asked Annie.

'I'm personal assistant to an advertising account executive,' said Valerie.

'Ah yes,' said Annie, none the wiser. 'And is that a very demanding job?'

'It is if you want to get on, like me,' said Valerie. 'A lot of girls

treat it like, you know, a normal job. But if you want to get promotion quickly, you have to put in the extra hours. It pays off in
the end.' She uttered the words glibly, as though this was a message she had memorized.

'Gosh,' said Annie. 'I suppose you're right. And what are you
aiming for?' Valerie looked at her blankly, as she spooned instant
coffee into mugs.

'Well, you know,' she said. 'To get on. While I'm still young.
Before I'm too far into my thirties. Before I settle down and have
children.' She giggled, rather embarrassedly. 'You have to plan
your career break in advance, you know. If you want to keep a
toe on the career ladder. You can't take time off just like that.'

'Wow,' said Annie. 'I am impressed. I never thought ahead
like that. I just went ahead and had children when I felt like it.'
She stared at Valerie, intrigued, as she poured hot water on the
coffee. 'I was never very good at planning ahead. When I married
Stephen, that was it, I wanted a baby straight away.' She laughed.
'I expect you're made of sterner stuff.'

'Ooh,' giggled Valerie. 'Well, actually, I haven't ever thought
about it.'

'But you obviously do want children? And your . . .' she
glanced at Valerie's left hand, 'your boyfriend?'

'Ooh,' exclaimed Valerie again. 'I haven't really had many
boyfriends. I had one at university, but he went to live in the
States. And what with my job, I don't really have time to meet
new people.'

'That's a shame,' said Annie.

'Not really,' fluted Valerie. 'The modern girl doesn't need a man. Men hold you back and let you down. A job doesn't. I don't need a man; I'm independent. If men ask me out,' she giggled, 'I usually say I'm too busy. That puts them in their place.' Annie stared at her in slight puzzlement.

'But you want children one day,' she said.

'Ooh, yes,' said Valerie. 'Just not quite yet. I want to wait till my career's more firmly established.'

'And before you have children, you'll want to find a man?'

'Ooh, yes,' said Valerie, and giggled excitedly.

'And are you so sure,' said Annie bluntly, 'that you'll find one?'

Stephen and Don were standing in the room that would become the hotel lounge. It was a long, low room, with bare boards and recently plastered walls.

'Well, this is a good-sized room,' said Stephen cheerfully. 'You should fit a lot of guests in here.'

'Yes, I suppose so,' said Don. 'It's funny, sometimes I forget that it'll be full of guests. I've got used to it being empty.'

'I suppose it's quite a good investment just as a house,' said Stephen.

'That's right,' said Don. 'It wouldn't really matter if it never opened as a hotel. Apart from the fact I wouldn't have any income!' He gave a chortle. 'But then, who needs money when you've got views like this?'

'I suppose so,' said Stephen, following Don's gaze out of the window.

'Thankfully I haven't got a mortgage to worry about,' said Don. 'Not yet, anyway. I may need one later.'

Stephen's insides contracted at the word mortgage. He was dreading having to ask Patrick to rethink the deal they'd made; reduce the loan he was taking out; basically chicken out of the world of high finance. It looked so feeble. And he was sure Patrick would shake his head at the opportunity Stephen was missing. But he couldn't help his nature, Stephen thought to himself. He was just more cautious than Patrick. And he was naturally nervous of debt. Which was all a mortgage was, really. Debt. It was a word that conjured up for him pictures of poorhouses, disgrace, wrecked lives. Ridiculous these days, when *everybody* seemed to have a mortgage. But that was just the way he was.

'Of course, that rascal Patrick tried to convince me to take out all kinds of fancy loans,' said Don amusedly. 'You know what he's like when he's got you cornered.' Stephen gave him a look of astonishment.

'Not that I'm knocking him,' said Don quickly. 'I know he's a friend of yours. No offence.'

'Oh, no, no,' said Stephen. Suddenly he wanted to hear more. 'What sort of deal did he try to do with you?' he said casually. 'Just out of interest.'

'Oh, he had some idea I should take out a mortgage on this place and let him make some money with it. I told him plain. I said that if he was about to start up a business like me, he'd be looking to decrease his debt, not increase it.'

Stephen felt a sudden wave of reassurance. So there was someone else in the world who didn't see a mortgage as a desirable ac-
cessory to life.

'He nearly got me,' said Don, grinning. Stephen's heart started
pounding.

'What did you do?' he said, trying to sound unconcerned.
Don looked surprised.

'Well, I told him I'd take it away and think about it. Then,
of course, I called him up the next day and told him no thanks.'
He gave Stephen a beady look. 'I never sign anything on the
spot.'

Stephen felt a wave of mortification rush over him. That's
what he should have done. He should have told Patrick he'd go
and talk it over with Annie. If he'd done that, if he'd left it a day,
he would have quickly come to his senses; and now he wouldn't
be in this mess. He looked at Don's amiable, sunburnt face. Don
would never have allowed Patrick to talk him into signing. Don
would have been cautious and prudent.

'Is anything wrong?' said Don. Stephen felt a stab of panic.
He couldn't let Don—or any of them—find out what a fool he'd
been.

'No, no,' he said quickly. He smiled—unconvincingly he felt—
and searched desperately in his mind for a way to change the subject. Don eyed him warily.

'I wouldn't like any of this to go back to Patrick,' he said. 'I
have actually done some business with him since then—and I do
think of him as a friend.' There was a pause, and Stephen realized that Don was looking at him expectantly.

'Oh, of course,' he said hastily. 'I won't say anything to him.'

'That's all right then.' Don grinned toothily. 'Aha. I think I hear our coffee coming.'

The beaming smile with which Stephen greeted Annie as she came into the room bearing two mugs of coffee hid a thumping heart and a sensation of sickness. He felt despair at himself. How could he have been so stupid? How could he have been so thoughtless? How could he have done something as momentous as that without even consulting her?

'Have some coffee,' said Annie. 'Careful, the mug's hot.' He smiled shakily at her, taking in her wispy brown hair, her cheerful, blue T-shirt, tucked into a floral, cotton skirt, her simple plimsolls. He looked down at himself, his old tweed jacket, unfashionable trousers, battered Oxford shoes.

What had he been thinking of? It was laughable to think he could ever be like the rest of them: rich, worldly, fashionable. He should have known he was on dangerous territory as soon as he entered Patrick's sumptuous study. He saw it clearly now. Patrick was the sort of person who would do something like take out a huge mortgage and invest it—and would probably make his money twice over. He would pick the right investments, time his manoeuvres well, use his hunches to good advantage. But Stephen was the type for whom such an enterprise was bound to go disastrously wrong, no matter who was advising him, who was carrying out his investments. He saw, with fatalistic clarity, scenes of stockmarket crashes, company failures, panicked decisions. It was no good. If he had been the sort of person who was going to make a lot of money in life, he suspected he would have made it before now. And if he wasn't, then it was probably better not to try. Better just to carry on as they were.

'You're looking very serious,' said Annie, smiling at him. 'Is everything all right?'

'Oh yes,' he said, effecting a cheery voice. *Please God, don't let her find out what I've done; how stupid I've been. Please let me somehow sort it out on my own.* He took a sip of heartening coffee and looked up, smiling gaily, distractingly at her. 'Yes, everything's fine,' he said. 'We were just admiring the view from here.' She turned her head to look, as he had intended, out of the window, and exclaimed with pleasure. It was so easy to deflect her, Stephen thought, watching the back of her head. She was utterly unsuspicious; she would be the easiest person in the world to deceive. But far from reassuring him, this realization suddenly made him feel like weeping.

Charles woke to blinding pain and a weight of misery around his chest. A pulse in his temple throbbed; with each throb the brightness from outside seemed to pierce his eyelids more strongly. He didn't dare open his eyes, but lay motionless, gradually locating other areas of pain in his body and wishing he could fall back asleep.

He remembered everything. It was almost as though he had never fallen asleep; as though he and Cressida were, in his mind, still in the middle of their conversation. Or rather, their fight. Now, he realized—from the weight on the mattress; the taut line of the duvet; the light sound of her breathing—she was in bed beside him. She must have stayed closeted in the bathroom for a good hour. He had sat up for a while, waiting for her to re-appear, then unwillingly crawled into bed.

He didn't open his eyes. He didn't want to see her. An un-bearable combination of guilt and anger was creeping through his body. He had screwed Ella. Oh God. He had wanted to screw her again. He still did. Cressida had a right to hate him for that. But then—she didn't know about it. And it was *her* finan-cial arrangements that were going to ruin them. Ruin them completely.

A vision of the future stretched ahead in Charles' mind; a dark, black road of debts and demands; of uncertainty. Unlim-ited liability; unlimited uncertainty. If Mr Stanlake's letter had stated the worst, if it had mentioned a definite total sum to be paid, then they would have had something to latch onto. They would have despaired for a while—and then set about tackling the situation. But the letter had mentioned only possible figures. Probable figures. Estimated figures. For how long would they wonder? How long before the next demand? The next set of esti-mated figures? The next smoothly ambiguous sentence, assuring them that the final demands might not be as large as expected—although, of course, they might be larger . . .

It was the uncertainty that would be the debilitating, wear-ing, endlessly nagging factor in all of this. It was the not know-ing; the continual threat; the knowledge that the sword was hanging over them—but might never fall. It was the hope. Per-haps worst of all was the hope. The tiny, insidious flicker of hope that it would all turn out much better than they had expected;

that this time next year they would be laughing about it all. He could feel it now, unwanted, unlooked for: a flame of hope that he couldn't get rid of; that would stay alive inside him, no matter how hard he tried to suppress it.

Cressida gave a little sigh in her sleep, and Charles' thoughts immediately changed track. A painful wave of resentment ran through him. This was his wife's problem, he thought, as though realizing it for the first time. Hers. Not his. It was she who had received the letter. Dear Mrs Mobyn, it had begun. His own fucking name. His own fucking stupid wife.

He lay perfectly still, trying to think rationally about it all. But nothing could stop the increasing surges of anger which filled his body with silent, furious, pumping adrenalin, driving reasonable thought from his mind. She was a Lloyd's Name and she hadn't told him. She'd allowed him to marry her, buy a house, behave as if nothing was wrong—while all the time, this disaster had been just waiting to happen. Everything they'd done in the last three years; all the money they'd spent; that holiday to Antigua . . . Charles could hardly bear to think about it. He'd been so confident, so sure of the future. If he'd only known. If he'd only fucking known. The stupid bitch.

He was fairly sure—no, completely sure—she wasn't lying when she said she hadn't realized what being a Lloyd's Name meant. Jesus, he should know she was thick. He was continually re-amazed at how completely—unbearably it seemed now—stupid she was. Even now, he was pretty sure she didn't realize the full enormity of the situation. But that bastard Stanlake had obviously kept things deliberately quiet. Some bloody misguided loyalty to Cressida, no doubt. Thought Charles wouldn't marry her if he knew she was a Lloyd's Name. That must have been it.

Charles stared straight up at the ceiling. The quiet room was driving him mad; he felt constricted and trapped inside the bed. So Stanlake had thought he wouldn't marry Cressida if he knew she was a Lloyd's Name. Well, perhaps he was right. Perhaps he would have taken another look at her insipid pale looks; listened one more time to her imbecile, brainless conversation—and got out as quickly as he could. To think he'd actually found her stupidity attractive. Jesus, if he'd known all this was going to happen . . .

He felt suddenly wary, as though Cressida, slumbering next to him, could read his thoughts. He opened his eyes and swivelled them quickly towards her. But she was motionless, buried under a rounded duvet. Dust motes were dancing in the sun above her. Once upon a time he would have burrowed down underneath the duvet with her, gently waking her with little kisses and whispers, until she gave that sudden, delighted half-asleep giggle. Today he wanted her to stay asleep, away from his thoughts.

He eyed her blond hair against the pillow, immaculate even in sleep. He should have guessed she was a Lloyd's Name. Of course she was. She was exactly the sort of person who would be. If he'd only once thought to ask her, to check, to bring the subject up. But he'd taken to filtering out difficult subjects of conversation when he spoke to Cressida, just to avoid seeing that stupid frown of utter incomprehension.

Oh God. He should have guessed; he should have known. And if he'd known, could he have done anything? Could he have prevented this thing from happening? Could he have stopped it all in time? Charles gazed at the ceiling. He didn't, wouldn't dare find out the answer. The discovery that, by acting then, he could have avoided this black pit of despair would be too much to bear. A million pounds. A million pounds. Charles whispered it quietly to himself. It didn't really mean anything to him.

The duvet rustled and Charles felt Cressida turning over. She opened her eyes and looked at him, at first with her normal sleepy early morning expression—then, as she recollected her thoughts, with sudden dismay. Her hand came up to her cheek and touched it lightly. She didn't wince as her fingers met the skin, but her touch was tender. Of course, thought Charles suddenly. That's where I hit her. He stared at Cressida, appalled. It was all so sordid. Her eyes scanned his face uncertainly, then she pulled back the bedclothes and slowly got out of bed. She tottered to the bathroom, a tall, willowy figure in her long, white nightdress. Charles watched her numbly. He couldn't bring himself to say anything, call out to her or go after her. She was part of the nightmare. Until she spoke, none of it seemed real; if he ignored her, perhaps it would all go away. He turned over, buried his aching head beneath his pillow, and stared blankly into the mattress, wishing himself into oblivion.

Caroline and Ella were having breakfast on the terrace. Caroline had made what she considered to be the supreme effort of getting up, making some coffee, heating up some croissants, and taking it all outside, only to discover that Patrick wasn't hungry, Charles and Cressida were still in bed, Martina had fed the twins, and all the others had breakfasted early before going to church.

'For Christ's sake,' she said to Ella, gesturing to the breakfast table, 'you must tell them I did all this. I can't believe no one's here to appreciate it.' She bit crossly into a croissant. 'These are good, aren't they?' she added. 'They're from the new pâtisserie in Silchester. You must try it out before you go.' Ella took a thoughtful sip of coffee.

'I probably won't be around long enough,' she said. 'I've decided to go to Italy sooner rather than later.'

'But you've only just come back to England,' objected Caroline.

'I know,' agreed Ella. 'But I think I've seen enough of it.'

'Seen enough of Charles, more like,' said Caroline bluntly. 'He had a bit of a nerve, didn't he? Dragging you off for moonlit walks in the middle of the night? I would have told him where to go.' Ella shrugged.

'It was nice to see him. No really,' she added, at Caroline's incredulous look. 'I needed to get him out of my system.'

'And have you?'

'Well,' said Ella, 'I'm not sure he was still in it. But if he was, he isn't any more.'

'Well, that's a relief,' said Caroline. 'As long as he didn't sweet-talk you back into liking him.' Ella's mouth curved in amusement.

'Perhaps he thought he did. He was very ardent.'

'Ardent?' Caroline stared at Ella for a few seconds. 'Ardent as in . . . ardent?'

'It was the middle of the night,' pointed out Ella. With a deft movement she brought her legs up beneath her cross-legged on her chair, and shook back her hair. Caroline clapped her hand over her mouth and gazed at Ella with sparkling eyes.

'I'm not even going to *ask* you my next question,' she said in an excited voice, 'because I don't want to know the answer.' She paused. 'Except I do,' she added hopefully.

'It's not important,' said Ella.

'How can you say that?' demanded Caroline. 'He's married now.'

'That's not my fault.'

'It's not his wife's fault, either,' pointed out Caroline. She took a gulp of coffee and lit a cigarette. 'Christ, I'd go barmy if Patrick did that to me.'

'You don't know what Charles did,' said Ella.

'No, but I can guess.' She gave a wicked cackle.

'It's nothing,' said Ella, spreading her hands deprecatingly. 'Over.' She poured herself a glass of orange juice. 'Poor Charles,' she added.

'Over?' said Caroline suspiciously.

'Maybe over,' conceded Ella. 'Maybe not. It's funny, I'd half-forgotten what he was like. I had a different image of him in my mind. Perhaps I'd created it on purpose. But now I feel I don't know him as well as I thought I did. And I would quite like to know him again. Know him as a person, rather than as a lover.' She gave a little smile.

'But what about his wife?' insisted Caroline.

'What about me? Where's the symmetry in all this? I might have a husband, or a partner that no one knows about. Charles might be the other man as much as I am the other woman.'

'Have you got a husband?' asked Caroline curiously. 'You can't have. You don't look married.'

'No, not a husband,' said Ella, smiling down into her orange juice.

'But someone. There is someone.'

'There is someone,' agreed Ella.

'And don't you feel bad, betraying them like that?'

'Betraying? I'm not betraying anyone. A quick fuck isn't the same as betrayal.'

'Ah!' said Caroline triumphantly. 'So you did sleep with him.'

'I didn't sleep with him,' said Ella. 'I fucked him. Something else altogether. His wife slept with him. Or so I imagine.' Caroline looked at her slightly puzzledly for a moment, then leant forward.

'And what's going to happen now?' she said, lowering her voice unnecessarily to a confiding, gossipy tone.

'Now?' Ella's voice rang like a bell through the garden. 'I'm going to have some more coffee.' She smiled at Caroline and reached for the *cafetière*. Caroline took a deep drag of her cigarette and looked around the garden. Ella obviously wasn't going to settle down to a good girly chat. She frowned in slight annoyance, and stretched out a tanned leg from under her dressing-gown, admiring the smooth, brown skin against the white satin.

'Oh I don't know,' she said suddenly, heaving a great sigh. 'What's it all about, anyway?'

'It?' Ella looked at her quizzically.

'Life. You know.' Caroline waved her cigarette vaguely in the air. 'Where are we all aiming?'

'Well, that really depends on your point of view,' began Ella.

'I mean, take Patrick,' interrupted Caroline. 'All he wants to do is earn money.'

'And all you want to do is spend it,' suggested Ella.

'Well, yes,' said Caroline, in slight surprise. She caught Ella's eye and gave a sudden cackle. 'But what do I want to spend it on?' she added. 'That's the difference.'

'You're not having a mid-life crisis, are you?' said Ella, her eyes twinkling.

'Christ, no,' said Caroline. She took a deep drag. 'The thing is, Patrick and I had a bit of a scene last night. About us paying Nicola's school fees. It just made me think.'

'What sort of scene?'

'He was furious with me for landing him in it. Which I suppose is fair enough.'

'Hadn't you talked about it already?' said Ella in surprise.

'Oh no. It was completely spur of the moment. Anyway, if I'd asked him beforehand, he would never have agreed. Patrick's basically a stingy bastard.'

'Well, I think it's a wonderful idea,' said Ella firmly. 'Not that I approve of private education in principle. But Nicola's a little bit different. And surely you can afford it?'

'I would have thought so,' said Caroline. 'I mean, what if we'd had two children? We would have been able to afford it then, wouldn't we?'

'Or three children,' said Ella.

'Or five,' said Caroline. 'Some fucking chance.' Her face suddenly clouded over and she stubbed out her cigarette in silence.

CHAPTER ELEVEN

By one o'clock, Patrick was presiding over a barbecue.

'I can't bear barbecues,' said Caroline at intervals. She was reclining on a white lounger, eating a plate of chocolate-fudge cake and smoking a cigarette. 'Bloody awful things.' She glanced provocatively at Patrick every time she spoke, but his face remained calm.

'Barbecues are lovely!' protested Annie in amazement. She was handing out hot dogs in buns to the children and had a smear of tomato ketchup on her cheek. 'They're such fun. Those spare ribs smell delicious,' she added encouragingly to Patrick.

'They're just about ready,' he said. 'Who's for a rib?'

'Who's for a rib?' echoed Caroline disparagingly. 'Who's for a burnt bone with a shrivelled-up bit of meat attached?'

'Come on, Stephen,' said Annie. 'Have a spare rib. You've hardly eaten anything. And you need something after all that tennis.' She giggled. The match between her, Stephen, Patrick and Caroline had been a desultory affair, undertaken only because of Patrick's insistence. It had lasted a mere forty minutes, during which time Stephen and Annie had managed to win only two games, despite rallying cries from Don.

'In a moment,' said Stephen, taking a swig of beer. 'You go ahead.'

Stephen wasn't feeling hungry. Now that he had decided to talk to Patrick about backing out of the deal, he wanted to get it over and done with. He was sure Patrick would make him feel stupid for pulling out of such an opportunity; perhaps it would be easier to leave it till later or even phone him once they were at home. But the thought of prolonging his mortgage commitment— by even a few hours—made Stephen nervous. He had stood for a while by the barbecue, trying to seize his moment to talk to Patrick. But the barbecue was soon surrounded by children, prodding the sausages and asking for ketchup and no mustard and no onion and no lettuce.

He watched Nicola grasp her hot dog awkwardly and take a huge, unguarded bite, and he winced even before she did at the burning-hot sausage inside. She gasped, instinctively opened her mouth to breathe in cool air, and turned pink—not with pain, he knew, but with embarrassment at having been caught out. Stephen felt a chord of recognition within him. She was like him in

nce they had made love so frenziedly, that he had
eager flesh with a strange, mixed feeling of famil-
wness, that he had shouted, that she had cried out,
elt like weeping. But the more he reminded himself,
all seemed like a dream. The sensations became more
he memories of her skin, her hair—even her lips—
his mind. He felt hollow and bland; a nothing.

, standing behind the barbecue, watched Charles,
staring at the ground, refusing to join in the party. He
ssida had obviously had some sort of barney last night—
y over Ella. Patrick didn't like to think what had gone on
n those two last night. But even if the worst hadn't hap-
, deciding to go for a midnight walk with an ex-lover
t exactly normal behaviour for a married man. Especially a
married to such a lovely creature as Cressida. Patrick's gaze
sferred compassionately to her. She was sitting all alone, like
ale moth on the grass, fiddling with the same chicken drum-
ck he'd given her half an hour ago.

At the sight of her, Patrick's antagonism towards Charles in-
reased. He was still smarting from their encounter yesterday;
still resentful at the way Charles had dismissed his offer. Since
marrying Cressida, Charles behaved as if he had been born and
bred into wealth; as if he was somehow superior to everyone
else. Of course, it wasn't his money, everyone knew that. If he
hadn't found himself a rich wife, he would still be in Seymour
Road, relying on his pathetic hippy arts centre for a living. Cressida had pulled him up a few notches—and in principle Patrick
didn't mind that. But look at the way he was treating her! Let-

so many ways. He would spill scalding tea over his hand at a tea
party and smile as though it were nothing; he would turn down
the wrong street and carry on rather than turn round. Of course,
children always take after their parents, he thought, watching her
as she quickly breathed in and out, trying to relieve the burning
sensation in her mouth, then, adopting a casual air, took a great
gulp of cold water. But what no one ever tells you is that your
children inherit just as many of your deficiencies and foibles as
they do your better characteristics. He smiled at Nicola.

'Is that good?' he said.

'Delicious,' she said stoutly. 'Really yummy.'

'Not too hot?' he said, in spite of himself.

'Oh no,' she said, as he knew she would. 'Just right.'

Charles and Cressida were sitting near each other on the grass.
They had somehow staggered through the morning, communi-
cating in short, polite phrases; avoiding each other's gaze. When
their eyes did meet, it was with disbelief. This couldn't be happening to them.

They had arrived downstairs for lunch with an assumed unity;
had mustered up smiles and excuses for their lateness with
enough good cheer to stave off curious looks. But the others
seemed intuitively to know that something was wrong. No one
had come to sit near them; no one had attempted to bring them
into the general barbecue banter. A tacit, perhaps unconscious,
avoidance area surrounded them; even Martina and the twins
were sitting away from them with the other children.

Cressida picked abstractly at blades of grass and took tiny bites of the chicken drumstick, which Patrick had pressed on her. The food was tasteless in her mouth; her mind was black with misery. She wanted to sit calmly somewhere and think it all out; but her thoughts were too confused; everything seemed to go round in circles. And there seemed to be a missing piece; an unexplained factor which, if she only knew what it was, would slot in to make things clearer. Something—a thought; a memory; an observation—kept tugging at her mind. She groped through her thoughts unhappily, but nothing tallied, nothing made her start with recognition.

She had almost successfully managed to block from her mind the scene last night. Of course Charles had not meant to hit her; he had simply been strung up. It was really her own fault for falling asleep and letting him discover the letter without her breaking the news to him first. In retrospect, it occurred to her, perhaps she should have kept it a secret until she had visited Mr Stanlake and checked that it wasn't all some awful mistake. Perhaps it had been wrongly addressed to her. Perhaps it should have gone to some other client. She imagined Mr Stanlake smiling at her, tearing the letter up and promising her he would have a stern word with whoever was responsible for worrying her in this way. She would smile gratefully back at him, and ask him to make quite sure no mistakes like that could be made in the future. He would pat her hand and order tea.

This scene was so comforting, Cressida dwelt on it a little bit longer. After all, people made mistakes every day, she reasoned. They dialled wrong numbers often enough; why shouldn't they

have sent out the
Charles' sullen face.
him it was all a silly
more she was convinc
thought was cheering.

Charles, sensing Cressi
and saw a little smile cross
drumstick determinedly, app
situation. A part of him wanted
could behave so naturally, when
But his senses seemed numbed; he
rouse himself to any strong feelings,
he deliberately reminded himself of the
that they might eventually owe, and pair
into terms of material goods, a huge grey
was an abstract terror; it was almost as thou
be terrified—so he was. In the same way tha
been able to believe that all that money in Cress
his too, so he was unable to relate a demand for
to himself. Other people dealt in that kind of mor

Every now and again, he glanced over at Ella.
he had seen her that day, the sight had brought back,
a memory of the night before. Now he couldn't stop t
himself—prodding his own sore spot like a small bo
bruise. But his senses were becoming numbed towards h
The more he looked, the more the pain was dulled. The pa
of last night had slipped away; try as he might, he couldn't rec
ture it. He reminded himself several times that it was on

ting her go upstairs to bed by herself like that last night; disappearing outside with Ella; even now, ignoring her completely.

Patrick eyed Cressida's pale skin, her fluttering eyelids, her delicate hands. She was a real lady, he reflected. She wasn't the sort to complain, or cause a fuss, or defend herself; she was the sort who would just suffer in silence. And she'd chosen as her protector that pretentious, arrogant Charles—who had only married her for her money, anyway. Patrick's chest burned in silent indignation, and without looking at what he was doing, he knocked a sausage onto the grass.

'Daddy!' cried Georgina. 'You clumsy!' She shrieked with laughter, and after seeing what had happened, Caroline joined in.

'Blast!' said Patrick, bending down and trying to pick it up with the tongs.

'That must be enough food now, anyway,' said Annie. 'Why don't you sit down, Patrick? You must be boiled.'

'Yes, come and sit down,' said Caroline, in a mollifying voice. 'Come and have a nice drink.'

As Patrick sat down, Don sidled over.

'I've been looking again at the chart,' he said.

'Oh yes?' said Patrick shortly. There had been a slight scene when Patrick announced that the finalists in the tennis tournament were himself, Caroline, Charles and Cressida. Don had looked shocked; Valerie had expressed voluble disbelief; Patrick had stalked off to light the barbecue.

'I see the way you've worked it out,' said Don. 'I suppose that is a valid method, although it's not one I've seen before.'

'Oh good,' said Patrick.

'And I suppose, with Val injured like that,' continued Don, 'we weren't likely to win all our matches.'

'No,' chimed in Caroline in a loud, sarcastic voice. 'And you certainly wouldn't have wanted to put her through a final. Not with an injury.' Don flushed slightly.

'What I was wondering,' he said dolefully, 'was whether you wanted an umpire for the final. Since I won't be playing, I thought I'd volunteer.' He shifted morosely from one foot to the other.

'Yes, well,' said Patrick. He looked around at the others for help. 'What do you think?'

'Oh, yes!' said Annie. 'That'll make it really special.'

'And since we do have an umpire's chair . . .' drawled Caroline.

'Exactly,' said Don. 'It'd be a shame not to use it.'

'Yes, you're right,' said Patrick, feeling an increasing enthusiasm for the idea.

The authentic Wimbledon-green umpire's chair that towered at the side of the tennis court had been an expensive purchase from a specialist sporting catalogue but was rarely put to use by anyone other than Georgina.

'We could get along the kids to ballboy,' said Caroline. 'Georgina, you were volunteering yourself the other night. How about it?'

'Actually,' said Georgina, 'it's nearly time for us to do our play.' She sprang to her feet, and called to the others. 'Get everyone sitting in a row,' she commanded Caroline.

'What about the ballboying?' said Caroline.

'Maybe,' said Georgina. 'Play first. We'll be down when we've put our costumes on.'

'All right,' said Caroline. 'There's no hurry!' she called after her. 'Why do kids always want to put on plays for their parents?' she addressed Annie. 'I was just the same.'

'So was I,' agreed Annie. 'I used to love charades. And we had a wonderful dressing-up box.'

Patrick seized his chance. Sauntering casually down to where Cressida was sitting, he smiled gently at her and said, 'The children are about to put on a play for us. Are you interested?'

'Our children?' Cressida seemed confused; her eyes darted about.

'They're inside, getting their costumes together,' explained Patrick. 'Georgina's been organizing them.'

'Oh, I see, yes, of course.'

'They'll be a while yet,' said Patrick, and sank easily onto his heels. 'Lovely day, it turned out,' he said, looking up at the sky.

'Yes, lovely,' murmured Cressida.

'I tend to lose my appetite in this kind of heat,' said Patrick. 'I don't know if you're the same.'

'Oh, yes,' said Cressida vaguely.

'And it makes it worse when you're the one in charge of the cooking!' He laughed pleasantly and eyed Cressida surreptitiously to see whether she was relaxing. He wasn't quite sure what all this was leading to; but somehow he felt an obscure need to show her that not all men were like Charles; that there were a few she could trust, perhaps even confide in.

Cressida stared fixedly at her fingernails and felt a pink tinge creep over her face. It had just occurred to her that Patrick's job was something in finance. Perhaps he would know whether the letter was a mistake or not. Perhaps she should ask him. It would be such a relief if he could reassure her. She opened her mouth to speak—and then shut it again. If she mentioned the letter, he might well ask to see it. Did she want him, a relative stranger, looking at her correspondence? Did she want him to know how much the demand was for? Could she perhaps bring up the subject in a more oblique way?

She glanced over her shoulder. Charles had got up, and was stalking off towards the terrace. No one was near.

'Actually,' she said, 'there was something I wanted to ask you.' She blushed, and looked down at her skirt.

Patrick's heart surged with a mixture of pride and terror. Cressida had chosen him to confide in. He had been right. She needed someone she could trust. But what was he to say if she asked him about Ella? He quickly prepared a few anodyne phrases in his mind. Of course, it wasn't right for Charles to have gone off with Ella like that—but on the other hand, had anything really happened? And although he would have relished Charles' embarrassment at any indiscretions, he couldn't bring himself to say anything that would hurt Cressida.

'It's about a letter,' said Cressida. Patrick's heart sank. Had Charles and Ella been writing to each other all this time? Had the affair never ended? He inwardly cursed Georgina again for having told Ella it was all right for her to come and stay with them. As far as he was concerned, it was never OK for that Jezebel to stay with them.

'A letter?' he said, in light tones, ready to downplay its significance. 'I've never been one for much letter-writing my-self.'

'But business letters,' said Cressida quietly. 'You do write business letters.'

'Well, yes,' said Patrick, surprised. Was she not talking about a letter from Ella, then? 'At least,' he added, 'my secretary does. If anything goes wrong, I blame her.' He gave a quick laugh. Part of him regretted having invited Cressida's confidences. Although, to be fair, he hadn't really invited them. But he had certainly welcomed them. And now he had a nasty feeling he didn't want to hear her troubles after all. What if she was involved in some sort of scandal?

'I received a letter yesterday,' said Cressida, 'which I think might be a mistake. In fact, I'm sure it is a mistake. But I'd just like to be sure.' She brought her head up, and stared at him with large blue eyes. Then her expression changed, and her attention shifted to over his shoulder. Patrick turned round, and saw Stephen striding towards them.

'Hello, you two,' he said, in a determinedly cheerful voice. 'Patrick, might I have a quick word? You don't mind, do you, Cressida?' Cressida's face had closed up.

'Oh, no, not at all,' she said politely. Stephen grinned.

'I think the youngsters are about to entertain us,' he said. 'But I wanted to catch you before they begin.' He stopped, clearly waiting for Patrick to rise to his feet. Patrick didn't know whether to feel annoyance or relief.

'All right,' he said eventually, struggling up and brushing

down his trousers. 'I'll talk to you later perhaps,' he said to Cressida, then wondered whether that sounded compromising. But Stephen wasn't the sort to wonder why he and Cressida had been chatting alone.

They walked off together in silence, and Stephen's face grew more and more scarlet. He could barely bring himself to say what he was planning. The whole subject covered him with embarrassment and shame; he would almost rather have just swallowed the mortgage commitment, managed somehow, and said nothing. But a growing conviction that he needed to sort this all out as soon as possible compelled him at last to speak.

'It's about that deal,' he said awkwardly. 'I've been having second thoughts.' He looked away, in acute embarrassment. Patrick's step barely faltered. He was used to this kind of thing.

'People do,' he said in a jovial tone. 'When did you ever make a big decision and not have doubts somewhere along the line? It's only natural. But I can assure you, you've really done yourself a favour.'

'Maybe,' said Stephen. 'But, actually, I don't think I really want to take out a huge mortgage. Not while I'm still doing my doctorate.'

'Hardly huge,' said Patrick. 'It's well within your means.'

'I know,' said Stephen. 'I'm sure you're right. But you know . . .' He forced himself to look at Patrick. 'I just don't feel comfortable with it. I'm not like you and Charles,' he added. 'I'm not used to dealing in big sums of money, and I'm not used to borrowing. I just wouldn't be able to sleep at night. So,' he paused, 'I've decided I'd like to pull out.'

'You really have got it bad,' said Patrick, giving an easy chuckle. 'You'll be laughing at yourself tomorrow, when you remember this conversation. But don't worry,' his eyes twinkled, 'I won't hold you to it!'

'No, really.' Stephen's voice was firm. 'I want to cancel the deal.'

'Well, that might be a bit difficult,' said Patrick in a thoughtful voice. 'The problem is, you see, the penalty charges for early surrender. You might come out with quite a bit less than you put in.'

'But I only put it in yesterday!' Stephen's voice rose in outrage.

'I know, silly, isn't it? These funds are all structured the same. They reward people who stay the course and penalize those who leave early.'

'And what counts as early?'

'For you, anything before ten years. But don't worry. I'm sure it won't come to that. If you like, I'll go through your accounts with you and work out how you can be sure of meeting the mortgage commitment each month.'

'Patrick, you don't understand. I want to cancel the deal.'

'I know you do.' Patrick's voice was sympathetic. 'But if you cancel the deal, you'll definitely lose out. You'll have to pay your charges straight away. They could be a good few thousand pounds. I really wouldn't advise it.'

'Oh.' Stephen looked crestfallen. There was a short silence.

'Actually,' Patrick said, in a thoughtful voice, 'there is an answer.' Stephen looked up. 'You could switch into our guaranteed investment fund.'

'Guaranteed?' Stephen looked up. Guaranteed. It had a comforting ring about it.

'Oh yes,' said Patrick. 'Utterly safe. I don't know why I didn't think of this for you before. It's designed precisely for someone like you, who isn't keen on risk.'

'That's me,' said Stephen, making a half-hearted attempt to joke.

'I understand completely. You're not one of the big-shot investors of our time, are you?' said Patrick in a sympathetic voice.

'Not really,' said Stephen. 'That's just it. I'm not happy with debt. Never have been.'

'Well then, that's the answer,' said Patrick, in a pleased voice. 'What a relief! You leave it all with me. I'll put your investment in our one hundred per cent guaranteed fund, and you sleep easy at night.' He grinned at Stephen. 'That way, you can't fail to cover the mortgage payments.'

Stephen felt uplifted, despite his reservations, by Patrick's enthusiasm.

'And you think that would be a better option?' he said cautiously.

'Christ, yes. I should have thought of it before. You get the best of both worlds with this fund. Investment and security. I'll go through it all with you on Monday, shall I?' Stephen gazed at him.

'All right,' he said eventually. There didn't seem to be any choice in the matter. He would just have to trust Patrick and hope for the best.

They walked along in silence for a few moments.

'Out of interest,' Patrick said casually, 'why the sudden panic?' Stephen flushed.

'Nothing really,' he said. 'I'm just a bit uneasy with such a big debt.'

'But it's not debt if you're making more than enough to cover it,' said Patrick, grinning at Stephen.

'I know that,' said Stephen. 'But I started thinking, I should have taken the papers away to think about yesterday, shouldn't I?'

'Not necessarily,' said Patrick easily. 'There's no point delaying something if it's to your advantage.'

'But most people would think about it overnight,' persisted Stephen. 'At least, that's what . . .' He broke off.

'Yes?'

'Nothing,' said Stephen. Patrick stiffened slightly.

'Has someone been talking to you?' he said casually. 'Giving you advice? I'm just interested to know,' he added, smiling at Stephen. Stephen looked uncomfortable.

'Not really,' he said. 'I mean . . .'

'Don't worry,' said Patrick. 'I know what it's like. People ask you not to let on what they've been saying.'

'Well, yes,' said Stephen. He looked away.

Patrick stared at Stephen, filled with a mounting, angry certainty. Charles. It had to be Charles fucking Mobyn. Patrick was almost sure of it. It would be just like that supercilious bastard to find out what Stephen had been talking about to him, and advise him to pull out. What the fuck did Charles know about it? A memory of Charles' smooth voice ran through his mind. *I think it's a bit much trying to do business with one of your guests. This is supposed to be a party, isn't it? Keep your charts for the office.* Bloody bastard. Thought he was doing Stephen a favour, no doubt. Thought he was getting him out of a fix. Well, he should fucking well mind his own business. Spend more time looking after his wife and less poking his nose where it wasn't wanted.

'You liddle pigs are too old to leev at home,' said Martina, waving her arms vaguely in the air. 'You must go to seek your fordunes. But beware of ze volf!'

Toby and the Mobyn twins, each clad in a pink T-shirt, stared at her, apparently amazed.

'Off!' hissed Georgina, from the side of the lawn. 'Go on, Toby!' Suddenly remembering what he had to do, Toby grasped a twin by each hand and led them off the lawn.

'Shall we clap?' whispered Annie.

'Yes, I think we should,' said Caroline, and began hearty applause.

'It's not over yet!' Georgina's blue eyes regarded them with disapproval.

'Oh, we know,' said Annie. 'We're just applauding the scene.'

The adults were sitting in a row of seats facing the lawn, each holding a drink. Annie and Stephen were in the middle of the row, but Stephen was not attending. The sense of enthusiasm which Patrick had transmitted to him during their conversation was quickly ebbing away and his situation was becoming starkly apparent to him. He was still committed to a huge mortgage. That much seemed plain enough. He couldn't afford the few thousand pounds, or whatever it was Patrick had said he would have to pay in order to pull out. But was this guaranteed fund really the answer? What was meant by guaranteed? Stephen felt confused. Patrick hadn't actually said anything about it. Everything was going too fast.

One of the twins appeared on the lawn. He stared vaguely at the audience and began to suck his thumb. He looks so sweet, thought Annie, and she turned to grin at Charles. But Charles was sitting, chin cupped in his hand, staring morosely at the ground.

'Hello, little pig!' Annie looked up in surprise. It was Nicola, dressed in what appeared to be a suit and tie, and with a moustache painted on her face. She grinned tremulously at Annie, then addressed the twin. 'Can I interest you in some extremely fine straw for your house? It's the finest straw around; you won't find better, mark my words.' She fumbled with her bad hand at the catches of the attaché case she was carrrying; the audience was silent. Finally the lid swung open, to reveal a caseful of straw. 'Look at that, sir,' continued Nicola. 'Finest quality house-building straw. Yours for only five gold pieces.' A snuffling sound came from the end of the row. Caroline was shaking with laughter.

'She's brilliant!' she exclaimed in a muffled voice.

'So is that a deal then, sir?' said Nicola. 'I assure you, straw is the best thing you can build your house out of these days. Bricks are old-fashioned. Straw's what you want.' She bowed to the twin, handed him the case and walked off the lawn. The adults burst into applause and Caroline burst into snorts of laughter.

'She's wonderful! She's just like you, Patrick!' Patrick's head jerked up in shock. Along the row, faces turned towards him, giggles were stifled; even Charles raised his head and gave a grin.

Patrick turned white with anger. Was that how everyone saw him? As a cheapskate salesman? He wasn't surprised at Caroline—it was the sort of comment he might expect her to make. But for her to say it in front of all of them—some of them clients—filled him with a hot, embarrassed fury. Especially Charles. Charles, who had told Stephen he should try to get out of the deal. Charles, who thought he was so fucking superior. Patrick could hardly bear to look at his smooth, tanned face. Stephen, after all, didn't know any better. But Charles did; and Charles knew Patrick had been desperate for the business.

And now they were all sitting there laughing at him. With the utmost control, he forced himself not to get up and walk out. He gave a stiff grin and took a swig of Pimm's. The other twin appeared on the lawn, and once more Nicola came on with an attaché case.

'Are you building a house, sir?' Her tone was confident now; she was clearly enjoying the humour of the part. 'Might I interest you in some lovely twigs? They really are the finest twigs for house-building. Completely wolf-proof. Guaranteed against wolves of all shapes and sizes. You won't have any complaints, sir.' She handed the attaché case to the twin; once again the audience collapsed in laughter.

'She's priceless,' said Ella, wiping her eyes.

'It's amazing, isn't it?' said Annie. 'I had no idea she could be so funny.'

Toby wandered onto the lawn.

'I want bricks,' he announced loudly.

'Not yet!' hissed Georgina. Nicola hurriedly made her entrance. 'Hello, little pig,' she said. 'Can I interest you in some twigs or straw?' There was a pause.

'Now!' hissed Georgina from the side. Toby's brow cleared.

'I want bricks,' he said.

'Not straw?' said Nicola hopefully. 'Or twigs?'

'I want bricks,' said Toby.

'What about some nice cardboard?' suggested Nicola.

'I want bricks,' said Toby. Nicola sighed.

'You're making a big mistake,' she said. 'Don't say I didn't warn you. Here you are.' She handed Toby a brick, and led him firmly off stage.

'Interval,' announced Georgina.

'Aren't they good?' said Annie, turning to speak to Cressida. But Cressida was staring straight ahead, with a taut expression and unshed tears glistening in her eyes. Annie quickly looked away, and inadvertently caught the eye of Patrick. His face was thunderous. She quickly looked away again. Stephen was talking to Don; Valerie seemed to be talking at Ella, who was looking surprisingly interested in whatever she was saying. She glanced at Caroline. But Caroline had also noticed Cressida, and was staring at her with blatant curiosity.

'Act two,' announced Georgina, in a ringing voice. She eyed Caroline sternly. 'And try not to laugh.'

Caroline took no notice. She was still gazing at Cressida. The sight of the younger woman sitting wanly, almost in tears, had struck a sudden chord of compassion in her. She and Ella had been laughing gaily that morning about Charles—but neither of them had to go through what Cressida did. The poor thing had quite obviously found out about Charles and Ella; perhaps she was contemplating leaving him; perhaps divorce. Suddenly Caroline felt remorse for her treatment of Cressida. She'd always taken her to be a cold, stuck-up bitch, but here she was, in a dreadful state because of that stupid Charles. A dim sense of feminism rose up in Caroline's mind. Why should that poor girl suffer because of a bastard who'd only married her because she was rich anyway?

Suddenly there was a roar of laughter, and Caroline looked round to the lawn. One of the twins had come on, and sat down in a big cardboard box covered in straw. Georgina entered behind him, wearing a long, black cape and looking more like Dracula than a wolf.

'Little pig, little pig,' she intoned, 'let me come in.' The twin looked blankly at her. He was clearly too young to have been given any lines; but from the side of the lawn came Martina's voice, high and squeaky.

'No no, by ze hair of my cheeny cheen cheen, I von't let you in!'

'Then I'll huff and I'll puff and I'll blow the house down!' yelled Georgina, and charged at the cardboard box. The face of the twin crumpled with fear, and he let out a piercing wail. Georgina, regardless, began to blow as hard as she could at the box and the twin's wail turned into terrified sobs.

Suddenly the sound was joined by a cry from the audience.

'Leave him alone!' sobbed Cressida, tears starting to flow down her cheeks. 'Leave him alone!' She leapt up, rushed onto the lawn and scooped up her son, who began to sob unrestrainedly against her shirt. From the side of the lawn came more sobs, from the other twin, who had decided to join in with his brother. Without looking right or left, Cressida picked him up also, strode towards the house and disappeared in through the terrace door.

Charles remained motionless in his seat for a few seconds, then, as everyone turned to look at him, he stood up, muttering something, and went after her. The others sat for a few minutes in silence. No one seemed quite sure what to say. It was an awkward moment. Then a voice came from the side.

'Oh dear,' said Ella in an expressionless voice. 'I hope I wasn't the cause of that.' Caroline looked at her sharply.

'So do I,' she said shortly. 'So do we all.'

CHAPTER TWELVE

'I'm so sorry,' said Cressida to Caroline. 'I don't know what came over me. Too much sun, I expect.' The two women were standing by the tennis court, waiting for the arrival of their partners for the grand finale of the tennis tournament.

'Too much bossing by Georgina, more like,' said Caroline. 'She's a little Nazi. In fact, it's me who should apologize, on behalf of her. She's already caused havoc once this weekend.'

'Really?' said Cressida politely. Caroline cursed herself.

'Well, yes,' she said awkwardly. 'Telling Ella it was all right for her to come and stay. She didn't say a word about it to Patrick or me.' She looked away uncomfortably from Cressida's face. How could she have been so crass as to bring up the subject of Ella? But Cressida had obviously got her feelings under control.

'Extra guests are always difficult,' she murmured. 'People don't realize; they just phone up at the last minute and ask if they can bring their great aunt, or their godson, and one can't just say no. It's very trying. I've taken to making an extra pudding or two each time, just in case.' She smiled tiredly at Caroline, who was overcome by a sudden, irrational feeling of guilt. Her eyes swept over Cressida's pale, drawn complexion; the shadows under her eyes; the slender hand gripping the tennis racquet.

'It's not really a problem for me,' she said frankly. 'Since I never do any cooking.'

'Really? But last night . . .'

'Caterers,' said Caroline. 'I thought you knew. Can you see me making seafood tartlets?' Her eyes crinkled humorously at Cressida. 'I'm crap at cooking. When I first invited Patrick round to my flat for dinner, I hired a caterer to do Beef Wellington. They delivered it to the back door, and I brought it up the stairs, through the kitchen and out to Patrick. He thought I'd been taking it out of the oven!' She burst into raucous laughter, and Cressida gave a shocked giggle. 'He still thinks I made it,' added Caroline. 'You're the only person I've ever told. You mustn't tell him!'

'Oh, no, I won't,' said Cressida. She stared at Caroline, wide-eyed. 'Did he really believe you?'

'Oh yes,' said Caroline. 'Men are so blind. He didn't even notice it was on a foil caterer's tray.' Cressida broke into giggles again.

'That's amazing,' she said.

'Sometimes he asks for Beef Wellington again,' said Caroline, 'and I tell him I don't want to make it because I want to keep the memory of that dish special.'

'So you haven't ever had it since?'

'Never,' said Caroline. She took out a cigarette, put it in her mouth and reached for her lighter. 'The caterers went bust,' she said. 'And I don't want to risk using another firm. They might do it differently.' She caught Cressida's eye and they both broke into laughter again. Cressida gave a few broken, almost painful giggles as she watched Caroline light her cigarette. Caroline looked up.

'Would you like one?' she asked.

'A cigarette?' Cressida paused. 'I haven't smoked since I was at school.'

'Do you good,' said Caroline. 'Calm your nerves.' She offered Cressida the pack. After a few moments, Cressida took one.

'They're menthol,' added Caroline. 'You may not like them.' Cressida took a few hesitant drags.

'Minty!' she exclaimed.

'Nice, aren't they?' said Caroline. She grinned companionably at Cressida. 'They clean your teeth as well.'

'Really?' began Cressida, then saw Caroline's face. She laughed. 'I always believe what people tell me.'

'I'm the opposite,' said Caroline. 'I always disbelieve what people tell me. It's a good habit to get into.'

'But what if they're telling the truth?' Caroline shrugged.

'Then you'll find out soon enough,' she said. Cressida nodded puzzledly and continued taking puffs on her cigarette. Caroline watched her, inhaling with shallow little breaths and quickly exhaling again, and suddenly felt a strong, almost maternal fondness for her.

'Have you ever tried to make it?' said Cressida suddenly.

'Make what?'

'Beef Wellington.' Caroline inhaled deeply, and looked at Cressida sardonically.

'Me make Beef Wellington? You're talking to the girl who got straight Es in cookery. I told you. I'm crap at cooking.' She blew out a satisfying cloud of smoke.

'I could teach you to make it.'

Caroline looked slowly round at Cressida, suspecting a joke.

'Teach me? What do you mean?' Her voice came out more sharply than she had intended.

Cressida's face fell slightly; but she carried on, in a slightly hesitant voice, 'I could come round—or you could come round to me—and I could show you how to do it. I've made Beef Wellington lots of times. And I'm sure you could, too.'

'Come round to your house?'

'Not if it's inconvenient, of course,' said Cressida. 'I could easily come here.'

'No, no,' said Caroline slowly. 'I'm always popping into Silchester. It would be easy for me to come to you. And you really think I could learn to make Beef Wellington?'

'I'm sure you could,' said Cressida. She smiled shyly at Caroline. 'You could cook it for Patrick. As a surprise.'

'Christ, he won't believe his eyes!' said Caroline. She grinned at Cressida. 'I have to warn you, I'm a bloody awful pupil. But I'll make a special effort to listen. Are you sure you can bear it?'

'Oh yes,' said Cressida. 'It'll be fun!' Her eyes sparkled and she looked for somewhere to stub out her cigarette.

'Cressida! You're not smoking?' It was Charles' stentorian voice. The light in Cressida's eyes dimmed; her eyes darted about distractedly. Even her skin seemed suddenly lifeless.

'It's all my fault,' called Caroline loudly. 'Bloody nerve,' she muttered under her breath. Charles approached the court briskly.

'I didn't think you smoked, Cressida,' he said. 'It's an expensive habit, you know.' Cressida was silent. He stared at her expectantly, his eyes cold; his face hard.

'I just thought I'd try one,' she said eventually, in a voice that trembled slightly. Caroline drew breath, and looked with a sudden fierce hatred at Charles. He met her gaze challengingly—then, with a sound of impatience, turned away.

'Hello!' The cheery voice of Annie reached them. 'Everyone's coming,' she called. 'Patrick was held up by a phone call.' She was carrying a number of bottles and a plastic ice bucket. 'I thought I'd bring a few supplies,' she added. 'Does anybody want a drink? I've got lemonade, and orange juice.'

'We should have some water on the court,' said Caroline. 'I'll go and get some.'

As she left, Cressida suddenly felt exposed, as though an insulating barrier between her and Charles had been removed. She looked surreptitiously at Charles' face. It was still harsh, with taut lines and shadows that actually made him better looking. He looked . . . she groped in her mind for the word . . . moody. Mean and moody. Of course. The sort of looks one was supposed to fall desperately in love with. But Cressida had never been attracted to that sort of man. She had fallen in love with Charles because of his easy good nature; his wide smile; his even temper. She had felt safe with him; protected and secure. And now she was, in spite of herself, frightened. She didn't want to be alone with him again; she didn't want to listen to his shouts and threats; she didn't want to experience again that tense, miserable silence.

'Aha! Our worthy finalists!' It was Don, striding briskly towards the court, with a straw hat on his head and a clipboard in his hand. He walked over to the green umpire's chair and deposited his clipboard. Then he produced a tape measure, went to the centre of the court and ceremoniously measured the net.

'It's a bit low,' he called. 'Annie, would you mind adjusting it?'

'Gosh,' said Annie, getting up obligingly. 'This is all getting a bit serious.'

Cressida stared straight ahead, avoiding Charles' eye, as Annie wound the handle back and forwards. Stephen seemed a cheerful, straightforward man, she thought to herself. Lucky Annie . . .

'A bit higher,' called Don. 'No, a bit lower . . . slow down . . . up a bit more, yes that's right, stop, stop!' He beamed at Charles and Cressida. 'Might as well get it right before we start.'

'Absolutely,' said Charles, in a taut voice.

Caroline and Patrick were coming down the path towards the tennis court.

'Listen,' said Caroline. 'We've got to beat that little shit.' Patrick looked at her in surprise.

'Who, Charles?'

'Yes, of course Charles. He's a complete bastard.' Patrick's eye fell on Charles, on his blond hair and insolent tanned face, and he scowled.

'I couldn't agree more.'

'Well, then,' said Caroline, 'don't play your usual crap.'

'You've got a nerve!' said Patrick indignantly. 'Anyway,' he added, 'I thought you quite liked Charles.'

'He's a complete two-timing bastard.'

'Ah,' said Patrick. 'I thought he might be. How did you find that out?'

'Ella told me,' said Caroline over her shoulder. 'They did it last night. In a field.'

'In *our* field?'

'I know. Taking liberties a bit, I thought.'

Charles and Cressida had gone onto the court.

'Hello,' said Caroline briskly. 'Just going to limber up.' She took up a position by the court and attempted a few rather flashy stretching exercises. 'My hamstrings are out of condition,' she complained loudly, catching Patrick's eye. She flashed a look at Charles. He was standing, scowling at the ground. Miserable sod, she thought. Can't even enjoy adultery.

Charles was wondering whether he could bear playing this match at all. All the others seemed so fucking cheerful, while his mind was clouded over with bleak misery. The only other person who looked as downcast as him was Cressida. And she was beginning to annoy him beyond measure, with her fluttering eyelids, and her pale face, and that stupid outburst of weeping. Everyone obviously blamed him. Christ. That was bloody ironic.

'Ready,' announced Caroline. 'Let's knock up.'

ballboy last

work,' said

Who's got

tennis balls and began slam-
trying to relieve his frustra-

aroline, as another ball went
n not Steffi Graf, you know.
single shot.' She deliberately
ent in the net.

d.

serve.'

u decide.'

to under-

in tennis.

there for

y covered

he court,

ve one in

d. Every-

waving to attract her attention.
language. It's against the LTA

m in amazement. 'You must be

for players and audience alike,'

turned to the audience. 'Is anyone
sked loudly. There was silence.
orgina politely, 'I am.'

line. 'Anyway, I thought you were

the op-

unds, he

th of the

long,' said Georgina. 'Nicola wants
she goes home.'

mistak-

. She sat

wins. A

nbered,

who is

g; who

oy until then,' said Caroline impa-

, 'we'll probably go straight away.
ow you're doing a bit later on,' she

ick,' she said.

said Caroline, as Georgina marched

off with Nicola and Toby. 'She was dead keen to be
week.'

'She's probably realized it's actually quite hard
Annie, laughing. 'She's not stupid, your daughter.'

'Let's get cracking,' said Patrick impatiently.
rough or smooth?'

'I'll toss,' said Don officiously. 'Heads or tails?'

'Tails.'

'No, heads. That means Charles and Cressida are t

'So we choose an end,' said Caroline. 'I'll let yo

Patrick stared at her crossly. He had never been able
stand the mentality that went behind choosing an end
What did it matter? It wasn't as if you were stuck
the whole match. He gazed up at the sun, temporaril
over with light, gauzy cloud, and looked back down at
none the wiser. What was it they always said? Let's ha
the sun. But which end was the sun? He looked aroun
one was waiting for him to decide.

'Let's have that end,' he said perversely, pointing t
posite end. If he couldn't decide on any reasonable gro
could at least make that bastard Charles walk the leng
court unnecessarily.

As Charles passed the net, he saw the figure of Ella, u
able in her blue dress, coming down the bank in bare fee
down beside Martina and began talking to one of the
cold fury went through him at the sight of her, unencu
free, with no responsibilities. She had the air of someon
only pausing on the way to somewhere far more exciti

has dropped in, considerately, to say a quick hello, but who is already anticipating leaving for much greater pleasures elsewhere.

And he had actually thought last night that he was going to be part of those pleasures. Watching her, it came to him that she didn't really care whether he visited her in Italy or not. She hadn't brought up the subject again, she hadn't given him any conspiratorial glances or expressive looks. She was just going to go off, to her idyllic Italian ménage, and leave him behind, with a wife, two children and possible ruin. Selfish bitch, he thought furiously.

As if aware of his thoughts, Ella directed her gaze towards him and took off her sunglasses to see better. Charles hastily turned his head away, and met the amused glance of Caroline, who was approaching the net.

'You're looking rather tired today, Charles,' she said. 'I hope you slept well.'

'Oh, yes,' said Charles hastily.

'Perhaps it was just the late night then,' said Caroline, following Cressida, who was walking round on the other side of the court, with her gaze. 'Ella tells me you made quite a night of it.' She brought her blue eyes round to meet his; her face was full of contempt. A jolt ran through Charles. She knows what happened last night, he thought. That fucking bitch Ella told her. Why? Why tell Caroline?

She was still staring fixedly at him, and he couldn't move his eyes away from hers. He felt pinioned, like a rabbit mesmerized by a snake. She had power over him, and she knew it. If she wanted to, she would have no hesitation in telling Cressida; perhaps even telling the whole assembled company. She was that kind of insensitive, vulgar, indiscreet woman. No wonder Cressida couldn't bear her. He should have listened to his wife; they should have refused the invitation to come here.

Eventually she let him go.

'I think they're waiting,' she said. 'We'd better go to our places.' Charles watched her sauntering off to join Patrick; her pony tail bouncing, her tasteless gold bracelets glinting in the sun. What did she know of the troubles he was in, he thought viciously. She and Patrick hadn't a money trouble between them; they had the easy, lazy sybaritic life while he had nothing but worries. He walked to the back of the court and scooped up a couple of balls.

'I'll serve,' he said shortly to Cressida.

'The final of The White House tournament,' intoned Don, 'between Caroline and Patrick Chance and Charles and Cressida Mobyn. Linesmen ready.' He turned to the audience. 'Any volunteers?'

'That's your job,' said Stephen lazily, his arm around Annie. 'We're here to applaud. Anyway, you're the expert.'

'I suppose I am,' said Don, in a pleased voice. He adjusted his hat and sat back in his chair. 'Players ready.' He glanced from side to side. 'Play.'

Cressida stood at the net, staring at the grass in front of her. She felt completely detached from the game, detached almost from real life. She stood in the correct position, holding her racquet ready, listening vaguely to Charles grunting behind her as he served each ball. The sound made her flinch; it sounded so angry and brutal. And when the ball came thundering into the net beside her, she physically started. The sound of racquets against balls was growing louder and louder in her ears; the shots seemed to be whizzing past her faster and faster. It was quite a threatening game, tennis, she thought unhappily. Quite violent, in its own way.

'Double fault,' announced Don resonantly. 'Thirty-all.'

'Bad luck,' whispered Cressida. But Charles hadn't heard her. He was swiping angrily at the air with his racquet.

His next serve went in, but it was weak. Patrick took a swing at it, and sent it to Cressida, standing stationary at the net, staring miserably at the ground. Too late, she stuck her racquet out with an instinctive, schooled action. The ball went sailing past her and landed just inside the baseline.

'What were you saying about my usual crap?' said Patrick to Caroline. Charles glared at Cressida.

'You could have got that, darling,' he said, putting a jovial veneer on his voice.

'Sorry,' she said, in a voice barely above a whisper.

'Thirty-forty,' intoned Don. Charles scowled, and threw the ball up high. He came down on it with all his weight, and hammered the ball into the service court. Caroline valiantly hit at the ball as it came thundering towards her, and sent it sky-high. Cressida began to prepare automatically for an overhead, but from behind her came Charles' voice.

'Leave it! It's mine!' He ran forward, brought his racquet back and smashed it down wildly.

'Out!' Patrick looked up and gave Charles a smug grin. That would take the smooth bastard down a bit. 'Long by about a foot,' he elaborated. 'Bad luck. I think that's our game.'

Charles glowered silently at Cressida as they changed ends. Now she couldn't even play a decent game of tennis. For Christ's sake. That was about the only thing she was supposed to be good at.

A sudden memory came to him of a long-forgotten tennis game, which must have happened sometime before they were married. He had sat and watched Cressida, playing in the dappled shade of a cedar tree. Where had that been? He couldn't remember anything about it except the way she'd looked, wearing an old-fashioned-looking tennis dress, with a dropped waistband, like a Twenties flapper. And the way she'd played. Neat, deft, confident without being aggressive. Afterwards, when she'd played her final winning shot, she'd caught his eye and smiled shyly, twisting the pearls she always wore around her fingers. He'd really loved her then. Or he'd thought he did. Perhaps it amounted to the same thing.

CHAPTER THIRTEEN

As the games progressed, Cressida's confidence was in shards. She couldn't keep her mind on the ball; her racquet shook in her hand; her shots were lame and tentative; her reflexes seemed numbed and slow. As she prepared to serve, she felt, to her horror, warm tears rising up in her eyes. She brushed them away with the sleeve of her tennis shirt, then, to stop the others from noticing, quickly threw up the tennis ball and hit it blindly.

'Fault,' said Don. Cressida tried to compose herself for her second serve. But the sight of Charles at the net, with his taut, angry legs and unforgiving neck, completely unnerved her. She threw the ball too low and hit it weakly into the net.

'Fault,' said Don. 'Love-fifteen.' Cressida quickly turned away to pick up the balls for the next point. She really had to pull herself together. She was playing so badly; they were already four-two down; Charles was furious with her.

Normally, she would somehow have managed to block everything out and keep hold of herself. But at the end of the last game, as they both approached the net to pick up balls, Caroline had put a warm hand on hers and winked at Cressida encouragingly. 'Bloody men,' she had said. 'They're all the same. Don't let them get you down.' Cressida had smiled tentatively back; forcing herself to keep her face composed. 'And tell that husband of yours,' Caroline had added in a louder voice, 'that if he shouts at you one more time, I'll kick him in the nuts.'

Caroline's warm, coarse friendliness overwhelmed Cressida like a wave of sea water. It revived her temporarily—but left her shivering and tearful; unable to return to her dry, controlled composure. She slowly picked up two balls and took a deep breath. It wouldn't last much longer. The set was nearly over. At least—it would be unless she and Charles started winning a few games. She walked back to the baseline and bounced one of the balls up and down a few times, staring at it in miserable puzzlement. Was it wrong to want to lose this set as quickly as possible? She couldn't remember if they were playing just one or the best of three. Maybe they would lose this set and that would be it. Over. Suddenly she was overcome by a fierce longing. She wanted to get home, to safety and familiarity.

Patrick watched Cressida's anxious face as she stood, bouncing the ball up and down before serving. Even if he hadn't had his own grudge against Charles, he thought, the sight of that poor miserable woman was enough to stir any decent man's heart. So what if her tennis was a bit off today? At least she knew how to behave on the court. She was unfailingly polite and courteous; she added a real note of elegance to the game.

Eventually Cressida served to him, a poor, pathetic serve. Patrick considered putting the ball deliberately into the net, as a token gesture. But the sight of Charles' smug face was too much to resist. Approaching the ball ponderously, he whacked it at Charles as hard as he could. Charles quickly jumped aside—but not, Patrick noted with satisfaction, before a fleeting look of terror had crossed his face. So he wasn't as cool as all that. They both watched the ball skim down the line.

'Out!' said Charles triumphantly. 'Just outside.'

'Are you sure?' Don's voice came querulously across the court. 'It looked in to me.'

'It was out,' said Charles, a note of steel creeping into his voice. 'Wasn't it, Cressida?'

'Well,' said Cressida, 'I'm afraid I didn't really see it.'

'You must have done! Was it in, or was it out?' Patrick flinched at the hectoring tone.

'All right!' he said hurriedly. 'It was out! OK, Don? Fifteen-all.' As he passed Caroline, he muttered, 'Let's give them a few points.'

'Give that bastard a few points? You must be joking.'

'Not *him* . . .' said Patrick impatiently.

'Ahem,' interrupted Don. 'Mrs Mobyn is waiting to serve.'

Cressida's first serve went in the net. Her second was long and deep.

'Good serve!' exclaimed Caroline, glancing at Patrick. She shot a bright smile at Cressida.

'I'm sorry,' said Don in slight reproof. 'But that really was out. By quite a long way.'

'No it wasn't!' said Caroline.

'I'm afraid it was.'

'It bloody wasn't!'

'It was!' piped up Valerie, who was sitting on the bank near to the court. 'It was well out. Sorry,' she added to Cressida. 'But I did see it.'

'Stupid cow,' muttered Caroline. 'All right,' she said aloud. 'Our point.'

'Fifteen-thirty,' said Don reproachfully. 'Mrs Mobyn to serve.'

Cressida sensed the atmosphere had changed. Patrick and Caroline were looking conspiratorially at each other; they kept hitting the ball out and exclaiming too loudly. Suddenly she had won her service game.

'Well served, Cressida,' said Caroline as they changed ends. Charles looked at her suspiciously.

In the next game, Caroline's serve became surprisingly weak each time she served to Cressida. And with each shot she hit over the net, Cressida felt her confidence return. After a few successful forehands, she felt positive enough to come forward to the net and smack a volley across court, past Patrick and into the corner.

'Game to Mr and Mrs Mobyn,' announced Don. 'Four games all.' Charles looked from Caroline to Patrick and back again.

'You're giving points away,' he said suddenly.

'No we're not,' said Caroline briskly. 'Charles, it's your serve.'
But Charles didn't move.

'You're trying to give us this game,' he said. 'What's the matter? Do you think we can't play tennis?'

'Charles,' said Cressida hesitantly.

'You're talking nonsense, Charles,' said Patrick.

'Like hell I am! I know what you're thinking. You're thinking
poor old Cressida's playing utter shit, let's give them a few points.'

'You bastard!' exclaimed Caroline. 'How dare you say that?'

'It's fucking well true, though, isn't it? You and Patrick have
decided to be charitable to us. Well, thanks very much, but
no thanks. I think I can probably do without charity from the
Chances.' He spoke the name scathingly, and a sneer came to his
lips.

'What the hell's that supposed to mean?' Caroline suddenly
challenged him, feet planted wide apart on the tennis court,
hands on her hips.

'I'll leave you to work it out.' The two stared at each other in
sudden fury.

'Now, calm down,' said Patrick quickly. He glanced towards
the bank. Everyone was sitting completely still, staring agog at
Charles and Caroline. 'Come on, Charles,' he said, trying to
adopt a jovial tone. 'Play the game, and all that.'

'What would someone like you know about playing the game?'
Charles retorted.

'Charles, really . . .'

'Charles, I don't think . . .'

'Take it easy . . .'

Charles ignored them all.

'What the fuck would someone like you know about playing the game?' he shouted. 'You fucking pleb *nouveau*, inviting us all here because you think we're smart, you think we've got money, you think we might buy one of your sodding, stinking little investment plans.'

He stopped to draw breath. But a frenzied, furious voice stopped him. It was Caroline.

'You shut the fuck up!' Her voice echoed around the tennis court and there was a pause, in which everyone tacitly reevaluated the situation. Stephen, who had been about to stand up, decided to stay put. Don, who had been about to utter a few calming words, closed his mouth and looked down at his clipboard. The others watched silently as Caroline walked slowly up to Charles. 'You fucking well shut the fuck up.' The words issued from her mouth in a slow, deliberate sequence. 'You think you're superior to us? You think you're a better person than Patrick? Well, at least he didn't marry me for my fucking *money*! And at least he has better manners than to go to someone's house, as a guest, and spend the night screwing around with some tart in a field!' Her voice rose to a shriek. 'Just because you went to some fucking public school, doesn't make you a better fucking person! Patrick's worth a million of you!' She turned to face Cressida.

'If I were you, I'd leave him,' she began. But Cressida was staring at her, white and physically shaking.

'What are you talking about? What field?' she whispered. Caroline gazed at her uncomprehendingly.

'You know—Ella,' she said without thinking. Too late she realized, as Cressida's face crumpled. 'Oh fuck! I thought you knew. Shit. I'm really sorry. I thought that's why you were looking so ill.'

Cressida felt as though she was in a nightmare. It was all happening. Their private life was being discussed on a tennis court. In front of an audience. She barely took in Caroline's renewed apologies. Her humiliation was complete.

Annie and Stephen, sitting on the bank, glanced at each other worriedly.

'Say something!' whispered Annie. 'This is awful!'

'I can't!' hissed Stephen. 'What am I supposed to say? Don should say something. He's umpire.' They both glanced at Don, who was studiedly looking down at his clipboard.

'Cressida, let's go,' Charles suddenly barked in a stentorian voice. 'We've had enough here.' Cressida didn't move. She didn't even seem to hear him.

'Cressida!' Charles was starting to sound rattled.

'Why should she go with you?' Caroline poked Charles in the chest. He staggered slightly, as though she had hit him, and glared at her. 'Why should she go anywhere with a two-timing bastard like you? Sorry, Cressida,' she added. 'I didn't mean to remind you.' Cressida looked up. Something like a smile appeared on her face.

'It's all right,' she whispered. Caroline grinned back at her.

'You stay here tonight with us if you want to,' she said. 'You don't have to go anywhere with him. You can stay all week if you want.'

Charles gave a short laugh.

'That's rich,' he said. 'Stay with Caroline and Patrick. See how many investment plans they can sell you in one week. You think they're your friends? You think Caroline's being nice to you? They'll be getting you to sign on the dotted line by breakfast time tomorrow. Jesus Christ.'

'Stephen!' hissed Annie. 'Say something. This is getting really nasty.' But Stephen was listening, agog, as Charles turned to Caroline.

'You think your precious Patrick's so wonderful?' he said. 'Try telling that to all the people he's conned out of their money.' His eyes flickered contemptuously to Patrick. 'Salesmen are all the same. He'd sell you like a shot, if he thought he could get a good price for you. Fucking con man.' He suddenly rounded on Patrick. 'Why did you ask us here? Not because you like us, or you wanted to see us. Christ no. Just so you could try to flog me your sordid little fund. Just so you could notch up a few more thousands on the bedpost. Is that how you get your kicks? Is that what turns you on?'

'Is that why you asked us here too?' Everyone looked up, startled. It was Stephen. He had stood up, and was staring, bright red in the face, at Patrick. 'Is that why you asked me and Annie here? To sell us that investment fund?'

There was a flabbergasted silence.

'What investment fund? What are you talking about?' Annie stared at Stephen, but he avoided her gaze. Charles slowly swivelled to face him.

'Christ, he didn't get you, did he? Stephen?' There was a silence. Stephen looked down. Charles turned back to face Patrick.

'You little shit,' he said softly. 'Do you really think Stephen can afford to invest in one of your fucking so-called unique investment opportunities? Do you really think he can afford to risk his money on speculation like that? Christ almighty.' He turned to Stephen. 'How much did he get you for?' Stephen was silent. 'Oh Christ,' groaned Charles. 'It was the whole fucking whack, wasn't it? I can't believe he talked you into it.'

'Oh fuck off!' burst out Patrick suddenly. 'You've already done enough! I know you've been talking to Stephen. I know you told him he shouldn't have signed. You needn't pretend you don't know anything about it.'

'What do you mean?' said Charles impatiently. 'I haven't spoken to Stephen.'

'Don't give me that,' said Patrick furiously. 'I know you said something about taking papers away overnight; not signing straight away. I know you told him not to trust me.'

'I haven't said a word to him,' said Charles. They both turned to face Stephen.

'Actually,' he said, shamefacedly, 'it was Don I was chatting to.'

'Don?' Patrick's look of shock was almost comical. Everyone looked up at Don, still perched on the umpire's chair.

'Sorry, what was that?' he said, looking up from his clipboard. 'I was just checking the score. You know, we've already had eighteen double faults.'

'Weren't you listening?' said Patrick incredulously.

'I don't like unpleasantness,' said Don, pursing his lips, 'either on court or off. Was there something you wanted?'

Patrick was so taken-aback he could barely speak. 'No, no,' he said quickly. He looked about. 'Shall we carry on?'

'What do you mean, shall we carry on?' Annie's voice was clear and resolute. 'I think a few things need explaining. What's this investment fund?'

'It's nothing you need to worry about,' said Patrick quickly. 'Stephen, it's OK. I'll tear up the documents. Pretend it never happened. Cancel it.'

'Cancel it? Are you sure?' Stephen gazed at him in amazement. 'But you said I couldn't pull out.'

'He told you you couldn't pull out!' Charles jeered in derision. 'He forgot to tell you that you've got two weeks to change your mind. The cooling-off period. That's right, isn't it, Patrick?'

'What, really?' Stephen looked at Patrick incredulously. 'You told me it was too late! You said it would cost me a few thousand to cancel!'

'Oh dear!' Charles' voice was vindictively triumphant. 'It looks like our gracious host hasn't quite been doing the right thing by his guests. Aren't there some regulations somewhere about selling investments? Isn't there some sort of complaints procedure?'

'Look, I said we'll cancel the whole thing,' said Patrick, avoiding Stephen's eyes.

'You deliberately misled me. You conned me.' Stephen tried to drum up some anger. But the relief he felt was so strong, it wiped out any other emotion. It was almost euphoria. The whole thing was cancelled. He was in the clear. It was all OK. Suddenly he felt his legs buckling underneath him.

Flopping down in the deck chair, he met Annie's stern gaze.

'Not now,' he said.

'Yes, now! Tell me exactly what's been going on!'

'It was nothing,' he said. 'I just said I'd invest some money with Patrick. But I'm not going to now.'

'What money? We haven't got any money!' Stephen was silent. 'Oh, come on. You might as well tell me, because I'm going to find out somehow.'

'I was going to take out a mortgage,' Stephen said quickly. 'But it's all cancelled now. Isn't it, Patrick?' Patrick nodded, his face expressionless.

'A mortgage? What were you thinking of?'

'Oh, don't you start,' said Stephen irritably.

'How much for?' Stephen was silent again. 'Stephen . . .'

'Eighty thousand.'

'What?' Annie gave a shocked laugh. 'You're not serious.' Stephen shrugged. 'Eighty thousand pounds? Eighty thousand pounds' worth of mortgage? When we haven't got any income?'

'Oh Christ! Shut up! Yes, I made a mistake. Yes, it was with a lot of money. Yes, I've realized in time. Could we just drop it?'

'Eighty thousand pounds,' said Annie wonderingly. She turned to Caroline. 'Can you believe it?' she said. Caroline tried, too late, to adopt an astounded expression. She gave Annie an apologetic look and Annie gazed at her with unbelieving realization.

'You knew all along,' she said flatly. 'You knew Stephen had signed away all that money. Didn't you?' Caroline shrugged.

'I can't help what Patrick does. I told him I thought it was wrong.'

'But we're supposed to be friends,' said Annie incredulously.

'That's what I said to Patrick,' said Caroline defensively. 'I said you were my only real friend.'

'Well, if I'm your only real friend,' said Annie, in a voice which was dangerously quiet, 'why didn't you tell me what was going on?'

'I couldn't,' said Caroline uncomfortably. 'Patrick said he'd lose his reputation if I went around telling people to pull out of deals.'

'So you think it's better for him to succeed in persuading people to take out mortgages when they can't afford to?'

'Well, you probably could have afforded it,' said Caroline, rattled. 'I mean, it's not that much. And with us paying Nicola's fees . . .' She stopped abruptly.

'Hang on a minute! That's why! That's why you offered to pay Nicola's school fees! I don't believe it!'

Nicola, running down the path to the tennis court to see who had won the match, heard her mother's distressed voice rising above the hedge, and didn't understand what she meant. Bursting out onto the bank, she looked around, from shocked face to shocked face, and, in a voice that trembled slightly, said, 'But I don't have school fees. I go to a state school. You don't pay fees at a state school.' She looked around, her glasses shining, but none of the adults seemed able to speak. Then Valerie took a breath.

'Your mummy was talking about a different school,' she said, in a sugary voice. 'A lovely school in the country, with kind teachers and lots of space to run about.' She smiled at Nicola.

'A . . . a special school?' stammered Nicola.

'Oh yes,' said Valerie gaily. 'A very special school. For special little girls.'

Nicola's face turned ashen, and she swallowed. She looked from Annie to Stephen and back to Annie. Then she turned on her heel and ran back up the path, her bad leg dragging pathetically behind her. As she turned the corner, she gave a huge sob.

'Oh Christ,' said Stephen, getting up. 'Nicola!' he called.

'I'll go,' said Annie angrily. 'Haven't you done enough already?'

There was silence when Annie had left. Stephen looked around. Valerie was still sitting in her chair, watching the events with gleaming eyes. Martina and the twins were nowhere to be seen; Ella had also absented herself. Patrick and Caroline were glaring at each other; Cressida had quietly sat down on the tennis court, and was curled up, hugging her knees. She ought to realize, thought Stephen, that her skirt was a bit too short to be sitting like that. But his thoughts were interrupted by Charles.

'Stephen, you're a fucking moron!' he exclaimed. 'What were you doing signing something like that? You're supposed to be the bright one around here.'

'Yes, well, it's all right now,' muttered Stephen.

'But it might not have been all right! You might have been ruined! I can't even bear to think about it! I don't know what could have possessed you.'

'How about simple envy!' exclaimed Stephen in a sudden angry retort. 'How about the simple fact that everyone here is rich, and we're poor? How's that for starters?' Charles stared at him.

'I never knew you felt like that . . .'

'I never did feel like that! I really didn't. But look at us! We're approaching middle age, everyone's getting on in the world, and I haven't even got a job!'

'You've got your thesis,' said Charles awkwardly. 'That's more than a job. It's an achievement.'

'That's all right for you to say! But it doesn't pay the bills, does it? We're not all in your privileged position, Charles.'

'My privileged position!' Charles gave a short bitter laugh. 'Christ, you have no idea what my position is.'

'It seems all right to me,' said Stephen shortly.

'That's because you don't know anything about it.' Charles paused, and took a deep breath. When he spoke again, it was in a different voice.

'I might as well tell you,' he said. 'We're as good as ruined.' He exhaled sharply; there was a stunned silence. Caroline's eyes darted quickly to Cressida, but she remained motionless, her head bowed. The others looked uncertainly at each other. Charles looked up at the sky.

'It's almost a relief to have said it,' he murmured. Patrick looked at him curiously. Was the man serious? Was he mad?

'What is it, the Print Centre?' hazarded Caroline. 'It can't have gone bust, surely?'

'I wish,' said Charles bitterly. 'At least then I'd go bankrupt and that would be it. At least it wouldn't be unlimited.' He enunciated the word carefully, with a self-mocking despair. 'Unlimited fucking liability,' he added. 'Never-ending liability. Oh Christ!' He gave a despairing, shocking cry, which echoed round the court. Nobody moved for a few moments. Then Patrick spoke.

'Lloyd's of London?' he said quietly. Charles' head jerked up in surprise. 'How on earth . . . ?' His eyes swivelled round to Cressida, still sitting, curled up on the court, as though trying to block the world out. 'I suppose she told you,' he said contemptuously.

'Actually, she didn't,' said Patrick calmly. 'It was just a guess.'

Cressida slowly lifted her head. Her face was pale, and she was shaking. 'Do you mean,' she said, in a voice barely above a whisper, 'that it's not a mistake?' Patrick's heart contracted.

'I'm not sure,' he said gently. 'But I should think it's probably not.'

'Of course it's fucking well not!' yelled Charles. 'You stupid bitch! Is that what you thought? You really are retarded, aren't you?' Cressida's face crumpled, and she huddled closer to her knees. Caroline looked indignantly at Charles, but naked curiosity kept her mouth closed.

'Go on, say it!' exclaimed Charles to Caroline, catching her expression. 'You think I'm an evil bastard who married Cressida for her money! Of course you do. Well, maybe I did. But all I can say now is much fucking good it did me.' Stephen flinched.

'Honestly, Charles,' he said solidly. 'You don't mean that.'

'Don't I?' Charles' eyes were glittering. 'What would you know? Christ, you start whinging about a mortgage of eighty thousand. Do you know how much we owe?' He paused for effect. 'I'll tell you. A million pounds.' He looked round, to see the effect he'd made. Caroline looked astounded. Patrick was looking unsurprised. Stephen was staring down at his knees uncomfortably. 'Maybe less,' Charles continued, in a calmer voice. 'Or maybe more. Our debt is unlimited. We could still be paying out when the twins are twenty-one. Christ knows if we'll be able to send them to proper schools. But I should think it's most unlikely.' His eyes glittered more brightly. 'How do you think that feels?' He looked around, and his glance fell on Stephen, bright red with embarrassment.

'You're the lucky one,' he said, without rancour. 'You've got friends who can afford to help you out.' He looked around. 'Has anyone got a spare million they can let us have?' he said, in a mocking voice. 'We'll be terribly grateful. And we'll try to pay it back. Honest.' He gave a short, painful laugh, tossed a tennis ball, and slammed it hard across the court. Then he threw his racquet after it, slumped to the ground and buried his head in his hands.

CHAPTER FOURTEEN

Nicola was sobbing uncontrollably when Annie found her, curled up on the ground, half hidden by a bush. She looked up, startled, at Annie's touch and tried to scramble to her feet. But Annie clasped her firmly in her arms and pulled her back. There was a brief, tacit struggle before eventually Nicola surrendered and buried her hot, wet eyes in Annie's shirt, shuddering and gasping for breath. Annie hugged her tight, not saying anything but rocking gently, stroking her hair, soothing away the sobs.

'Now,' said Annie, after a while, when Nicola seemed to have calmed down. 'What's all this about?'

'I d-don't want to go away!' Nicola's wail turned into a sob, and a fresh stream of tears landed on Annie's shirt. 'I don't want to g-go to a s-special school.'

'A special school?'

'You know, for people like me. For weirdos.'

'My darling!' Annie held Nicola away from her in shock and peered intently at her face. 'Is that what you thought? That we were going to send you to a special school?'

'Th-that's what the g-girls at school s-say,' shuddered Nicola. 'They say I'll b-be sent away to a special school for p-people like me. They say it all the t-time.'

Annie stared at Nicola in shock. Control your anger, she thought. It won't make it any easier for Nicola if you lose your temper.

'Listen to me,' she said, slowly and clearly. 'You aren't going to any special school. You're going to stay just where you are. Those girls are crackers.' Nicola gave a half giggle, but her eyes were distrustful.

'Valerie said . . .' she said.

'Valerie was talking about something else,' said Annie. She felt Nicola stiffen. 'Now listen,' she said. 'I'll tell you what Valerie was talking about. What we were all talking about. Then you can think about it. All right?' Nicola nodded, her body still tense. 'When you're a bit older,' said Annie, 'you'll go to senior school.'

'Marymount,' agreed Nicola.

'Maybe Marymount,' said Annie. 'Maybe somewhere else. Has Georgina told you about the school she goes to?'

'Yes,' said Nicola cautiously.

'Do you think it sounds nice?'

'Yes.'

'Well, just maybe, if you wanted to, you could think about going there.'

'St Catherine's,' said Nicola thoughtfully. Annie felt her relax slightly.

'That's right,' said Annie. 'But you'd have to think very hard about whether you want to go. It's a boarding school.' Nicola nodded.

'I know,' she said. 'You sleep in dorms. And you have exeats.' Annie tried to read her expression, but the afternoon sun was glinting on her glasses.

'Well,' she said, 'we won't talk about it any more if you don't want to. There's heaps of time to decide.'

'Can I really go if I want to?'

'I'm not sure yet,' said Annie honestly. 'It depends on a few things. Would you be disappointed if you couldn't?' Nicola gazed at her for a while. She shook her head, then nodded, then giggled.

'I don't know,' she said.

'You silly cuckoo!' said Annie, starting to tickle Nicola's tummy. 'You silly cuckoo! Are you still ticklish here? I think you might be!' Nicola shrieked with laughter.

'Stop, Mummy!' she gasped.

'Sorry, I can't hear you,' said Annie. 'Did you say something?' Nicola roared with laughter.

'Stop! Stop!'

Eventually Annie relented. She put her hands above her head.

'Look! I've stopped.' Nicola remained keyed up for a few

seconds, ready for another attack, then flopped down, still giggling. Annie looked down at Nicola.

'Shall we go back to the others? Or shall we stay here for a while?'

'Stay here,' said Nicola. She buried her head into Annie's lap and closed her eyes. After a while, she said, 'Why did Valerie say I was going to a special school?'

'She meant a lovely, pretty, friendly school,' said Annie. 'Special doesn't mean bad, you know. Lots of things are special because they're so wonderful.' She paused. 'Like you in that play this afternoon. You were special because you were so funny.' Nicola looked up, her cheeks rather pink.

'It was Georgina's idea,' she said.

'But Georgina couldn't have done it nearly as well as you.' Nicola went pinker and looked pleased. 'I think my favourite bit,' continued Annie, 'was when you told the poor pig that the sticks were wolf-proof.' Nicola suddenly gurgled with laughter.

'That was so funny,' she said. 'And then the wolf just came and blew them all away.'

'Poor little pig,' said Annie.

'Silly pig, more like,' said Nicola robustly. 'He shouldn't have believed me. He should have thought, Will sticks keep the wolf out? No, they jolly well won't.'

'I know,' said Annie. 'That's what he should have thought. But, you know, not everyone's as sensible as you.' She smiled down at her daughter and gave her a sudden, fierce bear-hug. 'Not everyone's as sensible as you,' she repeated quietly. 'Not by a long way.'

After a while, Nicola got to her feet. She pushed her hair back and sniffed.

'I was supposed to find out who was winning the tennis match,' she said. 'To tell Georgina.'

'I'm not sure anyone did,' said Annie. 'I think they decided to stop.' And thank God you didn't come along any earlier, she thought, feeling suddenly ashamed of the ugly bickering that had gone on; the screams and fighting by people who were supposed to be civilized friends.

'Well, I'll go and tell them that,' said Nicola. She looked suddenly anxious to be away, suddenly embarrassed, perhaps, Annie thought. Well, she was almost getting to that awkward age of embarrassment. And maybe it started younger these days.

'You go off then,' she said. 'You can tell Georgina the score was quite close.'

'All right.' Without looking back, Nicola ran off, leaving Annie with a damp patch on her shirt and a feeling of emptiness where Nicola's head had rested in her lap. She sat for a few minutes more, with her head thrown back, feeling the sunshine against her face, letting her mind wander, until a cloud moved slowly over the sun, turning the air cool, and a gust of wind blew at her skirt.

Slowly, feeling old and creaky, she got to her feet, and brushed down her clothes. She walked slowly and unwillingly back to the tennis court, wondering what dreadful scene of confrontation would await her. But the only person there was Stephen, sitting in a deck chair, sipping at a can of beer.

She went and sat down beside him. For a while neither of them spoke. Then Stephen said, 'Is Nicola all right?'

'She's all right now. She thought we were going to send her away to some special school.' Annie sighed. 'Those girls at her school have been saying she's going to be sent away. To a school for weirdos. Can you believe it?'

'I can believe anything of that lot.'

'I told her she might be able to go to St Catherine's.'

'And what did she think of that?'

'I couldn't really tell.'

There was a short silence.

'Christ, I'm a fool,' said Stephen suddenly. 'I don't know what happened to me this weekend. I wanted . . .' He broke off. 'I don't know, I wanted to be rich, and successful, and, you know . . . like the others. I thought Patrick might make me a bomb of money, and we could buy a bigger house or something . . .'

'But I don't want a bigger house,' said Annie.

'No,' said Stephen. 'Neither do I. But it's easy to forget things like that.' He smiled foolishly at Annie. 'I'm not level-headed like you.'

'Oh, I'm not level-headed,' said Annie surprisingly. 'I have my own fantasies.'

'Do you?' Annie flushed.

'You know. Silly things. Clothes. Jewels.'

'I'll buy you clothes and jewels,' said Stephen robustly. 'I'll buy you all the jewels you can eat.'

'Will you?' Annie's eyes softened.

'You wait,' said Stephen, 'till my thesis is published to widespread acclaim. We'll celebrate with a double order of clothes and jewels.' Annie giggled.

'How lovely. I can't wait.' Stephen took a slug of beer.

'I thought I might do some work on it tonight. I've had a few ideas.'

'Good idea,' said Annie enthusiastically. She looked around and surveyed the empty scene. 'Is the party over, then?'

'I suppose it is,' said Stephen, 'if all the guests have gone home.'

'Have they?'

'Don and Valerie have. They asked me to say goodbye to you. Actually, Don got in a bit of a huff. He thought we weren't taking the match seriously enough.'

Annie giggled. 'Poor Don. I don't think we came up to scratch.' She giggled happily for a minute or two, savouring the silly, childish humour; the warm afternoon sun; the peace of the moment. Then she gave a huge yawn, stretching and wriggling in her deck chair. She looked at Stephen.

'Is it time to go home?'

'I think so.' Stephen stood up, held out his hands and hauled Annie to her feet. 'Let's get our stuff together. I don't want to hang around here anymore.'

When they got up to the house, they found Caroline standing in the hall.

'Oh, Caroline,' said Annie nervously, 'we thought we might go quite soon.'

'Yes, I thought you might,' said Caroline pathetically. 'I suppose you hate me now.'

'Oh no!' exclaimed Annie. 'Of course not! We've had a lovely time. Haven't we, Stephen?'

'Lovely,' said Stephen.

'Even after what Patrick did?'

'Patrick didn't do anything,' said Stephen firmly. 'It was my own fault, for getting myself into something I didn't really want to be in. No harm done.'

'Oh good.' Caroline smiled widely at both of them. 'So we're still friends.'

'Still friends.'

'And you'll still let us pay for Nicola to go to St Catherine's?' Annie glanced at Stephen.

'Maybe,' she said cautiously.

'Oh don't say you won't,' wailed Caroline. 'Because then I'll know that you think I only offered because of what Patrick did. And it's not true. I love Nicola and I want her to have the best. Please? Say you'll let her go?' Annie smiled. Caroline was irresistible.

'Well, all right,' she said. 'If she wants to go, that is. It's her decision.'

'Of course she'll want to go.' Caroline was sweepingly buoyant.

'She may not,' warned Annie. 'We didn't exactly break the news to her very sensitively.'

'Oh.' Caroline looked crestfallen. 'Did she say she didn't want to go?'

'Well, not exactly,' conceded Annie.

'There you are then! She'll do so well there. I can't wait.'
Annie rolled her eyes at Stephen.

'The woman's mad,' she said.

'I'm not!' Caroline looked at them both. 'I just don't want to
lose my friends.'

'You won't lose us,' said Annie.

'But we do really have to go now,' put in Stephen. 'I'm sorry
the party came to such an unseemly end.' Caroline shrugged.

'A party isn't any good unless it comes to an unseemly end. I
hope you realize it was all carefully planned.' She broke into cack-
ling laughter.

'Oh yes,' said Stephen. 'Just checking.'

As they went up the stairs, Patrick came into the hall.

'Are they off?' he said to Caroline.

'Yes,' she said. 'You'll be glad to hear they don't hold you any
grudges. And you'll also be glad to hear they'll still let us pay
Nicola's school fees.'

'Oh good,' said Patrick sarcastically. He caught Caroline's
eye. 'Actually,' he said, in a different voice, 'that is good. She
deserves a bit of a chance, that kid.'

'That's what I thought,' said Caroline. Patrick carried on
looking at her.

'You really laid into Charles out there,' he said. 'I couldn't believe it.'

'He's a shit,' said Caroline briskly.

'I know,' said Patrick. 'But you didn't have to get involved.'

'He was slagging you off,' said Caroline. 'Of course I had to get involved.' She looked at Patrick; her eyes were surprisingly bright. A second later, Patrick had enveloped her in his arms.

'I really love you,' he said. 'You know that?'

'I had heard a rumour,' said Caroline. 'But I never believe rumours.' Then she was silenced as he fastened his lips to hers.

'Very touching,' came a voice from the doorway. It was Ella. The sunlight was behind her, turning her hair into a halo and her face into a silhouette. 'Sorry to interrupt. I've come to get my bag.'

'Oh, are you going?' said Caroline, with an unconvincing display of regret.

'I think so,' said Ella. 'Don't you?' The two women looked at each other for a few moments before Patrick disentangled himself from Caroline's arms. He nodded brusquely to Ella and walked out of the hall.

'I'm sorry I called you a tart,' said Caroline in a rush. Ella shrugged.

'I don't mind. Words like that don't mean anything to me.'

'How can you be so calm?' Caroline stared at her in bemusement. 'After all that's happened!'

'What's happened? I fucked Charles. Nothing more.'

'That's enough to be going on with.'

'You've changed your attitude,' said Ella. 'Interesting.'

'Yes, well,' said Caroline in an uncompromising voice. 'We all change.'

Ella's eyes surveyed Caroline's face quickly and she gave a little nod.

'I see. I really am unwelcome here, aren't I?' Caroline was silent.

'All right. I won't take long to get my things together.'

'Then what will you do?' Caroline's curiosity overcame her.

'Do? I should think I'll go straight to Italy. I've had enough of this country.'

'Oh well . . .' Caroline's curiosity vanished as quickly as it had arisen. Ella's life in Italy, as she had described it, was so far removed from Caroline's idea of what life should be like as to be uninteresting.

As Ella went towards the stairs, Caroline wondered whether this was really the same plump, friendly girl who had lived with Charles in Seymour Road and looked up to him like a god. They had all changed since leaving Seymour Road, she thought. Except perhaps Stephen and Annie. And, of course, they still lived there. Caroline stood and thought about this for a while, and almost felt as though she was on the brink of some startling revelation. But the effort of thinking it out was a bit too much. She shook her head irritably and looked around.

'Well, we're off now.' Cressida's tremulous voice came down from the landing. Ella looked at Caroline quizzically from halfway up the staircase and shrugged. The next moment, Cressida's blond hair appeared round the corner. She descended a couple of steps—then saw Ella and stopped. The two women stared at each other for a few seconds. Cressida recoiled slightly; Ella's shoulders became taut. Caroline was reminded of a couple of cats put in the same room with no warning.

Then Cressida smiled. It was the smile of a well-bred woman; a smile of duty; the sort of smile that could mask a thousand emotions.

'Goodbye,' she said. She paused, and seemed about to say something else—but then appeared to think better of it. Caroline nodded approvingly. There really wasn't anything else to say.

'Goodbye,' said Ella, in an easy voice. There was a slight pause, as neither seemed sure which way to move. But suddenly Ella bounded up the staircase, taking it two steps at a time. She reached the top and disappeared along the corridor. Cressida looked down, caught Caroline's eye, and smiled with unmistakable relief.

'You don't have to go,' said Caroline, eyeing Cressida's suitcase. 'You can always stay here.'

'I know,' said Cressida. 'But I think I'd like to get home. Try and sort things out.'

Charles came down the stairs, laden with bags. He looked anxiously at Cressida and then at Caroline. 'Thank you for putting up with us,' he said. 'And I'm sorry. That's all I can say.'

'Don't apologize to me,' said Caroline, more harshly than she had intended. To compensate, she gave him a kind look. 'Take care of yourselves,' she said. 'And let us know if—you know—if we can help or anything.' Charles nodded wordlessly.

Caroline followed them out into the drive to wave them all off in their Bentley. Charles' face looked haggard as he leant out of the window, and Caroline tried to find a spark of *Schadenfreude* to cheer herself up with. She usually found it possible to gloat over the misfortunes of even her closest friends. But somehow this situation was far too big for that. Just thinking about it caused the base of her spine to tingle unpleasantly.

When they had gone, she wandered aimlessly back inside and

wondered what to do. Everyone was gone, or getting ready to go. But it was still warm. She might be able to fit in some last-minute sunbathing.

She went to the kitchen and poured herself a glass of white wine, opened a packet of peanuts and poured them into a bowl. For good measure, she added a jar of marinated olives. She put all of these, plus the bottle of wine, onto a tray and took them out onto the terrace. Her steamer chair was in just the right position to catch the rays of afternoon sun, and soon she was agreeably ensconced, her eyes closed and her feet up. At least it hadn't rained, she thought idly. They really had been very lucky with the weather. And tomorrow, with any luck, it would be hot again, and she could sunbathe topless.

When Stephen and Annie shepherded Nicola and Toby onto the terrace to say goodbye to Caroline, they found her asleep on the steamer chair.

'Never mind,' whispered Annie. 'We can each write her a nice letter.'

Out by the car, Patrick was waiting to see them off.

'Thanks for a lovely weekend,' said Annie. 'It really was.'

'Thanks, Patrick,' said Stephen, rather shamefacedly. 'Sorry about all that bother.'

'Don't be silly,' said Patrick. 'It's your right to decide what to do with your own money.'

'Well, yes, I suppose it is,' said Stephen.

They carefully manoeuvred the car out of the drive and drove off, still waving.

'Well, thank God for that,' said Stephen.

'For what?' said Nicola at once.

'Nothing,' said Stephen.

'For a lovely time,' said Annie. 'That's what you meant, isn't it, Stephen?'

'Oh, er, yes,' said Stephen. 'For a lovely time.' He put his foot down and the car leapt forward, as though as eager as him to get away; to get away from the lovely time, back to real life and home.

Last to leave was Ella. She put her bag on the backseat of her car and looked around for someone to say goodbye to. But no one was about. Shrugging, she slipped into the front seat and drove quickly and neatly out of the drive. Her little car was soon zipping along the motorway; she opened the sunroof and began to hum. She had already forgotten Caroline and Patrick; Annie and Stephen; had forgotten about the tennis party. Her mind was on the hills of Tuscany, on her lover, Maud Vennings. Maud would now, perhaps, be sitting outside her villa, sipping Strega, wondering if Ella was going to return to her. Business in England, Ella had told her. Unfinished business. But now there was nothing to keep her.